ARTIN SAMUEL

THE RESURRECTION

EDWIN SIBI

Contents

Contents

Contents

Contents

Contents

Preface

Artin Samuel

The name *Artin* holds many meanings across languages.

In Aramaic, it means *resurrection*.

In Persian, it speaks of one who is righteous and pure — someone who always tells the truth and does what is right.

But this story does not glorify Artin. It does not seek to justify his choices.

He is no hero.

He is a dead man returned. A soul ripped from the grave.

Unbound by law. Unmoved by judgment. Untethered from the rules of man.

A being whose path to salvation is not clean, but rather questionable—and bloody.

And in the end, he is accountable to no one... except God.

The dead don't seek justice. They bring it.

This is only the beginning.

Prologue

<u>Lionsfield Pharma: The Shadow Empire</u>

Founded by Mortis Lionsfield, Lionsfield Pharma is a Laos-based pharmaceutical and bioengineering giant that presents itself as a pioneer in genetic engineering and chemical research. But beneath this facade lies a dark, intricate web of crime and corruption that spans decades. From the very beginning, the company was built on deception. Under the guise of medical research, Lionsfield Pharma secretly cultivated vast acres of illicit plants, including opium, erythroxylum coca, and papaver somniferum—all key ingredients in narcotics. Initially, the company manufactured legitimate medicines, but in the shadows, they produced synthetic drugs on an industrial scale. Just two years after its establishment, Lionsfield Pharma had already manufactured and exported synthetic drugs worth $5 million—an astronomical figure for 1990. With its newfound financial empire, Lionsfield Pharma launched a subsidiary: Sitrom Logistics Group operated under the cover of a diverse manufacturing business—producing everything from plastics to processed foods—Sitrom's true purpose was much more sinister. It acted as the perfect front for large-scale drug trafficking, illegal human experiments, and chemical weapons research. To solidify its monopoly, Lionsfield Pharma infiltrated the Laotian government, ensuring that officials turned a blind eye to their operations.

With unprecedented power, the company became the most influential corporation in Laos, effectively controlling both the economy and law enforcement.

<u>Divertine: The biggest jackpot of Lionsfield Pharma</u>

By 2023, Lionsfield Pharma had already built a criminal empire, but they needed one final push to cement their place in the global pharmaceutical market.

That's when they introduced Divertine—a revolutionary drug that claimed to treat PTSD, depression, autism, and various mental disorders. The drug in reality only had the ability to increase brain power, surprisingly it was able to cure all these mental disorders but it had to be continuously administered.

It became an instant global sensation. Doctors prescribed it in record numbers, mental health institutions embraced it, and patients swore by its effectiveness. The sales? Unbelievable.

$400 million USD—that's how much Lionsfield raked in within years of its release.

With Divertine, Lionsfield wasn't just a pharmaceutical company anymore—they were a global powerhouse. They had the trust of the medical community, the backing of governments, and the money to silence anyone who questioned them.

And with that kind of money?

They set their sights on their next target—India.

<u>The Expansion to India</u>

India was the perfect choice. A massive population. A booming pharmaceutical industry. And most importantly—an ideal location for smuggling.

They built Sitrom factories across South India, choosing states like Tamil Nadu, Kerala, Karnataka, and Andhra Pradesh. But Kerala was their real stronghold.

Why? Because of its seaports.

With easy access to international waters, Kerala became the central hub for Lionsfield's drug operations in India. They funneled chemical compounds from their labs all across South India into one main processing center in Cochin.

But they didn't stop at just processing drugs.

In Cochin, they did something far worse.

They began human experimentation.

Their so-called "medical trials" weren't about curing diseases. They were testing dangerous new compounds on people—turning missing persons into unwilling test subjects.

<u>The Kerala Conflict</u>

Despite its influence, Lionsfield Pharma's illegal activities did not go unnoticed. Over time, tensions grew between the company and the Kerala government. Authorities attempted to dismantle their operations, but with Lionsfield's deep political roots, shutting them down was nearly impossible.

In 2026, after years of investigation, the Kerala government launched a full-scale raid on all Sitrom factories across the state. This wasn't just any investigation—this was a direct assault on Lionsfield's illegal empire.

Knowing they were about to be exposed, Lionsfield scrambled to cover their tracks. In a desperate attempt to erase all evidence, they ordered an immediate and massive cleanup operation—burning documents, destroying lab samples, and shutting down key facilities.

But this cover-up came at a staggering cost.

The rush to erase evidence led to millions of dollars in damages and lost resources. Equipment was discarded, research was destroyed, and entire supply chains were dismantled overnight. Even after cleaning up a lot, the Kerala government managed to shut down one Sitrom factory in Cochin.

For the first time, Lionsfield suffered a major financial setback.

ACT I

THE FALL

CHAPTER I

4:30 AM

The shrill ringtone of his phone sliced through the heavy silence of the early morning. Circle Inspector Jayanth groaned, blindly reaching for his phone on the bedside table. His fingers fumbled before he finally answered.

"Sir! Sir, this is Sub-Inspector Rajesh!" The frantic voice on the other end jolted him further awake.

Jayanth sighed, rubbing his temples. "What is it Rajesh?"

"Sir, this is urgent!" Rajesh's breath was uneven, as if he is terrified after seeing something.

Jayanth sat up, with concern. "What happened?"

"A 17-year-old girl, sir... she committed suicide."

Silence. Jayanth felt his stomach sink.

His mind snapped into focus. "Where?"

Rajesh replied "Near St. Joseph Chapel road."

Jayanth threw off his blanket and swung his legs out of bed, already reaching for his uniform. "I'll be there in ten minutes." His voice was sharp now, all traces of sleep gone.

The police jeep rolled to a stop outside a massive house, its imposing gates slightly open. Even at this early hour, a small crowd of onlookers had gathered, whispering among themselves, their faces a mix of curiosity and unease. The house itself was eerily quiet except for the muffled sounds of sobbing from within.

Circle Inspector Jayanth stepped out of the vehicle, adjusting his belt as he took in the scene. The front porch lights cast a dull glow over the polished marble floor, reflecting the anxious faces of a few uniformed officers standing near the entrance. He strode inside, his boots clicking sharply against the floor.

CHAPTER II

In the living room, the girl's parents sat on the couch, their bodies trembling as they wept. The mother's face was buried in her hands, covered in tears. The father, disheveled and pale, clutched a blood-stained handkerchief, his shirt spotted with dark patches of dried blood. A few neighbors stood nearby, whispering in hushed tones, offering silent condolences.

Jayanth's sharp eyes immediately locked onto the bloodstains on the father's shirt. He turned as Sub-Inspector Rajesh approached him, looking exhausted but alert.

Jayanth: "Who made the first call?"

Rajesh: "The parents, sir. They arrived home around 4AM and found her."

Jayanth: "Where's the body?"

Rajesh: "Still in her room, sir."

Jayanth exhaled sharply and nodded. "Let's see it."

Rajesh led him up the stairs, and with each step, a heavy sense of unease settled over Jayanth. He had seen many crime scenes, but something about this case felt different.

As they entered the room, the air was thick with the metallic scent of blood. Jayanth's breath hitched for a fraction of a second before he composed himself.

The girl's body lay sprawled on the cold floor. The walls were streaked with blood—handprints smeared across the white paint as if she had shaken a lot in pain. A bloodied knife lay discarded a short distance away.

Jayanth remained motionless for a moment, absorbing the scene. The sight was brutal, but his years of experience kept his face unreadable. He pointed to the weapon.

Jayanth: "Is that the suspected weapon?"

Rajesh: "Yes, sir. Likely what she used to take her own life. We're waiting for the forensic team to arrive."

Jayanth let out a low hum, his mind racing.

Jayanth: "Where were the parents last night?"

Rajesh: "Sir, they claim they were out of Kerala for two weeks and returned back today morning. The girl was staying here alone."

Jayanth's head snapped towards Rajesh, his brows furrowing.

Jayanth: "A 17-year-old girl left alone in this huge house for two weeks? What kind of parenting is that?"

Rajesh hesitated before nodding. "I thought the same, sir."

Jayanth turned back to the lifeless girl, his jaw tightening. Something felt off.

Jayanth: "Did you take their statements?" (Referring to the parents)

Rajesh: "Yes, sir, but just a preliminary one. We'll take a more detailed one later."

Jayanth's mind raced back to the father's blood-stained shirt.

Jayanth: "And the blood on his shirt?"

Rajesh: "The father said he rushed to her and tried to check if she was still alive when they found her. That's how he got the stains."

Jayanth: "Hmmm... I need to update SP sir about this, so I want a full report on the case as soon as possible."

Rajesh: "Yes, sir. I'll have it sent to you."

Just then, the forensic team arrived, their white coats and gloves contrasting sharply against the darkened room. They moved with precision, collecting evidence, scanning the walls for blood splatter patterns, and photographing the scene. The flashing camera lights momentarily illuminated the lifeless body on the floor, making the room feel even colder.

The parents remained in the living room, still sobbing, their cries subdued into soft, exhausted whimpers. Jayanth observed them from a distance, his arms crossed.

He glanced at the clock on the wall. The red digits flickered to 6:00 AM.

CHAPTER III

Ring... Ring...

The scene shifts.

A dimly lit bedroom. A couple, Artin and Celine lying in bed—each on their own side, backs turned to each other.

The phone alarm breaks the stillness.

Artin's hand emerges from under the blanket, reaching lazily toward the nightstand. He groggily turns off the alarm, his fingers brushing against the screen before collapsing back onto the bed with a sigh. His eyes remain closed for a moment, reluctant to wake up, reluctant to face the day.

Beside him, Celine remains asleep, her breathing slow and undisturbed by the alarm. She sleeps quietly, her body barely moving beneath the sheets.

Artin gets up from the bed, rubbing his eyes as he drags himself toward the bathroom. The morning feels heavy, the kind where sleep still clings to his body. He turns on the tap, splashes cold water on his face. He lets out a quiet sigh before picking up his toothbrush and starting his routine.

The house is quiet except for the soft hum of the fridge and the occasional rustle of leaves outside. After brushing, Artin moves to the kitchen sink, washing last night's dishes, his movements automatic. The sound of running water fills the kitchen as he scrubs a pan, then sets it aside to dry. He prepares breakfast, the sizzle of eggs breaking the silence, the aroma of coffee slowly filling the air.

As the clock reaches 7 AM, he wipes his hands on a towel and heads back to the bedroom. Celine is still curled up under the blanket.

"Celine, wake up. It's 7 AM," he says, his voice calm but firm.

She groans, pulling the blanket tighter around herself. "Just five more minutes, please."

Artin sighs, shaking his head. "No, no. If I let you, those five minutes will turn into an hour."

Celine groans louder, burying her face into the pillow before finally forcing herself up, her movements sluggish, her hair falling messily over her face. She sits on the edge of the bed, rubbing her eyes in frustration.

Artin doesn't wait for her to complain—he simply turns and walks back to the kitchen.

Artin finishes cooking breakfast and wipes down the last dish, placing it neatly on the drying rack. The kitchen is spotless, the scent of fresh food lingering in the air. He glances at the clock—7:45 AM. With a sigh, he makes his way to the bedroom, expecting Celine to be ready by now.

But as he steps inside, he finds the bathroom door still shut. The faint sound of running water seeps through, a reminder that she's still inside. He doesn't bother calling out or telling her to hurry. Instead, he turns away and picks up the neatly folded clothes he had set aside for the day.

Walking into the other room's bathroom, he closes the door behind him. He takes off his T-shirt, letting it slide off his shoulders, then pauses. His eyes drift to the mirror.

The reflection staring back at him isn't the one he remembers from years ago. His body, once lean and full of energy, now carries the weight of time and exhaustion. His stomach isn't as flat as it used to be, his face looks a little sunken yet bloated at the same time, his skin showing the early signs of aging. He's in his twenties, but he looks older—like life has been dragging him forward faster than he can keep up.

He leans in, running a hand through his hair, noticing a few strands of gray that weren't there before. His fingers trail down to his jaw, where the rough stubble makes him look even more worn out.

This isn't how he imagined his life would be. He always thought he'd be somewhere better by now—stronger, sharper, more in control. But instead, he feels stuck, like he's running in place while the years move past him.

He exhales slowly, shaking the thought away. It's just another morning. Another day.

Turning away from the mirror, he steps into the shower, letting the water run over him, hoping it'll wash away the weight clinging to his mind.

CHAPTER IV

Meanwhile back to CI Jayanth sitting inside his office in the police station.

Jayanth sat at his desk. His office was cluttered—files stacked haphazardly, coffee-stained reports scattered across the desk. The air smelled of paper, sweat, and the faintest trace of burnt-out cigarettes.

His phone buzzed. Sub-Inspector Rajesh.

Jayanth sighed, rubbing his temples before answering. "Yes?"

"Sir, I've sent you the report," Rajesh replied.

"Alright. The inquest procedures—are they done?" Jayanth asked, his voice gruff from exhaustion.

"Yes, sir. The body's been sent for postmortem."

Jayanth exhaled and leaned back in his chair. "Hmm... okay."

As the call ended, he unlocked his phone and scrolled through the report Rajesh had just sent. His brows furrowed. Something about this case didn't sit right with him. Without wasting much time, he dialed SP Saleem.

The phone rang twice before connecting. "Good morning, sir. CI Jayanth here."

SP Saleem's voice came through. "Yes, Jayanth? What is it?"

"Sir, the suicide case I mentioned earlier—I've gone
through the preliminary report."

Saleem exhaled sharply. "Alright, tell me."

Jayanth glanced at the screen, reading off the details. "The deceased is Ameya P. Varghese, 17 years old. Her father, Varghese Jacob, runs a business in Vietnam. Her mother typically stays with her, but for the past two weeks, she had accompanied Varghese abroad—possibly for a visit or business-related reasons. That left Ameya alone in their house."

Saleem grunted. "A 17-year-old girl left alone in a massive house for two weeks? Irresponsible."

Jayanth nodded to himself. "Exactly what I thought, sir. She was studying in 11th class at St. Teresa Public School, Cochin. According to her principal and class teacher, she was energetic, didn't show any signs of distress, but she had been absent for the last three days, claiming she was sick. Her parents confirmed that she had informed them as well."

"Hmm..." Saleem's tone sharpened. "And what about her phone?"

"It's been recovered, sir. We've sent it to the cyber

forensic department. From what we know so far, she was quite active on social media—especially Instagram."

There was a pause before Saleem spoke again. "how did her parent find her? What was their statement?"

Jayanth's jaw tightened as he recalled the gruesome scene. "According to the parents they landed in Kerala early this morning—around 4 AM. They tried calling her to open the door, but she didn't respond. Assuming she was still asleep, they used a spare key to enter the house. When they checked her room..." (Jayanth's voice slowly tightens.) "She was lying there. Lifeless. Covered in blood. Her throat was slit, and the walls were smeared with blood. They claim she was already dead when they found her. And sir there was no signs of breaking in, no signs of any damage. Nothing has also gone missing in the house. At first glance it seems like a suicide. But we are puzzled about one thing that is, why did she slit her throat? Why such a gruesome way to end her life?.

A brief silence followed.

Saleem muttered. "Hmm... and the weapon?"

"A kitchen knife, covered in blood, was found near the body. The forensic team has taken it for analysis."

Jayanth heard Saleem shift, possibly sitting up straighter. "Jayanth, what about that missing girl—Diya? I'm getting pressure from the higher-ups. There's a protest happening, led by the mother of one of the missing victims. This is getting out of hand."

Jayanth ran a hand down his face. "Sir, we've checked everything—CCTV footage, phone records, last-known locations. No leads. No ransom calls. Nothing. This is the seventh missing case in just two months."

Saleem's voice dropped to a serious tone. "That's exactly my point. Seven girls missing, and now this so-called 'suicide'? Something isn't right, Jayanth. You know it. I know it. We need answers. Fast."

Jayanth stared at the reports on his desk, his gut tightening. "Yes, sir. I'll keep digging."

"Make it quick," Saleem said before ending the call.

Jayanth put his phone down, his fingers tapping against the wooden desk.

CHAPTER V

Meanwhile, Back to Artin

Artin stepped out of the room, freshly bathed and dressed. He ran a hand through his damp hair, sighed, while walking into the dining room.

Celine was already there, sitting at the table, picking at her breakfast with one hand while her other hand scrolled mindlessly through her phone. The dim glow of the screen reflected off her face, her brows slightly furrowed.

Artin sat down across from her, reaching for his plate, but his presence didn't seem to register with her. She was too lost in the curated fantasy of social media—her envious eyes stared at the lavish vacations, perfect bodies, luxury handbags, designer clothes, influencers sipping wine on balconies overlooking the ocean. The lives of her friends, celebrities, and strangers all seemed so perfect, shinier, more fulfilling than her own. A hint of jealousy flickered in her eyes as she scrolled past another post of someone showing off a new car, a new house, a perfect morning routine with an expensive coffee machine and a flawless view of the city skyline.

Artin, on the other hand, unlocked his phone and started scrolling through YouTube. Random videos flashed

before his eyes—some meaningless entertainment, a podcast he'd never finish, new trends and prank videos that only made him feel worse about this new degenerative society. His thumb moved in an endless loop, scrolling, tapping, watching, forgetting.

They sat in silence, both consumed by their screens, their minds sucked into the digital void. The food on their plates was secondary, their eyes ate more than their mouths, the degeneracy, the meaningless extravaganza. They don't seem to talk to each other.

There was a time when breakfast had been different. When they used to talk—about dreams, about the days ahead, about things that were important. But now, even though they sat only a few feet apart, just the dinning table between them, they seemed far away from each other.

So close, yet so far away.

As Celine scrolls through her phone, a message notification pops up—Sidharth.

"Hey babe, aren't you coming to the office?"

A subtle shift in her expression—her face lightens, lips curling slightly. Without hesitation, she types back, "Yep, I'm having breakfast. I'll be there soon."

She hastily finishes her food, placing the plate in the sink without a second glance, still holding her phone. "Come on, Artin! It's almost 8:45, we're going to be late," she says, her tone carrying a hint of impatience.

Artin, eyes glued to his screen, barely registers her words at first. At the top of his screen, the time reads 8:39 AM. He exhales, "Wait a minute, let me finish the breakfast."

He quickly shovels the last few bites into his mouth, his gaze flicking toward Celine as she adjusts her purse, preparing to leave. She doesn't seem like she's in the mood for conversation.

Swallowing the last bite, and rushes to the kitchen, placing his plate in the sink with minimal effort. He washes his hands, grabs his bag, and heads toward the door before taking the car keys. Both of them exit the house. Artin locks the front door.

They walk to the car, Artin taking the driver's seat. As he starts the engine, Celine is already back on her phone, thumbs dancing across the screen. The only sounds in the car are the hum of the engine and the distant morning traffic.

As they move along the road, Artin hesitates for a moment before slowly placing his hand on Celine's lap—just a small gesture, a quiet attempt to remind her of his presence. A touch she once loved, a touch that used to make her feel safe.

She feels it but doesn't seem to care. Her eyes remain locked on the screen of her phone, her fingers scrolling through an endless feed of filtered lives. The warmth of his hand on her thigh doesn't stir her the way it used to.

Artin glances at her, searching for even the slightest acknowledgment. Nothing. His expression falters for a second—just a flicker of disappointment in his eyes. He exhales softly, withdrawing his hand and returning it to the wheel, brushing it off like it doesn't matter.

The rest of the drive is silent.

CHAPTER VI

Eventually, they reach the office.

The massive four-story building stood like an unshakable fortress, a testament to power and control. Its sleek, black exterior reflected the world around it, giving off an aura of authority and secrecy. Towering above, the bold Lionsfield logo stood on the topmost floor, a symbol of dominance staring down at the city below. Artin pulls into the parking lot, shifting the car into park. Without a word, they both exit. Celine walks ahead of him, moving forward, not by his side, not waiting.

They step into the elevator. Artin presses the button for the second floor. The doors close. The soft hum of the elevator's music fills the silence between them.

Artin shifts uncomfortably, the silence growing heavier. He finally speaks up, his voice tentative, almost hopeful. "Hey... tonight, let's have dinner outside?"

Celine barely glances at him, her tone casual, almost absentminded. "Umm...there's a party tonight"

Artin blinks. "Party?"

"Yeah, because of the huge investment we're getting from Alliance. Sidharth organized it."

Celine speaks without thinking she just blew her cover.

Artin furrows his brows. "I... didn't know that. How did you get to know of it?."

Celine pauses, and then shrugs. "Sidharth told me"

Celine, sensing his disappointment, takes a more reassuring tone. "We can have dinner some other day."

Artin forces a small nod. "Hmm... okay."

Artin thinks to himself "why would Sidharth tell that to Celine, she is just a B grade scientist and he is Executive Manager.

"Whatever" Artin shakes off the thoughts.

The elevator dings. A robotic voice announces, "Second floor reached."

The doors slide open. Without another word, they step out, moving forward—together, yet miles apart.

As they walk toward their workstations, Artin's best friend, Arun, approaches them with his usual energetic smile.

"Good morning, bro. Good morning, Celine," he greets cheerfully.

Artin's face immediately brightens at the sight of his friend. But Celine? She barely acknowledges Arun, offering only a brief nod before continuing her way to her desk, uninterested in engaging.

Artin slows his pace, stopping to chat with Arun, while Celine walks off without a second glance. Artin watches her disappear into the workspace before turning back to Arun with a puzzled expression.

"Bro, is there a party tonight?" Artin asks.

Arun furrows his brows. "Party? No, I don't think so. Why?"

Artin hesitates, glancing in the direction Celine had walked off. "She told me Sidharth is organizing a party tonight because the Alliance investment got approved."

Arun scoffs, shaking his head. "Wait, how come she knows that much? That's pretty confidential news for a Grade B scientist to be aware of... Bro, I kinda feel like Sidharth is into Celine."

Artin exhales sharply, running a hand through his hair. "Dude... I've kinda felt that before."

They exchange a knowing look. Arun claps a hand on Artin's shoulder as they continue walking, their conversation trailing off as they reach their workstations.

Artin and Arun reach their workplace, which is right beside Celine's. The office hums with activity—keyboards clicking, machines beeping, and the distant murmur of conversations.

Celine is already seated, engrossed in her work

Arun leans back in his seat. "So, another day of the same grind, huh?"

Artin lets out a small chuckle. "Yeah. Just another day."

Their work continues as usual, switching between their desks and the lab. Research, reports, and lab tests fill their hours.

As the clock ticks forward, the routine remains the same, yet Artin can't shake the unsettling feeling growing in his chest.

CHAPTER VII

As the clock hits 1 PM, the office begins to stir with movement as employees prepare for their lunch break. Some head to the cafeteria, others unpack their homemade meals and head to the cafeteria, and a few linger near the vending machines, chatting about the morning's workload.

Suddenly, the office speakers crackle to life.

"Ahh ahhmm... for the kind attention of everyone."

A familiar, confident voice echoes through the workspace. It's Sidharth. The usual chatter dies down as everyone turns their attention to the announcement.

"Tonight, there's going to be a party at the Lionsfield Convention Centre. Now, you all might be wondering—why am I organizing this party?"

A dramatic pause follows, building suspense.

"Because our company is about to receive a huge investment from Alliance Limited!"

A wave of murmurs sweeps through the office. Some employees exchange surprised glances, while others nod in approval. A few even break into light applause.

The cafeteria buzzes with energy. Laughter echoes off the walls, and the clinking of cutlery against plates mixes with cheerful conversations. Employees chat excitedly about the party, speculating about the investment and what it could mean for their careers.

At one table, Artin and Arun sit together, eating quietly. Arun occasionally cracks a joke, trying to lighten the mood, but Artin remains distant. His eyes drift across the room, searching—until they land on Celine.

She's sitting with a group of female colleagues, laughing at something on her phone. She didn't even glance at him.

It wasn't always like this. Not long ago, she used to sit by his side, sharing bites of food, exchanging playful banter.

Artin stares down at his plate, pushing his food around with his fork. Should he say something? Should he ask her what's going on? But the words never leave his mouth.

Across the room, Celine continues talking as if everything is normal. Maybe for her, it is.

With the lunch over, everyone gradually returns to their workstations. The energy from the announcement still lingers in the air, but for Artin, it's just another reminder—he's being left behind.

CHAPTER VIII

As the clock strikes 4 PM, the energy in the office shifts. Employees gather their belongings, their conversations buzzing with excitement about the party later that night. Laughter and casual chatter fill the hallways as most of them file out, eager for the evening ahead.

But not everyone leaves.

The scientists at Lionsfield Pharma are structured into three groups—Grade A, Grade B, and Grade C. Grade C scientists, along with the general employees, are the first to leave, their absence making the office eerily quiet. Only seven Grade B scientists remain—among them, Artin, Celine, and Arun.

In another section of the building, the seven elite Grade A scientists also stay behind.

By the time the last of the regular employees leave, the office is silent, the lively atmosphere from earlier now replaced with an unsettling stillness. The remaining scientists make their way to the underground parking lot, their footsteps echoing in the emptiness.

Two black, unmarked vans wait for them.

Without a word, the scientists board. Artin and Celine sit together, a rare occurrence these days, and for a fleeting moment, Artin feels a quiet sense of happiness. But the atmosphere in the van is tense. No one talks much during these journeys. They never do.

The vans move through the darkening streets, weaving through the city before heading towards the outskirts. The surroundings become less urban—concrete buildings replaced by dense trees, abandoned plots, and roads that few travel at this hour.

Finally, the vans turn into a desolate path, passing through a pair of rusted, creaking gates. The area is overgrown with wild grass and weeds, reclaiming what was once a thriving industrial site.

At the center stands a massive, decaying structure—its walls cracked and stained, its name barely legible under layers of dirt and rust.

Sitrom Logistics and Manufacturing Factory.

A government-sealed facility, officially shut down years ago.

Yet, tonight—like every other night—it is anything but abandoned.

The scientists exit the vans in silence, their movements practiced, almost ritualistic. They proceed toward the factory, their faces void of expression, as if conditioned for what lies ahead.

Inside, the facility is divided meticulously.

Grade A scientists operate in complete secrecy, their labs and workspaces strictly off-limits to the others.

Grade B scientists, including Artin, Celine, and Arun, have their own designated labs—separate, but equally vital to the company's hidden operations.

No one from Grade B is ever allowed inside a Grade A lab.

No one questions why.

The driver of the Grade A van steps out, moving toward the control panel near the entrance. With a practiced motion, he flips the main switch of the facility.

Instantly, the factory comes alive.

From the outside, it's a decrepit, abandoned structure—forgotten by the world, left to rot. But inside, it is a fully operational laboratory. Bright white LED lights flicker on, casting sharp shadows across the walls. High-tech equipment hums to life. The air, thick with the pungent aroma of chemicals, carries an almost suffocating sterility.

The Grade A scientists walk off toward their restricted lab, disappearing behind a secured steel door. No one outside their circle knows exactly what they do in there.

Meanwhile, the Grade B scientists move toward their designated workstations.

CHAPTER IX

Artin and Arun work at the same station, a small, organized workspace lined with vials, petri dishes, and chemical analyzers. Across the room, Celine works alongside three other scientists, her back turned to Artin.

Artin and Arun are responsible for analyzing and cataloging experimental substances sent from Lionsfield Pharma's research facility in Laos. Highly classified samples.

Artin pulls open the laboratory refrigerator beside him. A wave of cold mist spills out, curling around his fingers as he reaches in.

Sitting in the frosted compartment, in a stainless-steel rack, are two vials of an unfamiliar liquid. The substance inside shimmers strangely under the light—thicker than water, almost oil-like.

Arun, having been on leave for the past two days, narrows his eyes. He hadn't seen these before.

"What's this new stuff?" he asks, leaning in slightly.

"These arrived two days ago," Artin replies, his voice low. He carefully lifts one of the vials, tilting it to examine its consistency. Artin speaks, "Both samples are something I've never seen before in my life."

Arun watches closely, his curiosity piqued.

He leans in closer, eyeing the clear, unassuming liquid in the vial.

"Like what?" he asks, his tone laced with curiosity..

"This one," Artin says, tapping the label on the vial, "is called PredaXine. Looks almost like water, doesn't it?"

Arun squints at it. The transparency is deceiving. If he had seen this anywhere else, he'd have mistaken it for saline.

"Yeah..." he mutters. "It looks... normal."

"Yeah and its chemical name is really confusing. Mind taking a look?" Artin says, smirking as he hands Arun the vial.

Arun takes it, squinting at the absurdly long string of chemical compounds printed on the label. His lips move as he attempts to read it aloud.

"(1R,2S,5R)-2-[(3-Hexylphenyl)amino]-5-methyl-1-(pyrrolidin-2-yl) cyclohexan-1-ol..."

He pauses, eyebrows knitting together.

He continues hesitantly, stumbling over the convoluted molecular structures.

"N-{2-[(2S,3R,4S,5S,6R)-3,4-dihydroxy-5-(hydroxymethyl)-6-(methylamino)tetrahydropyran-2-yl]oxyethyl}-1H-indol-3-carboxamide...

What the hell is this?"

Artin chuckles, watching Arun's growing frustration.

"1-Azabicyclo[2.2.2]octan-3-yl α-hydroxy-α-phenylbenzeneacetate...

Dude, this sounds like some wizard's spell."

Arun's eyes widen as he reaches the final part.

"(S)-N-methyl-1-phenylpropan-2-amine?

Bro, is this a drug or an interdimensional summoning ritual?!"

"Yeah but this stuff is really dangerous" Artin chuckles.

"This is a cocktail of several drugs," Artin says, rolling the vial between his fingers. "First up—phencyclidine, aka PCP."

Arun's eyes widen. "Wait, you mean the drug that completely messes with your pain perception?"

Artin nods. "Exactly. This stuff will make you never feel pain.Then, there's yohimbine and codeine —yep, the same codeine that triggers uncontrollable adrenaline spikes.

Arun whistles. "Damn, What else is in this nightmare mix?"

Artin holds up a finger, his voice dropping slightly. "3-Quinuclidinyl Benzilate."

Arun blinks. "What The hell is that?"

Artin leans in slightly. "It's a military-grade compound. Some countries experimented with it as a 'berserker drug.' It scrambles cognitive function while pushing aggression levels through the roof. Basically, it turns people into mindless, violent machines."

Artin smirks darkly. "Nope. To top it all off, we have some good old meth, methamphetamine."

Artin exhales slowly, his fingers still resting on the refrigerator door as the cold air seeps out.

"Bro, I'm actually scared," he mutters, his voice low enough that only Arun can hear. "I mean... it's not like this is my first time processing an illegal drug, but this one" He gestures toward the vial of PredaXine, the clear liquid shimmering under the lab lights. "This one is on a whole different level. It's not just dangerous—it's catastrophic."

Arun watches him, sensing the shift in his tone. "Yeah," he nods slowly. "This thing could turn a normal person into an unstoppable monster."

But Artin's expression darkens even more. He swallows, then lifts his hand to point at the other vial—a small glass container filled with a thick, black liquid.

"And that!" Artin's voice drops almost to a whisper. "That one is even worse."

A strange chill creeps over Arun as he stares at the ominous, ink-like substance, its consistency looking almost unnatural. His throat feels dry.

"What the hell is that...?"

Artin takes a deep breath, his fingers tapping anxiously against the cold metal of the workstation. He picks up the black vial, holding it against the light, watching how the thick liquid clings to the glass like oil mixed with ink.

"This," he says, his voice low but tense, "is ODFC-4—Oncogenic D-Factor Complex 4." He lets the name sink in for a second before continuing.

"It's got Tesamorelin—so yeah, testosterone levels are gonna skyrocket with this one. Then there's Leuprolide, a GnRH agonist, meaning hormones are gonna be pushed into overdrive. And if that wasn't enough, they've thrown in Yohimbine and codeine again, ensuring a constant adrenaline surge."

Arun listens, eyebrows furrowed, but Artin isn't finished.

"This thing also contains Clenbuterol—a performance enhancer. Basically, if you're not already shredded, you're about to be. But then..." He pauses, narrowing his eyes at the label. "Temozolomide... I have no idea what the hell that is."

He looks up at Arun, who just shakes his head, equally clueless. Artin continues, his voice quieter now.

"Then there's Erythropoietin—which stimulates red blood cell production. More RBCs mean more oxygen transport, more endurance, and—more time before the body gives out.

And finally, the worst part—this thing contains D-Factor."

Arun swallows hard, his fingers tightening around the edge of the workstation. "D-Factor??" His voice drops to a whisper, his eyes flicking toward the black vial. "Bro, we've only processed two D-Factor-containing drugs so far... and even those were insane. This—this is something else."

Artin exhales sharply, rubbing his temples. "Yeah," he mutters. "And I have this gut feeling... this isn't just some underground pharma experiment.

This feels like military-grade stuff—hell, maybe even worse. What if this ends up in the hands of terrorists?"

Arun looks at him, his expression darkening. "You really think so?"

Artin nods slowly, the weight of the realization pressing down on him. "Bro, I'm genuinely uneasy about this. I mean, I know why we're here—we're doing this for the five lakh a month they're throwing at us. But... is that really worth it? At what cost?"

His fingers tighten around the vial as he stares at the swirling black liquid inside.

"I don't know, man..." he murmurs. "For the first time, I feel like... maybe we should be choosing truth over money."

Suddenly, the overhead speakers crackled to life, breaking the steady hum of the laboratory. A firm yet hurried voice echoed through the sterile halls:

"Artin and Arun, please expedite processing of the given sample. Exec has requested the mice test results."

Artin and Arun got to work, their hands moving with finesse, a practiced rhythm born from years of handling delicate compounds.

CHAPTER X

Two hours later...

Artin takes a deep breath, his fingers hovering over the screen as he glances back at Arun. They had just spent two exhausting hours refining the ODFC-4 sample, carefully diluting its potency and purifying the compound. Unlike previous D-Factor samples, this one was different—alive in a way that unsettled them both. The last time they worked with a D-Factor drug, its molecular structure was almost unreadable, but this time... they found DNA strands—10,000 nucleotides long.

"Bro, do you realize what this means?" Arun mutters, wiping his forehead. "This isn't just a drug—it's some kind of engineered bioweapon."

Artin swallows hard but doesn't respond. Instead, he steps toward the thick, reinforced door leading to the Grade A lab. Right in front of it is a communication screen, the only way Grade B scientists can interact with those inside. He presses the button.

A few moments pass. Then, the screen flickers to life, revealing Dr. Vivek, one of the senior Grade A scientists. His face, usually blank and emotionless, creases slightly in irritation.

"What is it?" Vivek asks, his voice calm but clipped.

Artin clears his throat. "The ODFC-4 sample is ready for transfer." He hesitates for a second before adding, "This one is... different. We found something unusual in its molecular structure—long DNA strands, far stranger than anything we've seen before."

For a fraction of a second, Artin swears he sees a glint of recognition in Dr. Vivek's eyes. But just as quickly as it appears, it's gone.

Vivek nods once. "Noted. Bring it to the transfer chamber."

Then the screen goes dark.

Artin exhales sharply, glancing at Arun. "Did you see that?"

Arun nods slowly. "He knows."

Neither of them says anything for a moment. But the tension lingers in the air.

Artin carefully places the processed sample into a metallic storage box, a compact, high-tech mini-refrigerator no larger than a water bottle. The cold mist seeps out momentarily before the seal locks shut. With a deep breath, he lifts the box and walks toward the reinforced door leading to the Grade

A lab.

As the automated doors hiss open, a strange unease washes over him. The sterile white lighting feels harsher, the hum of the facility almost deafening in the silence. Standing just beyond the threshold is Dr. Vivek, clad head to toe in a protective biohazard suit, the reflective visor hiding his expression.

Without a word, he extends his gloved hands, and Artin carefully transfers the refrigerated box into his grasp. The weight of the exchange feels heavier than the actual vial inside. Dr. Vivek nods, his posture stiff, his movements calculated.

Artin walks out of the door and slumps into his chair, exhaling heavily, his body sinking into exhaustion. The fluorescent lights hum softly overhead as he rubs his temples, trying to shake off the mental weight of the day's work. Arun, equally drained, leans back, closing his eyes for a brief moment of relief.

CHAPTER XI

Meanwhile, inside the Grade A laboratory, a different kind of tension lingers in the air. The lab, cold and sterile, is illuminated by the dim glow of monitors. In the center of the room, a girl is strapped to a steel chair, her body limp, head hanging forward. Partially conscious, she barely seems aware of the men surrounding her in their protective suits.

Dr. Vivek steps forward, holding a small, metallic container—the vial of ODFC-4. With practiced precision, he hands it over to a scientist, who loads it into an injection gun. A camera positioned in front of the girl blinks to life. Dr. Vivek clears his throat, his voice cold and clinical as he addresses the recording.

"ODFC-4. Test Subject 1: Official name—Diya Gopal. Age—15. Administering 10% dose of processed sample number one."

The scientist pulls the trigger. The needle punctures her arm with a sickening precision. A soft hiss follows as the drug is injected into her bloodstream.

At first, there is nothing. Then, a flicker of movement. Her fingers twitch. Her head lifts weakly. Her lips part, trembling.

"I... I want to see my mom... please," she whispers, her voice barely a breath.

Silence. The scientists exchange uneasy glances. Dr. Vivek frowns. The girl isn't reacting as expected. His frustration grows.

"Administering 50% dose," he announces, adjusting the injection settings.

One of the scientists hesitates. His voice wavers. "Sir... that dosage is too high. Her body is already carrying 10%—"

"Shut up," Dr. Vivek snaps, his sharp gaze cutting through the protest. "I am the head here. I decide the dosage."

Without further hesitation, he presses the trigger. The second injection enters her bloodstream.

For a moment, nothing happens.

Then— a violent convulsion.

Her body jerks against the restraints. Her back arches unnaturally. A guttural scream tears through her throat.

Inside the Grade B lab, Artin and Arun jolt upright. The muffled scream slithers through the thick walls, sending a chill down their spines.

Back in Grade A, the lab descends into chaos. The girl's eyes roll back, her mouth foaming as her muscles spasm violently. The scientists scramble, fumbling for a sedative, but their hands shake too much to grasp it.

Then, in a burst of raw, inhuman strength—she snaps her restraints.

Dr. Vivek barely has time to react before her fist collides with his chest, sending him crashing into the table behind him. Vials shatter. Glass rains to the floor.

She stumbles forward, panting, wild-eyed, her mind trapped in a feverish madness. She turns toward the door.

Artin and Arun, still seated, hear rapid footsteps pounding towards them. Their breath catches. The scream is louder now—closer.

And then—

BANG.

The metal doors explode open.

The girl stands there, panting, her bloodshot eyes darting around the room.

The Grade B scientists freeze in horror. The sight before them is something out of a nightmare—her veins bulge beneath her skin, her muscles twitch unnaturally, her mouth foams with blackened bile.

Arun stumbles back. "What the hell...?" he breathes.

The girl takes a single step forward—then collapses.

Her body convulses on the floor, limbs jerking at disturbing angles. Her muscles ripple and twist, moving in ways the human body was never meant to. Then, she begins to vomit uncontrollably.

Black bile spills from her lips, pooling onto the pristine white tiles. Her breathing slows. Her body stiffens.

Then— she goes completely still.

Dead.

CHAPTER XII

The room is suffocatingly silent.

Artin feels his heartbeat pounding in his ears. His hands tremble. His skin crawls.

Dr. Vivek steps forward, his protective suit rustling against the sterile air as he approaches the still body of the girl. His expression remains cold, calculating—unbothered by the horror that just unfolded before him.

Suddenly Artin snaps.

"What the hell is this, Dr. Vivek?!" Artin's voice cuts through the silence like a blade. His breath is ragged, his hands balled into fists.

All the scientists freeze. Their wide eyes, filled with fear and uncertainty, slowly turn to Dr. Vivek, silently echoing Artin's question.

Dr. Vivek doesn't flinch. His gaze is sharp, indifferent. He looks at Artin as if he were nothing more than a nuisance.

"Clean it up," he orders, his tone void of emotion.

Nobody moves.

Arun, sensing Artin's growing rage, grabs his arm. "Bro, let it go," he whispers, his own voice shaken.

But Artin doesn't let it go. His fury spills over.

"Are you serious?! A kid just died! And you're acting like it's nothing?!"

Artin shoves Arun's hand away, stepping forward. The tension in the room thickens. The other scientists exchange nervous glances. They have seen things—terrible things—but this? This is different.

Dr. Vivek exhales, as if mildly inconvenienced. His eyes lock onto Artin's, dark and unwavering.

"You're paid to do your job, Artin. Not to question it."

That's it. That's the moment Artin snaps.

He lunges forward, rage exploding in his veins. Arun grips his shoulders, yanking him back with all his strength.

"Bro, stop!" Arun hisses, struggling to restrain him.

The other scientists remain motionless, trapped between fear and moral conflict. Their faces scream what their lips won't—What the hell are we doing?

Dr. Vivek merely dusts off his gloves. "Get him out of here," he mutters.

Without another word, Arun tightens his grip and pulls a seething Artin towards the exit.

Artin and Arun stand outside, the cool night air doing little to settle the storm raging inside them. Their minds race, still processing the horror they just witnessed. The weight of what they've been a part of feels heavier than ever.

Inside the facility, the cleanup is swift and mechanical. The body, the blood, the evidence—erased as if nothing ever happened.

CHAPTER XIII

Inside his office, Dr. Vivek wipes the sweat off his forehead before dialing Sidharth's number. His hands are steady, but his mind is racing. The call connects.

"What is it?" Sidharth's voice comes through, calm and composed.

Vivek takes a deep breath. "There was a problem."

"What kind of problem?"

"The test subject. She broke free."

A long pause.

"Explain." Sidharth's voice is lower now, carrying an edge of irritation.

Vivek swallows hard. "We administered the first dose—10% of ODFC-4. There was no immediate reaction. I increased it to 50%."

"50%?" Sidharth's tone sharpens. "Are you out of your damn mind?"

"We needed a reaction. And we got one." Vivek rubs his temples. "She went into a violent convulsion. Broke the restraints. Tried to kill me. She was strong—inhumanly strong, even with just that dose. She ran straight into the Grade B lab, but her body couldn't handle the drug. She collapsed and died before she could get any further."

Silence.

Then, Sidharth sighs.

"And the cleanup?"

"Already taken care of. No evidence left behind."

"And the others?"

"They're scared, but they won't talk. Most of them are too deep in this already." Vivek pauses. "Except Artin."

"What about him?"

"He snapped at me. He's getting too curious. Too restless."

Another long pause.

"Keep an eye on him," Sidharth finally says. "And for now, disperse everyone. Tell them to go home. And remind them about the party."

"Understood."

The call ends.

Vivek leans back in his chair, exhaling slowly.

A few minutes later, Dr. Vivek's voice echoes through the facility speakers.

"All scientists, today's work is over. You may leave and there's no work here tomorrow, you can return home after the work at office and don't forget about the party tonight."

The announcement feels surreal. Like a bad joke after a nightmare.

Artin doesn't move. His jaw clenches, his fists tightening. He is still burning with anger.

As the scientists gather their things and prepare to leave, a figure steps beside Artin. It's the same scientist who had tried to warn Dr. Vivek about the dosage. His face is tense, his movements cautious.

Without a word, he presses a small pendrive into Artin's palm.

"You wanted to know what's going on here, right?" His voice is barely above a whisper. "This has everything."

Before Artin can react, the man pats his shoulder—almost like a silent 'good luck'—and walks away, disappearing into the crowd.

Artin stands frozen, staring at the tiny drive in his hand. A key to the truth. But at what cost?

The van ride back is silent. Everyone is too shaken to speak.

As they reach the Lionsfield office, Artin and Arun exchange a weary goodbye before parting ways. Arun looks like he wants to say something, but words fail him.

Artin heads toward his car, his thoughts still clouded with rage and confusion.

Celine follows behind him, her usual air of confidence now subdued. She doesn't say a word.

She knows Artin is pissed. She also saw what happened inside that lab.

But she doesn't ask.

She just gets into the passenger seat, her expression unreadable.

The silence between them is suffocating.

CHAPTER XIV

Eventually they reach their house.

As Artin unlocks the door, the air between him and Celine is thick with tension. The house is eerily silent, amplifying the unspoken words hanging between them.

Artin turns to her, his voice firm, unwavering. "Celine, we are not going to the party."

Celine, already irritated, narrows her eyes. "Why? If you don't want to go, then don't. But don't try to control me."

Artin clenches his jaw. "Celine, you're my girlfriend. We're not going, and that's final."

Celine scoffs, shaking her head in disbelief. "Are you serious right now? I've been drowning in stress, and this is the only relief I have! Why are you always like this?"

Before Artin can respond, Celine's phone vibrates. A notification pops up. Sidharth: "Hey Celine, where are you? The party's about to begin."

Artin's eyes catch the message. His blood boils. His voice drops to a sharp, accusing tone. "Why is he messaging you ?"

Celine snatches her phone away. "Artin, shut up. We're just friends."

Artin exhales sharply, his patience thinning. "Friends?.

Celine rolls her eyes, already turning towards their room. "I don't have time for this. I'm going, whether you like it or not."

Artin's voice rises. "Then walk. I'm not giving you my car."

Celine spins around, her frustration reaching its peak. "FINE! I DON'T NEED YOUR DAMN CAR!"

Artin exhales sharply, shaking his head as he storms out to the porch. He needs to breathe, to cool down. He grips the railing, trying to steady himself, but the anger lingers, twisting into something heavier—something closer to heartbreak.

Inside, Celine pulls out her phone, fingers trembling slightly. She types quickly:

Celine: "Artin isn't coming. Can you pick me up?"

Ten minutes later, she walks past Artin without a single glance. He doesn't stop her. He doesn't say another word. The front gate creaks as she steps out.

CHAPTER XV

Artin sighs, running a hand through his hair before stepping back inside. He doesn't see the black Mercedes pull up, its sleek frame gliding to a stop. The tinted window rolls down just enough for Sidharth to smirk as Celine slides into the passenger seat. The car disappears into the night, leaving Artin alone in the quiet house, drowning in the silence she left behind.

Artin enters his room, the weight of the day's horrors pressing down on him. The air inside feels heavier than usual. He shuts the door behind him, locking out the world, but not the storm raging within him.

He takes off his stiff work clothes and slips into something more comfortable. His fingers absently reach into his pants pocket, and he feels something small and solid—the pendrive.

Pulling it out, he holds it between his fingers, staring at it. His pulse quickens. What did that scientist want me to see? What the hell is going on in that facility? He wants to check it immediately, but suddenly.

Ring Ring.

The sudden chime of his phone startles him. He glances at the screen. Father Rafael.

For the first time in hours, his face softens. A hint of warmth flickers through the chaos in his mind.

"Hello, Father," Artin says, his voice carrying a rare trace of relief.

"Helloooo, Artin, my boy! How are you?" Father Rafael's voice booms through the speaker, full of life and warmth, a stark contrast to the suffocating dread in Artin's chest.

Artin exhales, rubbing his temple. "Father... things are kinda tough right now."

There's a pause. Then, in that same steady, comforting tone, Father Rafael speaks.

Artin leans back against the couch, the tension in his shoulders easing slightly as he listens to Father Rafael's familiar voice. There's something about the old priest's warmth that makes everything feel a little lighter, even after the nightmare of the day.

"What's wrong, Artin?" Father Rafael asks, his tone shifting to gentle concern. But before Artin can answer, the priest's voice brightens with excitement. "Well, you don't need to worry much because... I'm getting transferred to your church!!!"

"Really?!" Artin sits up, his exhaustion momentarily forgotten. His face lights up with genuine happiness, a feeling he hasn't had in a while.

"Yes, my boy!" Father Rafael says with enthusiasm. "I don't know the exact date yet, but most likely, I'll be there in two days!"

Artin lets out a small laugh, shaking his head in disbelief. "That's amazing, Father. It's been too long."

Father Rafael softens his tone—

"Now, tell me, my son, what's been making things tough for you?"

Artin hesitates for a moment before exhaling heavily. "It's Celine, Father. She's been acting... different. Distant.

I don't know what's going on, but she isn't the same Celine I loved."

Father Rafael hums thoughtfully. "Hmm... how long have you two been together?"

"Five years," Artin replies, running a hand through his hair.

"Five years! And yet, I still haven't met her?" Father Rafael teases, laughing.

Artin chuckles despite himself.

"My son, five years is a long time. Don't you think it's finally time to propose to her?" the priest suggests.

Artin's expression falters. "I want to, Father, I really do. But... I don't know if this is the right time. Things between us feel so—"

"Artin." Father Rafael's voice is firm but kind. "Maybe that's exactly why you should. Perhaps she's feeling unappreciated, unsure of where she stands in your life. A proposal might be the reassurance she needs."

Artin leans forward, rubbing his chin, considering the idea.

"Listen to me, my boy," the priest continues. "Don't overthink it. Just propose to her tomorrow! And in two days, when I arrive, you can introduce her to me as your fiancée!"

Father Rafael's infectious laughter fills the speaker, and despite everything weighing on his mind, Artin finds himself smiling—genuinely smiling—for the first time in what feels like forever.

"Hmmm... maybe I will propose tomorrow," he murmurs, his heart feeling lighter, even if just for a moment.

"That's the spirit!" Father Rafael cheers. "Alright then, son, call me tomorrow and tell me how it goes."

"I will, Father. Thank you."

"God bless you, Artin," Father Rafael says warmly before the call ends.

As the silence returns to the room, Artin lays down back into his bed, staring at the ceiling. His mind is still cluttered, but for the first time in days, there's a small glimmer of hope within the chaos.

Artin slowly drifts into sleep, exhaustion finally overtaking him. His breathing evens out, his mind momentarily escaping the weight of the day.

CHAPTER XVI

Meanwhile, at the grand Lionsfield convention center, Sidharth's black Mercedes pulls up to the entrance, and Celine steps out. The party is already in full swing—luxurious decorations, dim golden lighting, and the rhythmic pulse of bass-heavy music filling the air. Waiters in black-and-white attire weave through the crowd, carrying trays of expensive liquor. The air is thick with the scent of perfume, cigars, and something else—something almost metallic, giving the whole event an eerie undertone.

Arun, who had reluctantly decided to attend, leans against the bar, sipping a drink, scanning the crowd. His eyes widen slightly as he spots Celine stepping inside with Sidharth. A heavy feeling settles in his chest. He quickly pulls out his phone and types a message to Artin:

"Hey bro, you aren't coming?"

He wants to tell him about Sidharth, about Celine arriving with him, but he hesitates.

The party continues, growing louder, more indulgent. Powerful people mingle—business executives, high-ranking officials, and among them, a figure that stands out: Superintendent of Police Saleem. His presence alone shifts the atmosphere, adding a layer of tension beneath the forced laughter and clinking glasses.

As the evening progresses, an exclusive group of guests, including Sidharth, SP Saleem, and a few other high-profile figures, retreat to a private dining area inside the venue. Arun, ever observant, catches a glimpse through the slightly open door. His jaw tightens when he sees Celine seated among them, smiling, engaged in conversation.

A bitter taste lingers in his mouth as he turns away, gripping his glass a little tighter. Something about all of this feels wrong.

The party finally winds up, the grand hall that was once filled with laughter, music, and clinking glasses now feels emptier. The energy has dulled, leaving only the scent of alcohol and cigarette smoke lingering in the air. Most of the guests have already left, the scientists long gone, and only a few remain, chatting lazily or finishing their last drinks.

Arun had left much earlier, unable to stomach the sight of Celine and Sidharth together. The unease in his gut hadn't faded, but there was nothing more he could do tonight.

Now, as the clock nears 1 AM, Celine checks her phone and sighs, rubbing her temple. The exhaustion is evident in her posture. She turns to Sidharth,

"Sidharth, can you drop me home?" she asks casually.

Sidharth smirks, setting his glass down. "Of course, Celine. Let's go."

They step outside into the cool night air. The once-bustling parking lot is now mostly empty, with just a few luxury cars still lined up under the dim streetlights. Sidharth leads her to his black Mercedes, unlocking the doors with a soft beep.

Celine slides into the passenger seat.

The roads remain silent, the dim glow of streetlights stretching endlessly ahead. Inside the car, an awkward tension lingers—partly from the weight of unspoken words, partly from the lingering effects of alcohol. The

air between them is thick, charged with something neither of them openly acknowledges.

Celine finally breaks the silence, her voice light but laced with curiosity. "So... are we getting a raise because of this new investment?" she teases, tilting her head slightly as she watches Sidharth's reaction.

Sidharth chuckles, gripping the wheel with one hand while his other lazily taps against the gear shift. "It's 100 crores to the company. Of course, salaries are going to increase." He glances at her, a slow smirk forming. "But when you get promoted to my life partner, maybe you'll get an even bigger raise."

Celine smiles at his words, but the awkwardness between them only deepens. A moment of hesitation passes, her fingers fidgeting slightly in her lap.

Because the truth is—Celine and Sidharth had been secretly seeing each other for the past five months.

The awkward ride continues in silence, neither of them saying much as the car glides through the dimly lit streets. Finally, they pull up in front of Celine's house. She exhales, pulling out her phone and dialing Artin. The call barely rings before he picks up, his voice groggy and disoriented.

"Artin, open the door. I'm at the front," she says, her tone neutral, almost cold.

A low hum escapes Artin's lips in response. He rubs his eyes, his body feeling heavy and weak as he forces himself out of bed. His legs feel unsteady beneath him as he stumbles toward the door, his mind still clouded with exhaustion.

With a sluggish motion, he unlocks the door, barely glancing at Celine before turning and walking away. He doesn't wait for her to step inside, doesn't say a word—just drags himself back to bed, leaving the door open behind him.

Celine changes into her nightwear and slips into bed, turning her back to Artin without a word. The silence between them is thick, heavier than the blankets that separate them. Artin exhales, staring at the ceiling for a moment before closing his eyes.

CHAPTER XVII

6 AM

Ring Ring— the alarm blares through the room.

Artin's eyes flutter open, his body instinctively moving to turn it off. He sits on the edge of the bed, running a hand through his messy hair, his mind hazy. The events of yesterday weigh on him. The experiment. The girl. The party. Celine.

He drags himself to the bathroom. As he looks up at the mirror. He doesn't want to go to work today. Not today. He makes up his mind—he'll take the day off. I should buy the ring today, he thinks to himself with some excitement.

After that he steps out of the bathroom and heads to the kitchen. Moving with practiced ease, he prepares Celine's breakfast like he always does—frying eggs, making toast, brewing coffee. The routine feels almost mechanical. Once everything is set, he walks to the bedroom and gently shakes Celine's shoulder.

"Celine, wake up. Breakfast is ready," he says softly.

She stirs, slowly opening her eyes, her expression neutral as she sits up. By the time she's ready and dressed for work, Artin is finishing up in the kitchen, wiping down the counter and placing the dishes in the sink.

As she walks into the dining room, he leans against the counter and says, "I'm taking a leave today."

Celine, halfway through pouring coffee, turns to him with mild curiosity. "Why?"

Artin exhales. "I don't feel okay after everything that happened yesterday."

Celine doesn't press further. She simply nods and takes a seat, slicing her toast. "Okay. Take rest. I'll take a cab to the office."

Artin with a hint of excitement says, "I'll pick you up in the evening."

She barely looks up from her plate. "Okay, as you wish."

The conversation ends there. Once she's done eating, she grabs her bag, adjusting her watch as she walks toward the door.

"Bye," she says simply.

"Bye," Artin replies, watching as she steps out. The door closes behind her, leaving him alone.

CHAPTER XVIII

He turns to head back to his room, inside his eyes land on the pendrive sitting on the drawer.

His fingers hover over it before finally picking it up.

He grabbed his laptop, powered it on, and plugged in the pendrive. A single file popped up on the screen as he opened the pendrive folder.

"Mephisto"

Artin frowned. What the hell is this?

He clicked on it. The screen flickered for a moment before a strange interface appeared—lines of code running across the screen.

Then, a message appeared:

"Hello, I am Mephisto, an AI designed by Lionsfield Corporation. To gain access, please enter your unique ID."

Artin's heart skipped a beat.

An AI?

This wasn't just files or evidence—this was something much bigger. Something connected to the very core of Lionsfield's operations.

Artin's mind raced, trying to think of a way in. A unique ID... what could it be?

His eyes darted around the room, searching for anything that could help. Then, his gaze landed on his office ID card, lying on the bedside table. He snatched it up, flipping it over.

On the back, printed in small, nearly unnoticeable letters, was a strange alphanumeric code:

"fkduohvzloouhwxuq1225"

His fingers hesitated over the keyboard. Could this be it? If he was wrong, the system could lock him out—or worse, alert someone.

But he had no other option. Taking a deep breath, he typed the code and hit enter.

For a moment, nothing happened. The screen remained still, the cursor blinking in eerie silence.

Then—

The screen flashed.

A message appeared in bold, white text:

"Welcome, Artin Samuel."

"B-Grade Scientist, Lionsfield Facility, Cochin."

Artin's stomach twisted.

It worked.

His heart pounded in his chest. This wasn't just some random software. It recognized him. It knew exactly who he was.

The screen flickered again, and new options appeared before him:

1. Research Logs

2. Clinical Trials

3. Restricted Documents

A cold sweat forming on his brow.

Mephisto wasn't just any AI—it was the key to Lionsfield Pharma's entire database. A system built to streamline research, providing instant access to vast amounts of classified data, from clinical trials to experiment logs. With countless research files, video recordings, and reports, Mephisto made it easier for scientists to retrieve information without sifting through endless documents manually.

Artin clicks on "Clinical Trials." The screen shifts, and a new set of options appears:

Test Subjects

Test Footage

Sample Records

His pulse quickens as he selects "Test Subjects."

The screen flickers. Seven photographs appear.

Each image is of a young girl, their faces blank, their eyes filled with silent terror. Under each photo, a status is listed:

Test Subject 1 – STATUS: DEAD

Test Subject 2 – STATUS: ALIVE

Test Subject 3 – STATUS: ALIVE

Test Subject 4 – STATUS: ALIVE

Test Subject 5 – STATUS: ALIVE

Test Subject 6 – STATUS: ALIVE

Test Subject 7 – STATUS: ALIVE

Artin's breath catches in his throat. They're all minors. A sharp pain stabs through his chest. His hands tighten into fists.

What the hell is this?

His fingers tremble as he moves the cursor, hovering over the next option—"Test Footage."

He clicks.

The screen changes.

"PLEASE ENTER THE PASSWORD TO ACCESS FILES."

Artin freezes. A password? He wasn't expecting that. His brain, still reeling from the photos, struggles to process. He needs to see these videos. He needs to know what happened to those girls.

But before he can think—

A new message flashes across the screen.

"ENTER PASSWORD IN 15 SECONDS OR DEVICE WILL SELF-DESTRUCT."

A robotic voice speaks, its tone eerily calm.

"15... 14... 13..."

Artin's heart slams against his ribs. Shit. Shit. Shit. He scrambles for ideas. His fingers twitch over the keyboard. Think! What could it be? A project name? A researcher's ID?

"12... 11... 10..."

His mind races, but it's like wading through quicksand. The shock, the fear—it's suffocating.

"9... 8... 7..."

His hands shake. There's no time.

"6... 5... 4..."

His breath is ragged. No choice.

In a flash, Artin lunges forward, yanks the pendrive from the port, and hurls it across the room—

BOOM!

A small explosion erupts, sending sparks and smoke into the air. Luckily nothing happens to his laptop. A faint burning smell lingers.

Artin stands frozen, his hands still trembling.

The evidence—the only proof—is gone.

Artin sits frozen in his chair, staring at the remnants of the small explosion. What just happened? His mind struggles to process it. His company—Lionsfield Pharma—was involved in something far darker than he ever imagined.

Slowly, he forces himself to clean up the mess. He shuts down his laptop and leans back, gripping the sides of the chair. Should he leave the company? The thought gnaws at him. Maybe he could propose to Celine and convince her to resign as well. Start fresh. Get away from all of this.

CHAPTER XIX

After a while, he pulls himself together and heads to the kitchen. He cooks lunch, though his hands feel mechanical, his mind still clouded. He barely tastes the food as he eats, lost in thought.

A glance at the clock—1:30 PM.

The ring.

The thought of buying the engagement ring offers a brief escape. Maybe this will clear his head. He washes the dishes quickly, changes into fresh clothes and exits his house.

He gets in his car. The drive to the store is quiet. Artin keeps his eyes on the road, trying to shake off the weight pressing down on him.

As he walks toward the store, he notices a protest encampment nearby. People holding signs, chanting—but he doesn't pay much attention. His mind is focused on the ring.

He enters the jewelry store.

A salesperson greets him with a warm smile. "Good afternoon, sir! How can I help you today?"

Artin replies, " hey, I'm looking for a diamond ring."

The salesperson nods eagerly and begins showing him different styles, different cuts, different price ranges. Artin goes through all of them all, but nothing seems to impress him. His mind slowly drifts away from the chaos of the day.

Then, the salesperson pulls out a tablet.

"Sir, this is our newest collection—these models haven't even arrived yet."

Artin scrolls through the designs, flipping through them one by one. Then he stops. His eyes fix on one. Simple, elegant, perfect.

"This one," he says. "I want this one."

The salesperson smiles. "Excellent choice, sir. This ring costs ₹7 lakhs. Would you like to pay now or when the ring arrives?"

Artin pauses for a moment, then pulls out his card. "I'll pay now. Deliver it to this address." He hands over his details and credit card.

As the purchase is being processed, he dials a familiar number.

Ring... Ring...

"Hello, Father Rafael."

Hearing the priest's voice brings him a small sense of comfort.

"Artin, my boy! How are you?"

Artin exhales. "Father, I have a small issue. I couldn't find the right ring, so I had to book one that hasn't arrived yet. The proposal will be delayed by about five days."

Father Rafael chuckles. "That's alright, son. No need to rush these things. Take your time."

"Thanks, Father. Also, when are you coming?"

"Most likely in three days."

"I'll be waiting for you."

"Good. Take care, Artin."

The call ends.

Artin tucks his phone into his pocket and steps toward the door, the weight in his chest feeling just a little lighter.

CHAPTER XX

As Artin exits the jewelry shop, his eyes dart to the protest outside, near the police station. Artin feels a spark of curiosity and wonders what the protest is about, but he walks towards his car. However, he can't resist. Seeing a man walk out of the protest encampment, he asks the man about it.

The man scoffs, "Do you not read any newspapers?"

Seeing Artin's embarrassed facial expression, the man understands Artin doesn't read any newspapers. He continues, "Just this month, five girls have committed suicide and seven have gone missing, all below the age of 18. A girl named Diya also went missing last week. The person hosting the protest is the mother of one of the girls who's gone missing."The man starts ranting and blaming the government. As Artin has no interest in politics, his eyes wander and he spots the photo of the girl on a poster held up in the protest encampment. To his horror, it's the same girl who died yesterday during the human trials of the drug. This revelation sends chills down his spine, he feels uneasy.

Seeing his reaction, the man asks, "Hello? Are you okay?"

Artin, pale, replies, "Yes."

He leaves the man and walks to his car, filled with despair and shock. His eyes slowly fill with tears as he can't take it anymore.Artin quickly gathers himself, realizing he's running late to pick up Celine from work. As he drives, his mind is elsewhere—he can't focus on the road. The revelation from earlier has shaken him to his core.

He finally arrives at the workplace, only to be scolded by Celine for being late. As they drive back home, Celine continues to shout at him, but Artin isn't paying attention. He is consumed by guilt and horror from the events of the day. Reaching home, Artin puts the food in the microwave before heading to the shower. As he washes himself, his mind races, and he thinks to himself, "No matter how much I try to clean myself externally, internally I'm filled with dirt from all my sins."

A deep suffocating guilt settles over him, he sits on the toilet seat, overwhelmed. He knows he must do something to stop this madness.

When Artin exits the bathroom, he finds Celine already eating dinner, watching television. He grabs a plate of food for himself and sits beside her. In a small voice, he says, "I want to tell you something."

Celine, without looking up, replies in a nonchalant tone, "What is it?"

Artin takes a deep breath and responds, "I think we should stop this." Celine, with an unpleasant expression, asks, 'What are you exactly talking about?' Artin says, 'I think we should resign from our jobs. We are literally being murderers! I don't want to continue this madness, no matter how much they offer us."Celine, who looks completely irritated by Artin's words, chimes back, 'Oh, come on, stop this nonsense, damn it! How many times have we had this conversation before?! What's gotten into you all of a sudden? Why are you trying to be a saint now? Do you think you can keep our lives flowing smoothly without this job? Huh? Everything was going so smoothly, and now, all of a sudden, you don't care about my happiness?"I do care about your happiness! That's why I signed up for this job in the first place!" Artin snaps. "Celine, this is not the way. We are not supposed to ruin others' happiness for the sake of our own!"

"Can you just stop caring about others? Be selfish sometimes in life!" Celine speaks with an angrier tone.

Artin replies, "I can be selfish for you, but not a murderer. We aren't being selfish; we are being literal murderers!"So what are you going to do, Saint Artin, plant a tree that grows money?" Celine replied mockingly.

"I am going to report all this to the police," Artin replied.

"Wow, amazing, absolutely spectacular idea, Saint Artin. You do realise the first people to be arrested will be us right?. So yeah, good luck with your path to grace," Celine said, her voice filled with sarcasm and threat.

Artin's frustration grew. "Celine, I am doing this for our future."

"Oh really? I don't know how that's going to help our future. Do whatever the hell you want," she snapped, storming off to their bedroom. She slammed the door violently behind her. Artin slowly tears up. He picks up Celine's plate. As he washes the dishes, a few drops of tears roll down his cheek. He sits alone in the kitchen, contemplating what to do next.

CHAPTER XXI

After some time, he goes to their room to apologize to Celine. As he enters the room, Celine pretends to be asleep. Mistaking her for being asleep, Artin does not disturb her. He sits at his work table in the next room and proceeds to work on his laptop. Slowly, his mind starts getting hit with more curious thoughts... He tries to brush them off at first, but eventually he gives in, he starts searching about the suicides and missing cases. Artin opens an incognito page on his browser, types "Kerala recent missing cases and suicides," and hits the search button. A headline from a national daily catches his eye:

"IS KERALA FALLING APART?"

He clicks on the article and begins to read.

Once known as "God's Own Country," Kerala is facing an alarming crisis. With a surge in drug overdoses, suicides, and disappearances, the state's safety is under scrutiny. This month alone, police have reported five suicides and seven missing minors, raising concerns about a deeper issue at play.

Victims of Suicide:

Ameya P Varghese – Age 17

Aradhya Manoj – Age 17

Shreya K Nair – Age 16

Satvika Manish – Age 15

Fathima Shiyaz – Age 15

Missing Persons:

Aleena Jacob – Age 18

Diya Gopal – Age 15

Aliya Muhammad – Age 16

Fidha Shareef – Age 17

Sara Ann Joseph – Age 15

Shameena Karim – Age 17

Mary Chacko – Age 15

Article by Ramesh Edapally.

Artin's breath catches as he scrolls down, his eyes locking onto the photos of the missing girls. All of them except for Diya are still alive!, kept as test subjects at the Sitrom factory.

A wave of panic crashes over him. His hands grow clammy, and his throat tightens. A cold sweat forms on his forehead. His heart pounds so hard he can hear it in his ears. His fingers tremble as he clenches his fists, his legs unsteady beneath him.

He grabs the water bottle in front of him, unscrews the cap with shaky hands, and takes a long sip, but the dryness in his throat lingers. The weight of everything—the suicides, the disappearances, the company's dark secrets—threatens to suffocate him.

His eyes dart to the drawer beside him. He pulls it open and retrieves a small bottle labeled Divertine. A drug synthesized by Lionsfield Pharma to help cope with stress and increase brain efficiency by many folds.

Without hesitation, he pops a pill into his mouth and swallows. His eyes flutter shut as he waits for the effect to kick in, for the chaos in his mind to settle, for the fear to dissolve into numbness.

But even as he sits there, waiting, he knows—this time, the pill won't be enough. Artin's eyes snap open as the pill kicks in, numbing his stress, his mind and body starts to calm down, and a faint sense of euphoria trickles through his veins. His mind, once drowning in panic, now feels sharper, more focused.

Lionsfield Pharma is behind the missing cases. He knows that for certain. But the suicides... they remain a mystery.

CHAPTER XXII

Determined, he keeps scrolling, his fingers moving faster across the trackpad. He skims through news articles, police reports, and social media discussions, searching for a pattern—something that connects the victims, something that makes sense.

Then, something catches his eye.

A Reddit post. **DRUGS ARE SOO EASILY AVAILABLE IN KERALA WTF?!**

Artin reads...

So this happened like two months ago. Me and my boys were having a sleepover, and for fun, we decided to check out the dark web.

At first, it was all fun. We found a lot of funny stuff there, like how to make homemade bombs—lol. But things took a dark turn when we entered a chat room called "Children of the Devil's Blood." Out of curiosity, we checked it out. To our horror, it was actually a drug market. They were selling a specific drug called Devil's Blood. We chatted with some of them for a while and found out that the drug causes extreme hallucinations and euphoria. They claimed that after taking it, you would literally float in the air and even meet the devil.

Ironically, one user said, "The drug feels like heaven."

They also dropped a link to a Chategram channel. That channel is like a community—there are around 60 users, I think—and it's all about Devil's Blood. People sell, buy, and share their experiences there.

But honestly, we were so freaked out that we didn't even check it out.

CHAPTER XXIII

Artin feels a connection between Devil's Blood and his company. When he first started working at Lionsfield Pharma, he overheard scientists talking about a drug called Devil's Datura.

Something tells him they're the same compound.

His curiosity deepens. Needing more answers, he scrolls down to the Reddit post's comment section.

To his surprise, the Chategram link is posted there too.

His hands hover over the keyboard, hesitating. His mind is sharp, but not sharp enough. He needs to be sharper.

His eyes flick to the drawer. Without hesitation, he pulls it open, grabs the Divertine bottle, and pops a pill into his mouth. He swallows dry.

Within seconds, a wave of focus washes over him. His senses sharpen, his thoughts accelerate—faster, clearer, more precise. The hesitation, the disgust—it all dulls, replaced by an eerie clarity.

He smirks.

Now, he's in control.

With renewed confidence, he quickly sets up his IP blocker and creates a new Chategram account under the name Aleena. His fingers move across the keyboard effortlessly, his mind two steps ahead of every action.

He clicks the link.

The page loads, taking him to a Chategram channel named Paradise.

A message appears instantly.

User: M or F? (Male or Female)

Artin exhales through his nose. He pauses, knowing exactly what answer will get him the most information. He types,

Aleena: F.

User: Age?

Aleena: 16.

A brief pause. Then—

User: Ohh cool, I'm 37.

Artin's smirk vanishes.

His fingers twitch over the keyboard. A sick, crawling feeling spreads through his veins.

He expected this. He knew the kind of filth lurking here. But seeing it spelled out so plainly in front of him makes his skin crawl.

A part of him wants to lash out, to type something vile, to expose his disgust. But he can't—not yet. He forces himself to inhale, slow and controlled, swallowing the revulsion clawing at his throat.

His grip on the table tightens. His stomach knots.

But he types.

The words feel like acid on his tongue.

He plays along.

For the next 30 minutes, he pretends to bond with the man, the conversation taking a darker turn.

User: I know you ain't here just to talk. So what are you really looking for?

Aleena: Just wanna get some fun inside my system.

User: What sort of fun we talking?

Aleena: I wanna try some new drugs.

The man immediately asks for a picture. Artin opens another incognito tab and uses AI to generate a disturbingly realistic image of a 16-year-old girl. His fingers press into the wood of the desk. His stomach twists, knowing exactly where this is going. He swallows down his disgust. He sends it.

Overjoyed, the user then asks for a voice message. Artin, using voice-changing software, records and sends a short clip.

The pervert falls for the trap completely.

User: Which drug you looking for, baby girl?

Aleena: I wish I got my hands on some Devil's Datura.

The user hesitates before replying.

User: That's kinda tough for you, baby.

Aleena: I thought we were friends? Please... can you help me?

Hook, line, and sinker.

The user sends a link.

User: This is a top-secret channel. You'll get all the drugs here, especially Devil's Datura.

User: But you need a passcode to get in.

Artin feels a rush of triumph—but it's short-lived.

Aleena: Oh? What is it?

User: I'll tell you... but only if you show me what's under your clothes.

Something in Artin snaps.

His fingers clench into a fist as pure disgust floods through him. But instead of engaging, he copies the link, switches back to his voice-changing software, and sends a final message—his voice laced with venom.

"Go die, you disgusting pedophile."

Before the user can respond, Artin blocks him, deletes the chat, and wipes the account from existence.

He quickly creates a new Chategram account under the same name, Aleena, refreshing his IP to stay untraceable.

Upon clicking the new link, Artin finds himself inside a channel named Devil's D is soo good.

A tingling sensation creeps up his spine. A wave of unease washes over him.

Suddenly, a user named Oldest Child starts typing.

Oldest Child: Hey, Girl. Lost? Wanna find a real fam for yourself?

Artin's breath catches. His hands grow clammy. His body feels cold.

But he forces himself to stay calm. Gathering his courage, he types back.

Aleena: Yes.

A moment later, the reply comes.

Oldest Child: First, you need to answer my question. Only then will you be allowed entry into this fam. Let me see if God sent you here... or the Devil.

Oldest Child: What is the code?

Artin remembers about the passcode the previous man mentioned. His mind races.

He hesitates but then types:

Aleena: Devil's Blood?

A pause.

Then—

Oldest Child: Haha, close... but not the answer.

Oldest Child: One more wrong guess, and you'll be blocked forever.

A brief pause.

Oldest Child: And just so you know... we have your IP address.

Artin's mind kicks into overdrive.

Frustration bubbles up, but then—

A thought strikes him.

Quickly, he types:

Aleena: Scopolamine D-factor 3?

A long pause.

Then—
Oldest Child: Congratulations. Welcome to the family.
A second later, a new invitation appears.
Artin reads the channel name.
His blood runs cold.
Hell in God's Own Country.
A crushing sense of dread tightens around his chest.

CHAPTER XXIV

The same overwhelming stress and anxiety from before resurface. His hands tremble, his breath quickens.

He needs relief.

Without thinking, he pops another pill of Divertine.

As the drug kicks in, a forced sense of calm washes over him.

His breathing steadies. His mind slows.

With dulled hesitation, he clicks on the link.

And enters the channel.

Inside, Artin is horrified by what he sees.

Drugs being bought. Secret locations exchanged. Videos on how to use them.

He keeps scrolling, stomach twisting with unease.

Then—his finger freezes.

A video and its title catches his eye.

*"The b**ch I was using suicided lol gotta find a new sl*t."*

Artin's breath hitches. His vision blurs. A wave of nausea crashes over him.

His body begins to shiver uncontrollably. His hands turn clammy, his heartbeat pounds in his ears.

Because the girl in the video...

Is none other than **Ameya P. Varghese.**

His breath turns shallow, strangled by the sheer horror unfolding before his eyes.

The video plays, shaky and raw—a selfie recording.

Ameya, her face drenched in tears, her voice trembling.

"Vishal, please... if you won't give me the drugs, I'll do it. I'll kill myself. Please, Vishal..."

Her pleas turn into desperate sobs, her body shaking uncontrollably. The video glitches for a second, then cuts to another recording.

This time, her face is twisted in pure anguish. Her eyes, swollen from crying. Her lips trembling. Her voice barely above a whisper.

"You're not gonna get me the drugs, right?!" she chokes out.

She shakes her head, slowly at first—then harder, as if trying to, will force reality itself to change. Then, suddenly—she slams it against the wall.

Once.

Twice.

A sickening crack echoes through the speakers.

"Alright then, I'm going to kill myself!"

She keeps hitting herself, harder, until blood begins seeping from her forehead, streaking down her face. Her sobs dissolve into broken whimpers. Her entire body trembles as she picks up a knife with unsteady hands.

Tears drip onto the blade. Her fingers tighten around the handle.

She stares into the camera, her lips quivering.

"This is what you wanted, right?" she whispers, her voice barely holding together.

And before Artin can even process what's happening—

She drags the blade across her throat.

A sharp, wet gurgle fills the speakers.

Blood gushes from the deep wound, spilling over her hands, staining her clothes.

She collapses.

The phone clatters to the ground, the camera still rolling—capturing her final moments. Her body twitches. Then stills.

Silence.

CHAPTER XXV

Artin shuts the laptop in disbelief.

For a moment, there is nothing. No sound, no thought. Just a vast, numbing emptiness.

Then—his breath hitches. The first sob rips through him.

He can't hold it back. He doesn't even try. His body shakes as the tears fall uncontrollably, his breath coming in broken, uneven gasps. He presses a trembling hand over his mouth, biting down hard to muffle the sounds—Celine is sleeping in the next room. She shouldn't wake up.

But the grief is unbearable. The horror. The guilt. It crashes over him like a tidal wave, pulling him under, drowning him in a suffocating darkness. His hands grip the edge of the table so tightly his knuckles turn white.

His nails dig into the wood. He grits his teeth, his entire body shuddering as the sobs wrack through him.

Then—

A violent convulsion rips through his body. A cold sweat breaks out across his skin. His heart slams against his ribs, erratic, too fast. His hands twitch. His muscles spasm.

The overdose. The stress. The horror. It's too much.

He stumbles to his feet, legs barely holding him up as he rushes to the bathroom. His knees hit the cold tile hard as he collapses in front of the toilet. He vomits violently, forcing everything out of him—his stomach lurching over and over until there's nothing left but dry heaves and pain.

His throat burns. Sweat drips from his temples as he slumps against the toilet, forehead pressed against the cold seat.

He barely has the strength to move. His breathing is ragged, shallow. Slowly, he slides down onto the floor, curling up against the cold tiles.

And then, he weeps.

Muffled, strangled sobs shake through him as he lies there—consumed by grief, by horror, by the trauma now stitched into his very being.

He can never erase what he saw. He can never undo what happened.

And worst of all—

He was too late.

CHAPTER XXVI

Artin staggers out of the bathroom, drenched in sweat and tears. His red, swollen eyes stare blankly ahead—haunted, hollow.

He moves like a ghost, slow and deliberate, back to the table. Collapsing onto the chair, he buries his face in his hands. Silent sobs shake through him. The weight of what he witnessed presses down on his chest like a crushing boulder.

Then—something shifts.

His sobs quiet. His breath steadies. He lifts his head.

With trembling hands, he reopens his laptop. His fingers move on instinct, scrolling through the Chategram channel once more. The horror doesn't stop. Video after video. More girls. More suffering. More deaths, laughed off as nothing.

His fingers curl into fists. His whole body shakes—not with fear, not with grief.

But with rage.

A fire ignites inside him, searing through his veins. Enough.

They all need to be exposed. Every last one of them.

But time is running out.

If he doesn't gather everything now, he'll be flagged as an intruder and locked out of the chatroom. He has one shot at this.

His gaze flicks to the Divertine bottle on the table. He knows the risk. His body is already at its limit. One more pill could push him over the edge.

But he doesn't have time to stop. Not now.

He hesitates for only a second before popping another pill. As it dissolves into his bloodstream, his pupils dilate. His mind sharpens. A terrifying, almost mechanical clarity takes over.

He grabs his old laptop—an untraceable relic, its IP encrypted beyond reach. Opening a blank document, he begins typing furiously. Names, messages, transaction records—every piece of incriminating evidence he can find.

His fingers blur across the keyboard, switching between both laptops, digging deeper, unearthing more. The report he crafts is airtight—solid, undeniable. A ticking time bomb, ready to take them all down.

Finally, he breaks through.

Hidden beneath layers of encryption, he finds them—the real IP addresses of every user in the channel.

No more anonymity. No more hiding.

His heart pounds as he opens his mail app. He attaches the files, his hands moving with urgency. He sends the report to every major national daily, to the Kerala police, to government agencies.

Then—just as he clicks send—

A wave of dizziness slams into him.

His vision distorts. The overdose hits like a freight train crashing into his skull.

His fingers twitch uncontrollably. His body starts shutting down.

His gaze snaps to the table drawer. The anti-Divertine. His only way out.

With fading strength, he yanks the drawer open, rummaging frantically. His hands shake violently as he digs through the clutter, breath coming in short, ragged gasps. His vision darkens.

Then—his fingers brush against the cold plastic bottle.

He grabs it, barely able to focus on the label. His consciousness teeters on the edge. With the last shred of willpower left in him, he forces the pill into his mouth.

His body goes slack. The room spins.

Darkness engulfs him.

CHAPTER XXVII

Artin's eyes flutter open, his body aching as if he had been hit by a truck. His vision hazy. For a moment, he doesn't recognize where he is.

Then he sees them.

Figures in black robes stand around him, their faces obscured by the shadows of their hoods. Their presence is suffocating, an unnatural energy crackling in the air.

Then—

"Artin... Artin... ARTIN!"

They chant his name in eerie unison, their voices deep and distorted. The sound drills into his skull, growing louder, faster. The figures close in, their hands reaching for him. His breath catches in his throat, his pulse skyrockets.

Panic grips him.

"No... no, this isn't real!"

He tries to move, but his body won't respond. His heart pounds as the figures reach out, their fingers just inches from his skin—

He screams.

And wakes up.

His body jerks upright, drenched in sweat, his chest

heaving. His heart slams against his ribs. He frantically looks around, to see if they are still looming over him.

But he's alone.

It was just a dream.

A sharp knock on the door makes him flinch.

"Artin!"

His breath still ragged, he turns to the door. It's not the robed figures calling his name. It's Celine.

Another knock, more urgent this time.

"Artin, wake up! We're late for work!"

He suddenly turns his head toward the clock on the wall.

9:00 AM.

Shit.

The realization slams into him—he never set an alarm. Celine always relied on him to wake her up, and since he had overdosed and stayed up all night... they both overslept.

Scrambling out of bed, his muscles scream in protest, his body still weak from last night. He swings the door open to see Celine standing there, a look of frustration and concern on her face. She looks at his face drenched in sweat and asks.

"Artin you look like you saw some kind of a ghost. Why didn't you wake me up?" she asks, tying her hair up hastily.

"I... I must've forgotten," he mutters, his voice hoarse.

There's no time to explain. No time to think.

They rush to get ready, throwing on their clothes in a frenzy. Artin moves on autopilot, his mind still sluggish, his body protesting every movement. Celine, equally frantic, pulls together her things, both of them moving with the urgency of people who know they're already screwed.

In a matter of minutes, they're shoving down their pre-cooked food, barely tasting it. Without Celine noticing Artin takes a tracker and puts it in his pocket. He grabs his car keys, and they bolt out the door.

CHAPTER XXVIII

The drive to work is silent, the only sound the hum of the engine and the occasional impatient honk as Artin speeds through traffic.

But in the back of his mind, the nightmare lingers.

And the echoes of the chant refuse to leave him.

As they reach the office, when Artin steps past the entrance, he hears a familiar voice.

"Dude, you look like hell" Arun says, stepping up beside him. His best friend, dressed in his usual button-up and blazer, eyes him with concern. "Didn't sleep?"

Artin forces a weak smirk, but it fades almost immediately. He exhales sharply, rubbing his temples.

"I'll tell you everything later," he mutters, his voice low and tired.

Arun raises an eyebrow, sensing the weight in his words.

As they head to their respective stations everything seems normal. The routine hum of work resumes, the sterile white lights buzzing overhead as employees shuffle between labs and workstations. Artin tries to look for the scientist who gave him the pendrive, only to find out the scientist is on leave disappointing him. He forces himself to focus, burying the events of the previous day deep within his mind. Celine, unaware of his turmoil, works beside him, lost in her own tasks.

The hours slip by uneventfully—until lunch break.

Just as Artin is about to step out of the lab for a short break, a message pops up on his work screen.

Sidharth (Executive Manager): All scientists, report to the main conference room immediately. Mandatory meeting.

A knot forms in Artin's stomach. Celine, sitting beside him, also receives the message. Their eyes meet, sharing the same confusion.

"Did something happen?" she asks.

"I have no idea," Artin replies, already pushing his chair back.

Arun joins them, asks "hey why is that idiot calling for a meeting?"

Celine replies "I don't know, it's not usual for him to call a meeting with all the scientists during this time of the day. Whatever"

The three of them walk toward the conference room, joining a stream of other scientists murmuring in confusion. The tension in the air is thick—meetings like this are rare, especially unannounced ones.

CHAPTER XXIX

Inside the room, Sidharth stands at the front, his expression unreadable. The large television screen behind him remains blank. As soon as the last scientist takes a seat, he clears his throat.

Without any introduction, he grabs the remote and turns on the screen.

A news broadcast.

Artin's stomach drops as the headline appears in bold red letters across the screen:

"EXCLUSIVE: SECRET DRUG RING EXPOSED—DEVIL'S BLOOD LINKED TO SITROM FACTORY?"

The air in the room shifts instantly. Some scientists gasp. Others exchange nervous glances.

Artin's eyes widen in shock, his pulse quickening.

On-screen, the news anchor speaks, her tone grave.

"Shocking new evidence has emerged regarding the distribution of a highly dangerous hallucinogenic drug, known as Devil's Blood aka Devil's Datura. Investigative reports suggest a connection between the drug and an underground network operating within the pharmaceutical industry. Sources claim that key compounds of this drug are being manufactured and supplied directly from the Sitrom Factory—"

A chill runs down Artin's spine.

He knew this would happen.

But not this fast.

Not this publicly.

Celine turns to him, eyes wide with disbelief.

"Artin... what the hell is going on?" she whispers.

But Artin can't answer.

Because right now, every pair of eyes in the room is glued to the screen.

And with every passing second, the walls are closing in.

Artin's breath hitches. His fingers twitch against the table as his mind races.

This wasn't supposed to happen.

In his report, he had never once mentioned Sitrom. He had deliberately left out any trace of it—because he and Celine worked there. He had exposed the users, their IP addresses, the channels, and their entire

61

network. But nowhere had he linked Sitrom to Devil's Blood.

So how the hell did the news find out?

Before he can process his panic, the anchor continues:

"Further investigations led to the raid of a suspected dealer's house late last night. Authorities recovered large quantities of Devil's Datura, packaged in small packets, all stamped with an unfamiliar symbol. Upon closer inspection, forensic analysts confirmed that this symbol once belonged to a logistics company Sitrom."

A murmur spreads through the conference room. Scientists exchange bewildered and uneasy glances. Some whisper to each other in disbelief.

Artin clenches his fists under the table. He feels his heart pounding against his ears

"But Sitrom shut down in 2026," the anchor continues. *"So how did its branding appear on drugs that surfaced just this year? Could it be that, in the shadows of this closed company, production never truly stopped? Is there a secret operation still running, manufacturing and distributing these deadly substances?"*

Artin glances at Celine, whose expression is frozen shock.

Sidarth, taking control of the entire situation, steps forward, his voice low yet commanding. "We are all in danger now." His sharp gaze sweeps across the room, his expression grim. "The police are closing in. There's going to be a raid."

A murmur of unease spreads through the gathered scientists, but Sidarth silences it with a single raised hand. "We need to clear out the factory before they get

there. I'll delay the raid as much as I can, but we don't have much time. Everything needs to be erased—every trace, every record, every experiment. We will shift everything to the new factory. "

Artin could have attached the information about the missing girls in the report but he feared doing so as he and his girlfriend still worked at the facility but he feels guilt for his selfishness.

So Artin's eyes light up hearing about the raid.

For the first time since this nightmare began, there's hope.

If the police storm the factory, they'll find everything. The missing girls—the test subjects. If they move fast enough, they can be saved.

His pulse quickens, but he keeps his expression neutral, hiding the flicker of anticipation rising in his chest.

Sidarth continues, unaware of Artin's silent revelation. "Grade B scientists—except Celine—you all head to the factory immediately. I'll be sending some... extra hands along with you." Artin knows exactly what that means. Goons. Enforcers who will make sure nothing is left behind—or no one.

"They'll help clear everything out faster," Sidarth goes on. "I want all the test subjects alive. Every document, every sample, every second of footage—pack it all up. Not a single scrap of evidence should remain."

His voice lowers even more, his next words slow and deliberate. "We were never there."

The weight of his command settles over the room, thick and suffocating. A cold sweat forms on Artin's back, his hands still clenching under the table.

Sidarth exhales sharply. "Move. Now."

The room erupts into motion. The 6 grade B Scientists including Arun and Artin scramble to their feet, chairs screeching against the floor. Some whisper in hushed, frantic tones, others move in eerie silence, already resigned to their orders.

CHAPTER XXX

Artin and Arun, both Grade B scientists, descend to the ground floor along with the others. The tension in the air is thick, almost suffocating. They step outside, where a black van waits for them.

The security guard—who is actually the designated driver—climbs into the front seat. Without a word, the scientists file into the back. Artin and Arun sit across from each other. The doors slam shut.

The van lurches forward, speeding towards Sitrom Factory.

Inside, no one speaks. The only sound is the hum of the tires against the road, the occasional jostle from a bump. Some of the scientists sit stiffly, staring out the window. Others exchange nervous glances, clearly unsettled by how fast things are moving.

Artin, however, has one mission.

He pulls out his phone under the cover of his lab coat and quickly types a message.

Artin: Turn on chat encryption. I have something to say.

He subtly glances up at Arun. Their eyes meet. Arun, frowning, gives him a questioning look.

Artin gives a small, barely noticeable nod.

Arun hesitates but then unlocks his phone. A few quick taps, and the chat encryption is activated.

A second later, Artin's next message appears.

Artin: I'm the one who leaked all the information.

Arun's fingers tighten around his phone. His head snaps up, eyes wide in disbelief. His jaw clenches like he wants to say something, but Artin subtly flicks his eyes toward the screen—read first, react later.

Arun lowers his gaze, his pulse picking up speed as he watches more texts appear.

Artin: I'm sick of this madness. I want to end this company once and for all.

Arun's heart pounds. His fingers hover over the keyboard. What the hell is Artin doing?

Arun: What happened all of a sudden to you?

Artin: Trust me, Arun. Stand with me now.

Arun exhales sharply. He types fast.

Arun: Dude, you're my bro. I will always stand with you no matter what. I'm just asking—what's with this whole rebel move?

Artin's fingers move swiftly over his screen.

Artin: You know we're all murderers. I'm sick of it. I can't pretend anymore. And I have a lot to tell you.

Arun's fingers tighten around his phone. His throat feels dry. He stares at Artin for a moment before typing back.

Arun: I know we're murderers, man. You think I don't hate this too? You know I'm only here to pay for my mom's treatment. I've always wanted to see this company burn to the ground.

Artin: I promise you, Arun. Your mom's treatment will not be interrupted.

A long pause.

Then—

Arun: It's okay, dude. I'll stand with you no matter what.

Artin finally breathes.

He grips his phone tighter. For the first time in this nightmare, he's not alone.

Arun is with him.

The van skids to a halt in front of Sitrom Factory. The place looks as lifeless as ever, its cold, grey exterior hiding the horrors within. The moment the doors slide open, everyone rushes out—scientists, goons, all moving with purpose.

Sidarth's orders are clear: Clear everything out. Leave no trace. Take all test subjects alive.

Artin's pulse hammers in his ears as he pushes through the main doors. The fluorescent lights flicker above them, barely illuminating the metallic walls and rows of abandoned equipment. Scientists and goons scatter in different directions, grabbing hard drives, wiping servers, stuffing documents into bags.

But Artin's focus is elsewhere.

The Grade A scientist's room.

He moves swiftly, Arun at his side, but as they approach, another scientist—one of the higher-ups—follows them inside. Artin clenches his jaw. Damn it. He was hoping to do this alone.

Inside the dull cold room, all the six girls are lying unconscious, fortunately alive.

A single overhead light flickers, casting eerie shadows across the room. The moment Artin sees them—alive—he exhales a silent sigh of relief.

His fingers dig into his lab coat pocket, feeling for the tracker he had prepared. He has to act fast.

The other scientist starts unlocking the restraints, his attention solely on the chains.

Artin kneels beside one of the girls. She barely reacts, her face hollow from dehydration, her lips dry and chapped. He reaches out as if to brush a strand of hair from her face—and in a swift motion, he tucks the tiny tracker into her hair.

His hand lingers for a brief second.

A silent promise.

Then he stands.

The scientist nods at him, confirming the girls are free. They pull them up, guiding them towards the exit.

The moment they step outside, the goons descend.

Artin grits his teeth as he watches them roughly shove the girls into another van. Like cargo.

His fists clench.

The scientist next to him doesn't react. Just another day at work for them.

Artin forces himself to stay calm, to not react.

Because soon—

All of this will end.

CHAPTER XXXI

The clearing-up is nearly complete. The factory—once a hub of horrifying experiments—is now stripped bare. Documents burned, data wiped, vials and samples packed away.

Artin watches as the last of the equipment is loaded into the van.

A goon—one of Sidarth's most trusted men—steps forward, cracking his knuckles before addressing the scientists.

"Listen up." His voice is rough, commanding. "We're shifting everything to another location outside the city. Keep your mouths shut and follow orders."

Arun, standing beside Artin, nods slightly. A silent confirmation. He's in. He's ready.

Slowly, the scientists pile into the van. The metal groans under the weight as the last few push their way in. Artin watches as Arun winks at him before squeezing into the crowded space.

Then—the realization hits.

There's no room left for Artin.

He turns to the head of the goons, the man in charge of transporting the test subjects. The van carrying the girls.

"There's no space," Artin says, keeping his voice casual. "Mind if I ride with you?"

The goon's face twists in hesitation.

He looks at Artin with doubtful eyes and says "boss doesn't like it when things that he haven't commanded happen".

A tense pause.

Then—finally—the goon exhales sharply and nods.

"Fine," he mutters, rubbing his jaw. "Just don't try anything stupid."

Artin climbs into the passenger seat. The door slams shut.

All the vans begin to move.

CHAPTER XXXII

Meanwhile, back at the office...

Celine steps into Sidarth's office, her expression tense.

"I have something important to say," she begins.

Sidarth barely looks up from his phone, tapping his fingers anxiously on the desk. His face is pale, beads of sweat forming on his temple.

"Not now, babe." His voice is curt, distracted. "Brother Charles will call at any moment. I'm sure he's been informed about the news."

Celine hesitates, studying his face. There's a flicker of something in her eyes—doubt? Suspicion?

"Alright. Call me when you're free. I'll be at my station."

With that, she turns and exits the room, leaving Sidarth alone in the tense atmosphere.

Then—the phone rings.

Sidarth freezes.

A cold sweat breaks out on his skin. He stares at the screen, the name glaring back at him.

Brother Charles.

His hands tremble as he reaches for the phone. He knows what's coming.

He presses accept.

A deep, bone-chilling voice fills the silence.

"Brother Charles here." A pause. Then, in a razor-sharp and menacing voice—"What explanation do you have for this, Sidarth?"

Sidarth swallows hard. His throat is dry. Words stumble out, barely coherent.

"S-Sir, I—I'm sorry. But we're taking every measure to cover our tracks. We won't be caught, I swear."

Silence.

Then—an explosion of fury.

"SHUT UP!"

Sidarth flinches as if struck.

"DO YOU HAVE ANY IDEA WHAT WILL HAPPEN IF THIS GETS OUT?" Brother Charles roars. "DO YOU HAVE ANY IDEA WHAT FATHER WOULD DO? HUH?"

Sidarth grips the edge of the table as he hears the name Father. Even hearing the name sends a shudder down his spine.

Brother Charles' voice lowers into something even more terrifying—a cold, emotionless whisper.

"Clear out everything."

Sidarth nods frantically, though the man on the other end cannot see him. "Y-Yes, sir. We're already moving everything out of the factory."

A pause. Then—

"Do we still have any test subjects?"

Sidarth hesitates.

His stomach turns.

"Yes, sir... six girls."

A slow exhale from the other side of the call.

Then, with chilling finality—

"Kill them. They are useless now. Just get rid of them."

The words settle into Sidarth's bones like ice.

His breath catches.

He stammers out—"O-Okay, sir."

The call ends.

Sidarth's hand is still gripping the phone, his skin clammy, his heartbeat erratic.

Slowly, he places the phone down, his mind racing.

The order has been given.

And now—there's no turning back.

CHAPTER XXXIII

As the call ends, the scene shifts.

The frigid winds of Russia's barren outskirts howl through the emptiness. Snow-covered plains stretch endlessly, the sky a dull gray.

A black luxury car sits in the middle of this wasteland.

Inside, bathed in dim light, sits Brother Charles.

A tall, athletically muscular man with a face of a hunter, there's something unsettling in his sharp blue eyes. He exhales a long drag from his cigar, the embers glowing in the dim interior.

There's a knock at the door.

A henchman opens it.

Charles steps out, the cold biting at his skin, though he doesn't flinch. He adjusts the cuff of his sleek black coat, exuding confidence.

Ahead, a group of Russian mafia members stand waiting. Behind them—thirty armed men and five black SUVs.

The tension is palpable.

The Deal Begins.

One of the Russian bosses, a broad-shouldered man with a thick beard, steps forward. His icy glare meets Charles' smirk.

"Your price is too high, Brother Charles," he says in a thick accent. "This is robbery."

Charles exhales a cloud of smoke. "Oh? I call it exclusivity."

The Russian scoffs. "We're not desperate enough to be cheated."

He signals to one of his men—who immediately draws his gun and aims it at Charles' chest.

Instantly, Charles' henchmen tense up, hands twitching toward their weapons.

But Charles?

He doesn't move. Doesn't even blink.

Instead, he smirks.

Then—the low roar of engines fills the air.

From behind the Russians, five more cars appear, speeding onto the scene.

The Russian men barely have time to react before—

Gunfire erupts.

The hidden reinforcements unload rapid, merciless rounds into the Russian bodyguards.

Men collapse. Blood stains the white snow.

Amid the chaos, the Russian boss panics—his grip tightening on the trigger. He fires.

A direct hit to Charles' chest.

But Charles doesn't flinch.

The bullet bounces off his bulletproof vest.

His smirk widens.

Before the Russian can react, Charles grabs the gun from his hands.

His voice drops dangerously low.

"I am very disturbed today..." He cocks the gun, pressing the barrel under the man's chin. "You just made the biggest mistake of your life."

The Slaughter Begins.

Most of the Russian bodyguards are already dead.

The five Russian mafia bosses stand frozen in horror—held at gunpoint by Charles' men.

Charles exhales, rolling his shoulders. "Don't kill these five." He cracks his knuckles. "I will."

His men step aside.

The five Russian bosses tremble, realizing what's coming.

Then—Charles charges.

What follows is not a fight.

It's a brutal execution.

Charles fights like a madman.

Bone-crunching punches.

Skulls caving under his fists.

Blood spraying the snow.

He moves like a beast unchained—grinning, laughing, ripping them apart with his bare hands.

One man tries to crawl away—Charles grabs his head and slams it onto the icy ground, again and again, until it stops moving.

Another begs for mercy—Charles stomps his face in.

The last man spits blood, barely breathing. Charles kneels beside him, voice eerily soft—"You should've taken the deal."

With one final punch, he crushes the man's skull.

Silence.

Charles, now bathed in blood, straightens up, breathing heavily.

Then—he laughs.

A low, hysterical chuckle that echoes in the cold air.

Charles turns to his men. "Burn the bodies. Execute the survivors. No loose ends."

His henchmen nod. The remaining Russian bodyguards—terrified, injured—are lined up and shot in the head.

The area is wiped clean.

Charles, still smirking, flicks his half-burnt cigar into the snow, before getting in to the car he orders one his henchman "get the private jet ready I am going to India" saying this he strides back to his car.

As he slides into the back seat, he wipes blood from his face with a silk handkerchief.

"Drive."

The car pulls away, leaving nothing behind but corpses and the scent of death.

CHAPTER XXXIV

Scene shifts back to the office.

Sidharth sits at his desk, his knee bouncing anxiously under the table. The weight of the situation presses down on him like a vice. His fingers hover over his phone before he finally dials. (The goon driving the van carrying girls)

The line rings.

Click.

A deep, gruff voice answers. "Yeah?"

Sidharth swallows hard. "Execute those girls. Get rid of the bodies."

A brief pause.

Then—a cold, indifferent reply.

"Hmm. Okay, sir."

The call ends.

Back to the Van.

The night is eerily silent as the van speeds down a deserted stretch of road.

Artin sits in the passenger seat, hands clenched into fists, his mind still racing from everything that's happened. The girls in the back—six of them laying unconscious.

Then—the van slows.

Stops.

Artin's brows furrow. "Why are we stopping?"

The driver—the head of the goons—doesn't answer.

Instead, he reaches for his gun from the dashboard.

Artin's stomach drops.

"Hey... what the hell are you doing?"

The goon grabs the door handle.

He finally speaks. "Don't get out of the vehicle."

His tone is flat. Final.

Artin's pulse spikes. "What? Why?!"

No reply.

The goon steps out, loading his gun as he moves toward the back of the van.

A sickening realization crashes down on Artin.

He's going to kill them.

A surge of adrenaline kicks in.

Artin throws the door open and jumps out.

"WHAT ARE YOU DOING?!" he yells, panic lacing his voice.

The goon doesn't even turn. "Shut up."

He reaches the back of the van and unlocks the doors.

Inside, the girls now conscious flinch, their terrified gazes darting between the armed man and Artin.

The goon raises the gun.

Artin lunges.

He slams into the goon's side, grabbing at his arm, desperately trying to knock the gun away.

The goon snarls, shoving Artin back with brute force.

Artin stumbles, his back slamming against the side of the van.

He doesn't care.

He lunges again, trying to stop him—but the goon swings.

A fist connects with Artin's jaw.

Pain explodes through his skull.

He barely has time to react before—another hit.

Then another.

Blood fills his mouth. His vision blurs as he is thrown out of the van.

Artin get on his knees, coughing, spitting crimson onto the dirt.

Through his haze, he sees the goon stepping into the van.

The girls inside begs in weak voice "water, please give me some water"

"PLEASE DONT KILL THEM!!" Artin cries, voice breaking.

But it's too late.

The goon raises the gun.

BOOM.

A gunshot rings through the night.

Then another.

And another.

The sound of screams—cut short.

Artin's heart stops.

His body trembles violently as the realization sinks in.

They're dead.

They're all dead.

The goon steps out of the van, wiping blood splatter from his sleeve.

Artin stares at him, his world collapsing.

His chest tightens. His hands shake.
A scream—pure anguish, pure rage—tears from his throat.
The goon's face darkens.
Then—a punch.
Artin collapses to the ground.
Another punch.
Another.
Blood pools beneath him as his consciousness starts to slip.
His vision darkens.
Then—
Nothing.

CHAPTER XXXV

Meanwhile, at the office, Sidharth calls Celine to his room.

Celine enters, still slightly tense from the earlier meeting. Sidharth, his fingers tapping impatiently on the desk, looks up at her.

"You wanted to tell me something earlier," he says. "What was it?"

Celine hesitates for a moment, then sighs. "It's about Artin."

Sidharth narrows his eyes. "What about him?"

Celine looks conflicted but finally speaks. "Yesterday... Artin and I had an argument. He was acting strange the whole evening, and then he said he wanted to quit the job."

Sidharth's jaw clenches. "Quit?"

Celine nods, lowering her voice. "He said he couldn't take it anymore. That he wanted out. And... and he even said he would report all of this to the police."

A heavy silence fills the room.

Sidharth leans back in his chair, his expression darkening. His fingers stop tapping. His hand tightens into a fist.

His voice, when he finally speaks, is dangerously calm.

"Are you sure he said that?"

Celine, nods. "Yes."

"Can you go to your house and investigate?" His voice is calm, but there's an underlying sharpness to it. "Check if Artin is the one behind this chaos"

Celine hesitates for a moment but then nods. "Okay. I'll go now."

As she leaves, Sidharth's phone buzzes. He picks it up, and the rough voice of the goon on the other end greets him.

"Sir, while getting rid of the bodies, we found something."

Sidharth frowns. "What?"

"A tracker," the goon says. "It was hidden in the hair of one of the girls."

Sidharth's grip on the phone tightens. His mind races—who could have planted it? Was someone watching them this whole time?

His voice turns cold. "Bring it to me. Now."

"There's one more thing, sir," the goon continues. "Artin... he tried to wrestle with me when I was executing the girls. He put up a damn fight." The goon lets out a short chuckle. "But I knocked him out. He's lying unconscious right now. What should I do with him?"

A slow smirk spreads across Sidharth's face.
"Bring him to me."

CHAPTER XXXVI

Scene shifts to Celine at Artin's house.

She steps inside, her heart pounding as she moves toward Artin's desk. She opens his laptop and starts searching through his files, but there's nothing suspicious—no reports, no documents.

A sense of frustration creeps in. Could she be wrong?

Then, suddenly, a memory flashes through her mind.

That morning, when she entered Artin's room, she noticed something—his old laptop was on the table.

Her breath catches.

She immediately begins searching the room. After rummaging through drawers and under the bed, she finally finds it. She takes it to the table and powers it on.

A password prompt appears.

Celine stares at it. Her fingers hover over the keyboard.

This laptop... it was the same one Artin used back in college.

Back when they were deeply in love.

A lump forms in her throat. Then, slowly, she types:

C-E-L-I-N-E

Her heart skips a beat as the laptop is unlocked and freezes seeing the screen.

For a moment, she just stares. The wallpaper is an old photo of them together—back when things were simpler, before the darkness of Lionsfield Pharma consumed them both.

Her fingers tremble, but she pushes past the emotions and clicks through the files. She scans document after document until—

Her breath catches.

There it is.

The report.

Everything. Every name. Every detail.

Celine's eyes widen as she scrolls through Artin's investigative notes. The weight of the betrayal settles deep in her chest.

Before shutting down the laptop, Celine's eyes land on a folder named "Celine and Me."

Something about it makes her pause. Her fingers hover over the touchpad, her chest tight with hesitation. But curiosity tugs at her, and before she can stop herself, she clicks it open.

What she sees knocks the air out of her lungs.

The folder is full of photos—their photos. Every moment they had captured together, frozen in time. Artin had saved them all.

Her breath catches as she clicks through them, each picture dragging her back in time. The laughter, the stolen kisses, the late-night drives. Their love—raw, real, untainted. She can almost hear his voice, whispering sweet nothings into her ear, promising her forever.

A tear rolls down her cheek. Then another.

For a second—just a second—she wishes things had stayed that way. That they had never walked into this darkness. That they were still just Artin and Celine, two lovers against the world. She wipes her tears away, forcing herself to pull back.

That world is gone.

It had been gone the moment she met Sidharth.

When Celine first joined Lionsfield Pharma, she was ambitious, full of dreams. That was when Sidharth

noticed her. Not just as a scientist, but as a woman. He saw something in her—her beauty, her fire, her hunger for more.

And he wanted her.

At first, it was just attention. He treated her differently, spoke to her with charm, made her feel special. She told herself it was harmless, that Artin was the only man she loved. But then Sidharth pulled his most dangerous move—trust.

He made her feel like she could rely on him. That he understood her in ways Artin never could.

Then 5 months ago, came the night that changed everything.

A party, disguised as a celebration. A ritual, hidden under flashing lights and flowing champagne.

She didn't understand at first, but the moment she stepped in, she felt it—the power, the dominance, the presence of something far greater than herself.

The room was bathed in deep red light, the scent of burning incense thick in the air. Strange symbols lined

the walls, carved into wood and painted in blood. A group of hooded figures chanted in low, guttural voices, their words unknown but haunting.

Then, the music stopped.

One by one, the figures turned toward her, their eyes gleaming under the hoods. A single voice broke the silence—deep, commanding, otherworldly.

"Are you ready to give yourself to the darkness?"

She should have said no.

She should have run.

But something inside her—some part of her she never knew existed—wanted this.

The chanting grew louder. The air grew heavy. She felt something pulling at her mind, her soul.

And she let it in.

That night, she became one of them.

Sidharth stood beside her, his hand on hers. "Power," he whispered. "Beyond your imagination. This world will bow before us one day."

And she believed him.

That night, they whispered to her about limitless control, world domination, the throne she could sit on. She saw herself there, ruling over a world that bent to their will.

And Sidharth? He promised it to her.

But he wanted something in return—her.

She let him have her.

And just like that, she crossed the line. The betrayal began.

Over time, Artin became an afterthought. Sidharth had consumed her mind, her heart, her body. The rituals, the power, the promises—they had taken everything she was and turned her into something else. She had stepped too deep into the cult's darkness, and now, she didn't want to leave.

But there was still one loose end—Artin.

If she told Sidharth the truth, if she confirmed that Artin was the traitor, they would get rid of him. He would be out of her life. She could finally be with Sidharth, free from the past.

Her heart pounded. She sat frozen in front of the screen, her mind spinning, tearing itself apart.

She had promised to love Artin forever. They had sworn to take their love to the grave.

But now...

She closed her eyes, and when she opened them again, the decision was made.

She picked up her phone.

She swallows hard and pulls out her phone.

With shaky hands she dials Sidarth.

The call barely rings before Sidharth picks up.

"It was him," she says, voice hollow. "Artin sent the report."

On the other end, there's silence. Then—

A low hum of amusement.

"Hmmm..." Sidharth murmurs, his voice laced with something unreadable.

Celine exhales shakily. She closes the laptop, ready to leave—when something catches her eye.

A small packet on the floor.

She bends down and picks it up. The label reads:

Tracker Chips.

Her stomach twists.

A creeping realization dawns on her.

Artin didn't just betray the company.

He planted a tracker.

Her fingers tighten around the packet, her mind racing with the implications.

She exhales, slipping it into her pocket before standing up.

Without another glance at the laptop, she turns and exits the house.

She needs to get back to Sidharth.

CHAPTER XXXVII

Celine gets in the car and drives to the office, but her mind is elsewhere. Distracted by the weight of her actions, she struggles to focus on the road, her grip on the wheel unsteady.

Finally, she reaches the office. She picks up her phone and dials.

"Sidharth, I've reached."

"Hmm. Come to the basement," he replies.

Celine enters the building and steps into the elevator. She swipes her access card, and the panel blinks green, granting her entry to the basement level.

Alone in the lift, she tries to drown out her thoughts by listening to the soft elevator music playing through the speakers. But it does little to calm her.

"Basement reached."

The robotic announcement makes her heartbeat quicken. A wave of unease washes over her.

Reaching into her handbag, she pulls out a small bottle—Divertine.

She twists the cap open and pops a pill just as the elevator doors slide open. The anxiety dulls, her mind regaining composure.

Straightening herself, she steps out of the elevator.

The dark, silent basement is dimly lit by flickering lights. Shadows dance across the cold concrete walls as Celine walks toward the storeroom.

As she steps inside, her mind falters—a split-second of disorientation. Her foot catches, and she nearly stumbles, as she sees him.

Artin, strapped to a chair, unconscious. A single overhead lamp casts a harsh glow on his face.

Behind him, Sidharth and the head of the goons stand in silence. The air is heavy, thick with tension. The room is quiet, yet every corner is occupied by Sidharth's men, their presence suffocating.

From the shadows, Sidharth steps forward, a cold box in his hands, its surface catching the dim light.

He smirks. "So, here's the black sheep."

He lifts the box slightly, letting its metallic sheen glint under the lamp.

"I called Brother Charles. And according to him, there's only one punishment for betrayal."

He pauses, his voice chillingly casual.

"Death."

Celine nods, her expression unwavering as she speaks with a chilling confidence. "Do it. Hail Father Mortis."

Sidharth smirks, his eyes gleaming with amusement. He opens the box, a syringe sits inside of it, covered in the cold fog.

"Do you know what this is?" he asks, his tone dripping with irony. "It's funny, really—because this is the ODFC sample Artin himself processed. As you know, Celine, within three hours, he'll slip into a coma. In five hours, he'll be dead from cardiac arrest."

He chuckles darkly before adding, "Don't worry—I'll make sure it looks like nothing more than a natural death."

Sidharth takes the syringe in his hand and presses the needle into Artin's arm. A faint noise escapes Artin's lips as the sharp tip pierces his skin. Celine watches, her eyes devoid of guilt or hesitation.

Almost instantly, Artin's body jerks—his muscles tightening as violent convulsions take over. His vision blurs into darkness, panic surging through him as he struggles against his restraints. But the goons hold him down with ease. Moments later, his body goes limp, his consciousness slipping away.

The goons lift Artin's unconscious body and shove him into the back seat of Celine's car. Sidharth takes the driver's seat, while Celine settles beside him in the passenger seat. The silence is deafening, the vehicle speeds through the night, heading straight for Artin's house.

Upon arrival, Sidharth and Celine carry Artin inside, his weight heavy between them as they drop him onto his bed. His breathing is shallow, his fate seemingly sealed.

Sidharth turns to leave, but Celine follows him to the door. He pauses, looking back at her, his gaze lingering. The tension between them thickens, an unspoken desire crackling in the air. Without another word, they lean in, their lips crashing together in a feverish kiss. One touch leads to another, their restraint unraveling.

Moments later, they disappear into the room next to where Artin lies unconscious—succumbing to their darkest impulses.

The sound of the rain muffles the remnants of their reckless night.

CHAPTER XXXVIII

As morning breaks, Celine stirs awake, her body still heavy with exhaustion. Slowly, she rises and walks toward the room where Artin had been left unconscious. But the moment she steps inside, her body turns to ice.

Her breath catches in her throat.

Artin is sitting up on the bed—disoriented, his face pale and drenched in sweat. His fingers press against his temple, his eyes squinted in pain. His other hand absentmindedly scratches at the spot on his arm where the syringe had pierced his skin.

Then, his gaze lifts.

He sees her.

"...Celine?" His voice is weak, strained, as if speaking takes every ounce of his remaining strength.

Celine stands frozen, disbelief gripping her. This isn't possible. He should be—

Snapping out of her shock, she blurts out, "I—I'll be right back. I left the front door open." Without waiting for a response, she turns and bolts out of the room.

Her heart pounds as she rushes to the other bedroom. She shakes Sidharth awake, panic lacing her voice. "Wake up. Wake up now."

Sidharth groggily blinks at her, annoyed. "What the hell, Celine?"

"Hide in the bathroom," she hisses urgently.

Still half-asleep, Sidharth frowns. "What? Why?"

"Just do it," she whispers fiercely, shoving him toward the bathroom door. "Now!"

Sidharth grumbles but obeys, disappearing inside.

Celine barely has a second to collect herself before stepping out of the room, her breaths shaky.

But the moment she turns the corner, her stomach drops.

Artin is standing there, weak and dazed, swaying slightly. He looks at her through half-lidded eyes, his body barely holding itself together.

Celine lets out a startled gasp, clutching her chest. "You nearly scared me to death!" she blurts. Then, regaining composure, she quickly adds, "Why are you even up? You shouldn't be straining yourself."

Without giving him time to think, she wraps her arm around his and guides him back to his bed. Artin collapses onto it, his breathing shallow.

"What happened yesterday?" he groans, his voice barely above a whisper. "I feel... so sick. My head is spinning."

And then, without warning, his body lurches forward, and he begins to gag.

Celine quickly grabs him, leading him toward the bathroom. Artin falls to his knees, violently vomiting into the toilet.

She kneels beside him, rubbing slow circles on his back as he heaves, his body trembling with exhaustion.

Minutes pass before the retching stops. Artin's body slumps, drained. Celine helps him clean his face and guides him back to bed.

He curls up, wincing in pain. His breaths are uneven, but he's alive.

Terrfying Celine more than anything.

Celine rushes back to the other room, her heart pounding, only to find Sidharth standing there, still half-dressed, gripping his pants with a look of utter confusion. He looks like an idiot.

She barely stops to catch her breath before blurting out, "Artin... he isn't dead."

Sidharth's face twists in disbelief. "What the f—?! Are you kidding me?!"

"We don't have time for this. You need to leave—now." Panic sharpens her voice.

Sidharth runs a hand through his hair, still struggling to comprehend. "How the hell am I supposed to leave?!"

"I don't know! Just go!" she snaps, frantically pulling open the wardrobe. She grabs a random t-shirt and shoves it into his chest. "Put this on and get out—I'll come to you as soon as I can."

Muttering curses under his breath, Sidharth throws on the shirt, grabs his shoes, and bolts out of the house.

Now standing outside, he realizes he looks like an absolute mess—barefoot, in a wrinkled t-shirt and professional dress pants. He sighs in frustration, running a hand down his face.

Spotting an approaching auto-rickshaw, he waves it down. The driver slows to a stop, sticking his head out to get a good look at him.

His gaze sweeps Sidharth from head to toe. He frowns.

Sidharth clears his throat. "Asset Apartments. Near Lionsfield Pharma office."

The driver pulls back, his nose wrinkling in disgust. "Did you even brush?"

Sidharth glares. "Just drive."

Rolling his eyes, the driver mutters something in annoyance before pulling away, leaving Sidharth slumped in the back seat, feeling both embarrassed and absolutely done with this morning.

Sidharth sits in the rickshaw, completely stunned. His mind is spiraling, trying to process what just happened. How the hell is Artin still alive? His grip tightens on his knees as the vehicle jerks through traffic, his stomach churning with unease.

CHAPTER XXXIX

Back at the house, Celine steps into Artin's room. His voice is weak, barely above a whisper.

"Make some hot water for me... I need to shower. I smell like garbage."

Celine nods quickly. "Okay, I'll prepare it." She heads to the kitchen, filling a pot with water to heat. As she waits, she leans against the counter, trying to catch her breath. Her mind is racing. This is f*ing impossible. How is he alive?! This is bad. This is so, so bad.

Once the water is hot, she pours it into a bucket and carries it back to the room, her hands trembling slightly. Artin slowly gets up, still disoriented. Celine helps him to the bathroom, supporting his weight.

Artin turns on the tap, letting cold water mix into the bucket until it reaches a comfortable temperature. As he does, he catches a glimpse of himself in the mirror. His breath falters. His body looks... different. He looks leaner, like he's lost weight overnight. Confusion flickers across his tired face.

Shaking the thought away, he takes a mug, scoops some water from the bucket, and pours it over his head. As the hot water cascades down, his muscles tense. His eyes squeeze shut.

Then—flashes.

Vivid, disjointed images from the previous night flood his mind. His breath quickens. His fingers twitch. His heartbeat rise. But he keeps pouring the water, hoping—desperately—that the heat will wash away whatever is clawing its way to the surface.

Artin finishes cleaning himself and wipes his body with a towel, feeling slightly better. His head is still foggy, but at least the warm water has helped ease some of the discomfort. Wrapping the towel around his waist, he steps out of the bathroom.

"Celine, can you get me a T-shirt and shorts?" he asks, his voice still a little weak.

From the kitchen, Celine replies, "I'll get it, wait a second." She walks to the other room, rummaging through his wardrobe. She pulls out a plain T-shirt and a pair of shorts before heading back.

As she approaches, her eyes unintentionally land on him—standing half-naked, his damp skin still glistening from the shower. Her gaze lingers for a second longer than it should. He... he looks different. The thought sneaks into her mind before she quickly shakes it off. "No, it's nothing. Just stress. Exhaustion. That's all."

Artin takes the clothes from her and starts putting them on while Celine turns toward the kitchen, trying to distract herself. She opens the oven and places some food inside to heat it up, her mind still unsettled.

Celine calls out from the kitchen, "Food's ready...!" before quickly taking a plate for herself and heading to the shower, biting into her breakfast as she walks. She doesn't waste a second—there's no time to think. She needs to get to the office.

As she showers, Artin heads to the kitchen. His stomach aches with hunger, and the moment he sees the food, he starts eating—almost too fast, shoveling the bites in like he hasn't eaten in days.

Celine finishes her shower, quickly dries off, and gets dressed in record time. As she steps out of the room, fixing her hair, she stops in her tracks—Artin is sitting at the dining table, eating with an unusual intensity. Something about his posture, the blankness in his eyes, makes her uneasy, but she pushes the feeling away.

Artin finally stops chewing and looks up at her, his voice eerily flat. "They killed those girls. I tried to stop it, but I couldn't... After that, I don't remember anything. What the hell happened, Celine?"

For a moment, Celine freezes. Then, instinct kicks in—she quickly crafts a lie.

"Sidharth found out that you fought with the goon. He was furious when he heard about it. He even reported it to Brother Charles, and..." she pauses, faking hesitation. "Brother Charles ordered them to kill you."

Artin's face remains unreadable, so she continues, her voice softer, more desperate. "I begged Sidharth to let you live. I pleaded with him, and he—he was merciful. He let me bring you back home." She lowers her gaze, playing her final card. "For the sake of our relationship, please, Artin... stay out of this. Stop fighting them. I don't want to lose you."

A tear slips down her cheek. A fake one, of course.

Artin sighs, his resolve visibly crumbling as he reaches out to hold her hand. "I'm staying out of this. Stop crying... I'm sorry. I'll stop everything."

Celine wipes away her tears and nods. "Okay..." She exhales, as if relieved, before grabbing her bag. "I'm going to the office now. Stay here and rest."

Without waiting for his reply, she walks out, shutting the door behind her.

CHAPTER XL

Artin sits at the table for a moment something Celine said doesnt sit right. He thinks to himself "will Sidharth really call brother Charles just to inform about a fight i had with one the goon?" He feels a bit suspicious but brushes it off. Then, slowly, he gets up, leaving the plate in the sink. He turns on the tap, letting the cool water run over his hands. As he washes, his eyes drift to the mirror above the sink.

His breath catches.

The wounds on his face, the bruises on his arms—already fading. The cuts from the scuffle last night should have been fresh, raw. Instead, they were closing up as if days had passed.

His fingers trace over a deep scratch on his jaw. What the hell...?

A creeping sense of unease settles in his chest, but his body feels too drained to care. Shaking off the thought, he dries his hands and walks back to the bedroom. The moment he hits the bed, exhaustion crashes over him. His mind is too battered, too overwhelmed to keep up with the thoughts racing in his head.

He just wants to sleep.

He just wants to forget.

Just as his eyes begin to shut—

RING! RING!

The sudden vibration of his phone jolts him upright. He glances at the screen.

Father Rafael.

Artin's distressed face finally lights up at the sight of the caller ID. A wave of relief washes over him as he picks up the call, his voice cracking with emotion—happiness laced with pain.

"Father..."

On the other end, Father Rafael's warm, familiar voice carries a note of concern. "Artin, my boy, you sound troubled. What happened, again had a fight with Celine?"

Artin hesitates for a moment, swallowing the lump in his throat. "It's nothing, Father. I just... I wish I could see you right now."

Father Rafael chuckles gently. "Well then, I have some happy news for you. Guess where I am?"

Artin's voice, suddenly filled with hope and surprise, "You're here...?"

"Yes, my boy," Father Rafael confirms, his tone light and reassuring. "I arrived at St. Paul's Church this morning."

Artin sits up, his fatigue momentarily forgotten. "Father, just wait for 15 minutes—I'll be there."

"Okay, but don't rush," Father Rafael says with a laugh. "Drive safe, hmm?"

Artin manages a small smile. "I will, Father."

CHAPTER XLI

Cutting back to Sidharth—

The auto-rickshaw comes to a halt in front of his apartment. Sidharth steps out, still reeling from the shock of what happened. His mind is a mess. He barely registers handing the driver the fare before trudging inside.

The moment he enters his apartment, he heads straight for the shower, hoping the hot water will clear his head.

It doesn't.

Even after getting dressed, as he sits at his dining table, absently chewing on his breakfast, his thoughts remain tangled. Should he call Brother Charles?

His fingers hover over his phone. His stomach churns at the thought. No. If Brother Charles found out that Artin was still alive, he wouldn't just be angry—he would be furious.

Sidharth shoves his phone aside. Not yet.

He heads to the company.

By the time he arrives, Celine is already there, engaged in conversation with Arun.

Arun's brows furrow. "Where's Artin?"

Celine doesn't hesitate. "He's sick. Fever, I think."

As she speaks, her gaze locks onto Sidharth's. He doesn't say a word, but his expression is enough. She knows—he wants to talk. Now.

A few minutes later, Celine makes her way to Sidharth's office, closing the door behind her.

Sidharth exhales sharply. "How the hell is this possible? He was supposed to die. Did I inject the wrong syringe?"

Celine's face is frozen. "Sidharth, I have no idea how he's still alive. Did you tell Brother Charles?"

"No. Should I?"

Celine hesitates, then shakes her head. "Let's wait until evening. See if he even makes it till sunset."

Sidharth leans back, rubbing his face. "And what if he does something stupid in the meantime?"

"He won't," Celine assures him. "I convinced him to stay out of this. For now."

Sidharth exhales through his nose, shaking his head in disbelief. "I can't believe this. Brother Charles will kill me if he finds out I failed."

Celine studies him carefully. "Are you sure you injected him with the right sample? Not the placebo?"

Sidharth lets out a sigh. "There is no placebo for

ODFC-4. The sample was sent from Laos two weeks ago. It's already killed fourteen test subjects there. And one here. How the hell is he not dead?"

CHAPTER XLII

Meanwhile at the house, Artin for the first time in what feels like forever, feels like he has a reason to move forward.

Artin quickly gets ready and steps out of the house with his weak legs, only to realize—Celine took the car to work. Frustration washes over him. He doesn't have the strength to walk far or wait around for an auto-rickshaw, he tries to walk forward but his legs are still powerless. Standing at the front door, he sighs in disdain, feeling utterly drained.

Then, an idea strikes him.

Divertine.

If it enhances his mental state, could it also help his physical condition? He rushes back inside, grabs the bottle from his bedside drawer, and pops a pill. The effect is immediate—his body collapses for a brief moment as if his body is trying to reanimate his dying state, but within seconds, he jolts back to full awareness. His senses sharpen, his muscles feel less fatigued, and his posture stabilizes.

Just in case, he grabs the Anti-Divertine bottle and shoves it into his pocket before heading out again.

He waits anxiously by the roadside, scanning for a ride. After what feels like forever, an auto-rickshaw finally pulls up.

"St. Paul's Church," he tells the driver.

The rickshaw speeds through the streets, but Artin's mind is elsewhere. He debates with himself—should he tell Father Rafael everything? Would the priest understand? Could he even help?

By the time the rickshaw reaches the church, Artin is no closer to an answer. He pays the driver through his phone and steps out, his heart pounding.

Walking through the church's grand wooden doors, he immediately spots Father Rafael sitting in the front pew, speaking to the parish clerk. Artin's eyes slowly tear up seeing father Rafael, he looks at Father Rafael and feels sense of holiness. Despite being blind, the priest sits with an air of wisdom and peace.

Artin takes a deep breath and approaches.

"Father."

At the sound of his voice, Father Rafael's face brightens. He gets up, his arms instinctively reaching out, searching for Artin. The moment his hands find him, he pulls him into a tight embrace.

"Artin!! My son, it has been so long. Hmm... you feel slimmer than the last time we met." The priest runs his hand over Artin's face, then chuckles, "Ew, why is your beard so overgrown?"

But as his fingers brush against a wound on Artin's cheek, his expression darkens. His tone shifts.

"What happened son?"

Artin takes a deep breath, his voice trembling. "Father, I need to confess."

Hearing the weight in his words, Father Rafael immediately signals the parish clerk to leave. Artin gently takes the priest's hand, guiding him toward the confession booth.

As Rafael settles into his chair, Artin steps inside—only to feel a sudden dizziness. His vision swims, his limbs go weak. He grips the wooden panel for support, but the world tilts.

His body gives out.

He crashes to the ground, his breath hitching as a violent tremor wracks his muscles.

"Artin?! Son?!" Rafael's voice rises in panic. The priest drops to his knees, blindly reaching for him. His hands find Artin's shoulder, then his face—cold sweat, clenched jaw, convulsing muscles.

Artin's thoughts are frantic. No—no, not now! Not in front of him!

His fingers fumble desperately in his pocket. He finds the Anti-Divertine bottle, but his grip is weak. The cap won't budge. His body jerks again, and it slips from his grasp, rolling across the floor.

"Artin, what's happening to you?!" Rafael pleads, hands still on him.

With sheer willpower, Artin lunges forward, snatching the bottle just before it rolls out of reach. His shaking hands finally pry it open. He shoves a pill into his mouth and nearly chokes, his throat dry.

CHAPTER XLIII

Seconds pass. His breathing stabilizes. The tremors fade. But Rafael has seen everything with his blind eyes.

A long, terrible silence.

Rafael kneels beside him, his face shadowed with something deeper than concern—fear. His fingers brush Artin's cheek, tracing over a healing wound.

His voice is low, almost a whisper. "What have you done to yourself, my son?"

Artin breaks.

Tears well up, unbidden. His chest tightens, his hands clutch his head, his whole body trembling—not from the drug this time, but from the weight of everything.

"Father, I'm in so much pain..." His voice cracks.

"Please... help me."

Rafael's heart clenches.

"Tell me, my son. Whatever it is, just tell me."

And Artin does.

Not all at once—but piece by piece.

He speaks about Celine first. The argument.

Then, Lionsfield Pharma. Their experiments. Their power. The truths they buried.

Rafael exhales sharply. "...This is much worse than I thought."

Artin hesitates before revealing the executions. The girls. Their screams. The blood.

Rafael goes still. The air in the booth thickens.

"God have mercy..." the priest murmurs. His voice is resonating pain, he is hollow like a man staring into the abyss.

Artin presses his palms to his face. "I don't know what's happening anymore, Father... I feel like I'm losing my mind."

Another silence.

Father Rafael suddenly hugs Artin tightly, pressing a reassuring kiss to his forehead. His voice is gentle but firm.

"Artin, if you push forward like this, you won't make it. You need time—to think, to recover. Let the dust settle, but don't let your guard down.

When the time is right, we will fight back."

He makes the sign of the cross over Artin.

"All your sins have been forgiven in the name of the Lord and our Saviour, Jesus Christ."

Father Rafael, holding Artin's hand speaks,

"Jesus carried a cross far heavier than we can imagine. With every step, it grew heavier—burdened by the sins of the world. But he did not give up. He endured. One must carry his cross inoder to attain greatness. And Jesus is always with you."

His voice softens.

"Go home, my son. Rest. Take the Bible and read it. Let His words be your strength."

Father Rafael calls the parish clerk and asks him to drop Artin home. As Artin settles into the car, a faint sense of relief washes over him. The weight on his chest hasn't lifted completely, but for the first time in a long while, he feels like he can breathe.

As they drive, the parish clerk tries to break the silence. "So, how do you know Father Rafael?"

Artin stares out the window for a moment before answering. "My father died when I was young. My mother... she wasn't well. Father Rafael took me in. He raised me like his own."

The driver shifts uncomfortably, realizing he's touched on something heavy. "Oh... ayyo, sorry for asking."

Artin shakes his head. "It's fine."

The Driver (glancing at Artin through the mirror) trying to lighten the mood asks "You look like you haven't slept in days, Work stress?"

Artin (quietly): "Something like that."

Driver: "That's why I left my last job, the stress will kill you before old age does, so what do you do for a living?" the driver asks.

Artin hesitates. He doesn't want to talk about it—doesn't even know what to say. After a long pause, he finally mutters, "I don't work anymore. I used to be in pharma."

Driver: "Pharma? Big money, ah?"

Artin (after a long pause): "Yeah... too big."

The driver nods and doesn't press further.

Eventually, they reach Artin's house. His legs feel weak as he stumbles to the front door. His hands tremble, making it difficult to fit the key into the lock. After several tries, he finally gets the door open and steps inside.

His stomach was making weird noises while he was stepping in without thinking much of it, he heads straight to his room. He pulls open a drawer, rummaging through it with shaking hands. His fingers finally touch something familiar—a book coated in dust. His Bible.

CHAPTER XLIV

Artin grips the Bible, his fingers trembling as he wipes away the dust. He hesitates before opening it, the pages dry and stiff from years of neglect. His eyes land on the first verse that catches his gaze. He decides to read whatever page appears first.

As Artin opens the Bible, his tired eyes land on a passage—Deuteronomy 20:1-4.

Going to War

"When you go to war against your enemies and see horses and chariots and an army greater than yours, do not be afraid of them, because the LORD your God, who brought you up out of Egypt, will be with you.

When you are about to go into battle, the priest shall come forward and address the army.

He shall say: 'Hear, Israel: Today you are going into battle against your enemies. Do not be fainthearted or afraid; do not panic or be terrified by them.

For the LORD your God is the one who goes with you to fight for you against your enemies to give you victory.'"

Artin's breath catches in his throat. His hands tighten around the book.

Was this a coincidence? Or was God speaking to him directly?

He keeps reading, flipping through the pages, letting the words soak into his soul. His mind, once a storm of doubt and pain, begins to calm. The weight on his chest doesn't feel as suffocating anymore. His heartbeat steadies.

For the first time since waking up, he doesn't feel lost.

Suddenly, a sharp, stinging pain shoots through Artin's stomach. His entire body weakens, his limbs trembling. A hunger—deep, primal, and unbearable—consumes him. It's unlike anything he has ever felt before.

He gasps, clutching his stomach, his breath shallow. The Bible slips from his hands, hitting the bed with a soft thud. But even in his desperation, he refuses to leave it on the floor—he grabs it, placing it on the bed before collapsing onto his knees.

His vision blurs. His body screams for food. He tries to stand, but his legs fail him. Crawling, dragging himself across the floor, he makes his way to the fridge, every inch forward feeling like a battle against his own body.

Reaching the handle, he yanks the fridge open. Inside, stacks of frozen processed meat. His hands move on their own, tearing into a packet with his teeth. The cold flesh meets his tongue, but he doesn't care. His body demands sustenance.

He devours one pack. Then another. And another. The hunger doesn't stop.

By the time he's done, twenty packets—nearly ten kilograms of raw meat—have vanished into his stomach.

A deep, guttural burp escapes him. He leans back against the fridge, his chest rising and falling, sweat dripping down his face.

Something is wrong.

Something is very, very wrong.

CHAPTER XLV

Artin dozes off after devouring the ungodly amount of raw meat. Time moves forward, the sun dips below the horizon, and evening sets in.

His sleep is restless. Flashes of the previous night invade his dreams. Blurred images, distorted voices—then suddenly, a sharp, vivid vision.

Celine, she was standing in front of him. He sees her face. He sees the syringe.

Artin jolts awake, drenched in sweat. His body feels different—stronger. His breathing is ragged. He hears a car pull up outside.

Celine.

She enters the house cautiously, her heart pounding. She wasn't alone—Sidharth is waiting in the car, watching. She steps inside, expecting to find Artin unconscious or dead.

But then—he opens the door.

Celine freezes.

Something about him looks... wrong. He's sickly pale, but there's a dangerous energy in his stance. His eyes are dark, sunken, yet burning with something primal. He looks like a starved animal.

She forces a smile, avoiding his eyes. "How are you feeling, honey?"

Artin doesn't answer right away. His gaze is locked on her, searching. Then, in a cold voice—

"Celine. What happened yesterday?"

She lets out an awkward chuckle. "Didn't I tell you? Sidharth forgave you and let us go."

Artin's expression darkens. His fingers twitch. "You're lying."

Celine stiffens. "Artin, just calm down, okay?"

"SHUT UP!" Artin's voice shakes the walls. "I REMEMBER EVERYTHING!"

His breathing is erratic, his pupils dilated. He grips his forearm, nails digging into the faint injection mark. "YOU TRIED TO KILL ME. YOU INJECTED ME. WHAT THE HELL WAS IT?!"

Celine takes a step back. Artin takes a step forward.

His hands tremble. His eyes glisten with rage and betrayal.

His voice drops, lower, pained— "You were betraying me, right?"

Celine stammers. "No, Artin, I wasn—"

"DON'T LIE TO ME!" Artin roars.

Hearing the shouting from outside, Sidharth grips the metal rod on the car floor.

He moves fast, stepping inside without Artin noticing, picking up a metal rod from near the doorway. Artin is too blinded by rage to hear his footsteps.

BANG!

A metallic clang echoes through the room. A sudden, searing pain explodes at the back of Artin's skull.

His vision distorts. The world spins.

He turns—slowly.

Sidharth stands behind him, panting, clutching the rod, his face twisted in fear.

Artin blinks, staggering. His head throbs, blood dripping down his temple. His knees buckle.

Everything goes dark.

CHAPTER XLVI

Sidharth pulls out a small bottle from his pocket, his hands still shaking. He uncaps it, leans over Artin's unconscious body, and sprays the sedative directly onto his face.

Celine watches, her breathing uneven. "We need to be sure," she mutters.

Sidharth nods and sprays more.

Artin lies sprawled in the backseat, his face ghostly pale, his clothes soaked in sweat. His smartwatch vibrates weakly, flashing a dangerously low heart rate alert.

Celine grips the steering wheel and starts driving.

Sidharth, still panting, pulls out his phone. "I'm calling Brother Charles," he says, his voice edged with fear.

Celine doesn't hesitate. "Do it. End this madness once and for all."

Sidharth swallows hard and dials.

After a few tense rings, the line clicks.

Brother Charles.

"Brother Charles here. Speak."

Sidharth grips the phone tighter. "Sir... it's about that B-grade scientist—the one who caused all this chaos."

Brother Charles's tone sharpens. "Artin?"

"Yes, sir. Him."

A brief silence.

Then, Brother Charles's voice drops to a lethal coldness. "Didn't I already tell you to kill that bastard?"

Sidharth flinches. "We tried. We injected him with ODFC-4, but..." He hesitates, his throat dry.

"But he's not dying."

A sudden, deadly silence.

Then—Brother Charles explodes.

"What?! What do you mean he's not dead?!"

Sidharth stammers. "I—I don't know, sir! We followed protocol! The dose was straight from Laos—it killed 14 test subjects there and one here too! But Artin... he just won't die."

Brother Charles breathes heavily on the other end, his anger palpable. He pauses, debating whether to inform Father Mortis.

But the thought alone sends a chill down his spine.

No. If Father Mortis finds out about this failure... it'll be more than just Artin's life on the line.

Finally, his voice turns cold, decisive.

"I'll kill him myself."

Sidharth's stomach drops. "Sir, are you here?"

"Yes. I reached Cochin this morning—because of your incompetence, you f-cking idiot!"

Sidharth grips the phone in terror.

"Bring him to the new Sitrom factory where you shifted everything."

Without waiting for a response, Brother Charles hangs up.

The line goes dead.

They speed off toward the new Sitrom factory on the outskirts of Cochin. The car cuts through the darkness, headlights slicing through the misty night.

CHAPTER XLVII

As they drive, Sidharth grabs his phone, his hands still trembling. He dials a secure number.

"Get to the facility. Now."

A cold voice on the other end answers, "How many men?"

"Everyone. And bring the A-grade scientists."

Without another word, the call disconnects.

By the time they arrive, a small army of goons and scientists is already waiting.

The moment the car stops, the goons pull Artin's body out, dragging him like dead weight.

Artin, barely conscious, fights to stay awake. His vision is hazy, his ears ringing. Through sheer instinct, his fingers flicker over his smartwatch, discreetly turning on the voice recorder.

The goons strap him to a metal chair, binding his wrists and ankles.

A scientist plugs in a vitals monitor. The screen flickers—his heartbeat is dangerously slow.

Then—the sound of roaring engines.

Everyone in the facility turns their heads as two cars screech to a halt outside. The engines snarl, their presence signaling the arrival of something far more terrifying than just another man.

A henchman rushes forward, opening the car door.

And then—he steps out.

Brother Charles.

Dressed in a pristine white suit, a lit cigar dangling between his fingers. His devilish eyes concealed behind dark sunglasses.

He walks with slow, deliberate confidence, exuding an aura so oppressive that the entire room falls into silence.

His men follow behind him like a pack of wolves.

Inside, the scientists freeze.

Then, one by one, they lower their heads and kiss his hand as he walks past.

Sidharth and Celine follow suit, their lips brushing against his knuckles in fearful obedience.

Brother Charles stops before Artin.

Without hesitation, he grabs a fistful of Artin's hair, jerking his head up.

Then, with the other hand, he takes a slow drag from his cigar.

And plunges it into Artin's forearm.

A sharp sizzle.

A faint "Ahhh..." escapes Artin's lips. His eyes flutter open.

Brother Charles grins, his voice silk-smooth, dripping with menace.

"You want to destroy my company?" He chuckles. "This is not a company, you fool."

He leans closer.

"This is a family. The Lionsfield Family. Devil's Family."

His grin widens. "And when someone touches my family... I finish them off."

Artin lifts his head, his gaze dark and unwavering.

Then—he spits in Brother Charles's face.

Silence.

Brother Charles's smile vanishes.

Slowly, he lifts a hand—

And strikes.

A brutal punch crashes into Artin's face, blood spraying onto the cold floor.

Artin spits out a tooth. His expression remains emotionless. Dead inside.

Brother Charles's breathing turns ragged, his rage boiling over.

"Bring me another ODFC sample!" he barks.

A nearby scientist flinches and scrambles toward the storage unit. With shaking hands, he retrieves a **syringe gun—**one capable of injecting three doses at once.

Brother Charles grabs the gun.

Without hesitation, he slams it into Artin's chest.

And pulls the trigger.

A searing shockwave of pain explodes through Artin's body.

His scream tears through the air.

Brother Charles watches, his eyes gleaming with sick pleasure.

He pulls the trigger again.

Artin's body arches violently, veins bulging. Another agonized scream rips from his throat.

Then—one final trigger pull.

The syringe gun clicks empty.

Artin convulses violently, his heartbeat skyrocketing.

210... 211... 212...

The vitals monitor screams its warning.

His veins pulse. His body trembles.

Artin lets out one final, ear-splitting scream.

The vitals monitor spikes violently—270... 280... 290... 300.

Then—silence.

A single, piercing beep.

The line goes flat.

His body slumps, lifeless.

The scientists hesitate, staring at the monitor. One of them, with shaky hands, steps forward, checking his pulse.

"He's... dead."

CHAPTER XLVIII

Brother Charles exhales, a slow, satisfied breath. His lips curl into a smirk.

"Good."

He straightens his suit, then turns to his men.

"Get the body. Take it to Medicity Hospital."

His voice is calm, cold, matter-of-fact.

"I've arranged everything. They'll stage it as a cardiac arrest. Make it look like he tripped and fell in his bathroom."

As the goons unstrap Artin's wrists, Brother Charles continues, his tone suddenly shifting—casual, almost amused.

"Sidharth, I'll be staying here for five days."

Sidharth, still shaken, nods.

"On the third, I'm hosting a party," Brother Charles says, adjusting his cufflinks. "We need to clean up the chaos this bastard caused. I'll be inviting government officials, powerful people, my mercenaries..."

His smirk widens.

"Bring your men and the scientists too. They'll love it."

Then, his expression darkens slightly.

"After the officials leave, we'll have a ritual."

Sidharth tenses.

"We need a sacrifice," Brother Charles adds, his voice dripping with eerie finality. "For protection."

He steps forward, placing a firm hand on Sidharth's shoulder.

"Oh, and no weapons."

His smile returns, unsettling.

"No one brings weapons inside. Understood?"

CHAPTER XLIX

After Brother Charles left the facility, the goons carried

Artin's lifeless body into a blacked-out van, the air thick with the scent of sweat and old leather. Sidharth and Celine followed behind in their car, their silence heavy with unease.

As they approached Medicity Hospital, the area felt disturbingly quiet. The dim, flickering streetlights cast long, unnatural shadows over the cracked pavement.

At the main gate, the van rolled to a slow stop, its tires crunching against gravel. The driver lowered the window, the stale air inside mixing with the damp night breeze.

The security guard, a frail man with dark circles under his eyes, barely reacted. His expression was blank, like he had done this a hundred times before.

"Delivery from Brother Charles," the head goon muttered.

The guard exhaled through his nose, his breath visible in the cold air. He glanced briefly at the van but didn't ask questions. Instead, he spoke in a low, almost robotic tone:

"Back gate."

Then, his sunken eyes flicked toward Sidharth and Celine's car. "That vehicle with you?"

The goon nodded once. "Yes."

A slow pause. The guard's lips barely moved. "Alright. They go through this gate. You—back entrance."

The head goon leaned out the window, signaling Sidharth to reverse. Then the van's engine rumbled as it backed up, disappearing into the dark alley that led to the rear of the hospital.

Sidharth and Celine drove forward, passing through the front gate. From the outside, Medicity looked ordinary—fluorescent lights, uniformed nurses, the sterile bite of phenyl in the air. But something felt off.

As the van rumbled through the back entrance of Medicity Hospital, its tires splashing through shallow puddles on the cracked asphalt, the place felt unnervingly still. The only source of light came from a dim, flickering bulb above the back door—its weak glow barely cutting through the darkness.

Waiting under the sickly yellow light were a nurse and two hospital staff, their faces blank, almost emotionless. They stood in perfect stillness, like silent sentinels, their eyes already fixed on the black van rolling to a stop.

The van's engine groaned to silence as the goons climbed out, their movements quick but practiced. The hospital staff wordlessly wheeled a stretcher closer, the wheels squeaking against the damp pavement. No questions were asked. No hesitation.

One of the goons opened the van's rear doors, and a cold gust of air seeped out—carrying the stifling scent of sweat, iron, and something else... something off.

Artin's pale, lifeless body was still strapped, his skin clammy under the weak glow of the hospital light. His chest no longer rose and fell. His smartwatch remained silent, the last recorded heartbeat long gone.

The goons grabbed Artin's limp body and hoisted him onto the stretcher, the thud of dead weight unnervingly loud in the quiet night.

That's when the doctor arrived—walking briskly, his white coat billowing slightly. Unlike the nurse and staff, his face showed no tension, no concern. His movements were precise, as if this was nothing more than another routine case.

His cold, calculating gaze swept over Artin's body for less than two seconds before he raised a single hand—a silent gesture that spoke volumes.

Leave.

The goons exchanged quick glances before stepping back, knowing their part was over. The doctor didn't wait. Without a word, he turned on his heel, motioning for the nurse and staff to take the stretcher inside.

As the hospital doors hissed open, an odd sterile chill poured out—a sharp contrast to the humid night.

CHAPTER L

As the stretcher rolled through the bustling hospital corridors, the usual sounds of a late evening in Medicity Hospital filled the air—patients murmuring, the beeping of monitors, the occasional distant cry of a baby from the maternity ward. The fluorescent lights shone steadily, casting a pale glow over the tiled floors, which carried the faint scent of disinfectant.

A few bystanders and hospital staff loitered near the reception desk, some waiting for updates on their loved ones, others scrolling through their phones. No one paid much attention to the stretcher being wheeled past, the body on it covered up to the chest with a thin white sheet.

From an adjacent hallway, The Chief Doctor, Mr Ali joined them. His expression unreadable, his white coat crisp and spotless. As his gaze landed on the stretcher, his face didn't betray a single flicker of concern.

"So, this is the delivery?" he asked, his tone even.

The other doctor, walking just behind the stretcher, gave a small nod. "Yes. Arrived just now."

The nurse walking alongside kept her eyes ahead, silent. The hospital staff pushing the stretcher moved with steady efficiency, guiding it toward the restricted area near the mortuary.

Dr Ali spoke again, his voice just above the hum of the hospital's background noise. "And what's the official story?"

"Cardiac arrest" The other doctor's voice remained neutral. "They also want it to look like he tripped in his bathroom and hit his head."

Dr Ali gave a slow nod as they reached an unmarked door. "Alright. That should be simple enough." He gave a glance toward the unmoving figure on the stretcher before looking at the nurse. "Make sure he's tagged accordingly. No unnecessary procedures."

The nurse only nodded as the door swung open, swallowing the stretcher into a quieter, more restricted part of the hospital. Behind them, life in the hospital went on as usual—people pacing, doctors making rounds, and the low murmur of conversations blending into the sterile, routine chaos of the night.

CHAPTER LI

Sidharth and Celine stepped into the hospital lobby, the sterile scent of antiseptic thick in the air. The soft murmur of bystanders and the occasional ring of a telephone filled the space, but for Celine, it all faded into the background. She sat down on a chair at the reception, her leg bounced anxiously, her fingers gripping the armrest of the chair.

The beeping monitors behind the reception desk made her tense. The rhythmic pulse of the machines dragged her back to the facility, to the monitor's frantic beeps as Artin's heartbeat skyrocketed beyond human limits. The memory made her stomach twist. He's dead now. It's over. Then why does it still feel like he's here?

Sidharth, however, showed no hesitation. He walked straight to the Chief Doctor Ali, exchanging a few quiet words before turning back to Celine.

"Wait in the car," he muttered, tossing her the keys. His voice was firm but slightly strained.

Celine didn't argue. She took the keys and left, feeling the weight of the moment pressing down on her chest.

Inside the restricted room the chief doctor, the previous doctor, and a new one dressed in surgical gear stood around Artin's lifeless body, with Sidharth standing at the edge of the room. The air was eerily quiet except for the soft rustling of latex gloves and the faint hum of medical equipment.

They began removing Artin's clothes, preparing to clean the body for its staged accident. As they worked, the Chief Doctor's hand suddenly froze.

His sharp gaze landed on a sleek, black smartwatch strapped to Artin's wrist.

The room went still.

The Chief Doctor exchanged a quick glance with the others before silently unbuckling the watch and handing it to Sidharth.

Sidharth took it, his fingers gripping it tightly as an uneasy feeling crept into his chest. The screen was dark, but if Artin had been recording...

His pulse quickened as he pulled out his phone and dialled.

Brother Charles answered almost immediately.

"He had a smartwatch on him," Sidharth said, his voice low, almost a whisper. "I think he was recording us."

A brief silence. Then, a slow, amused chuckle crackled through the receiver.

"Just bury it with him," Brother Charles said. "So the evidence is gone forever just like him." Another short laugh.

Sidharth hesitated for a second before shoving the watch into his pocket.

Outside the room, he slumped into a chair, rubbing his face with his hands. The doctors continued their work behind the doors—meticulously cleaning Artin's body, closing wounds, and smoothing out bruises.

Everything needed to be perfect. A body that looked clean. A story that sounded clean.

CHAPTER LII

It was almost 4AM, Sidharth had dozed off in the dimly lit hospital hallway, the exhaustion from the night catching up to him. His head bobbed forward slightly, but before he could sink into sleep, a hand firmly gripped his shoulder.

He jolted awake.

Standing over him was the Chief Doctor, his face as impassive as ever.

"The work is done," the doctor said, his voice calm but clinical. "You can inform the relatives or anyone else who needs to know and we have recorded his death so from today 4 AM onwards Artin Samuel is dead, I have informed the reception so anyone can visit and see the body under your presence."

Since the death was ruled as a cardiac arrest, no police investigation would follow. There would be no inquiries, no suspicions—just a routine documentation of another life lost too soon.

Now only one thing remained, to inform everyone and close this chapter forever.

Once the calls were made, the messages sent, and the condolences acknowledged, it would all be over. Artin Samuel would be officially dead, his name fading into the past, erased from their lives as if he had never existed.

The hospital staff wheeled Artin's lifeless body through the cold, sterile corridor leading to the mortuary. The hum of fluorescent lights filled the air, blending with the faint echoes of distant voices and the occasional rattle of a stretcher being pushed elsewhere. The hospital never truly slept, but to Sidharth, the place felt eerily detached from reality.

He walked out through the back door, his steps slow and heavy. His mind wandered aimlessly.

CHAPTER LIII

Outside, the air was thick with humidity, the remnants of the previous day's heat lingering in the morning. He spotted Celine in the car, her head tilted against the window, her breathing steady. She had fallen asleep.

Sidharth knocked on the car window. A sharp tap.

Celine jolted awake, her eyes darting around in confusion before she spotted him. She fumbled to unlock the door.

He slid into the driver's seat, exhaling deeply as he leaned back against the headrest. His body felt like a hollow shell, his voice barely carrying any strength as he spoke.

"The cleanup is complete," he muttered. His hands trembled slightly as he reached into his pocket and pulled out Artin's smartwatch. The cold metal pressed against his palm.

"Here." He handed it to her, avoiding eye contact. "I took this from his body. Brother Charles told me to bury it with him—so tomorrow, when they dress him up for the funeral, give this to them. Make sure he's wearing it when they put him in the coffin."

Celine stared at the watch in her hands, the weight of it sinking into her palms. The screen was dark, lifeless, just like the man who had once worn it.

She swallowed hard, nodding without a word.

Sidharth exhaled, rubbing his temple and continued. "Does Artin have a family? Just inform whoever you know, and let's arrange a proper funeral so that no one gets suspicious."

Celine, still shaken but composed, nodded. "Actually... he doesn't really have any close family. His father passed away when he was only ten, and that left his mother mentally unstable. She was never really there for him."

She hesitated for a moment before continuing. "But... there's a priest, Father Rafael. He practically raised Artin. Artin mentioned last week that Father Rafael was being transferred to the church here. I'll call him—he might know if Artin has any distant relatives. I'll also inform his college friends."

Sidharth considered this for a moment, his expression cold and even though he is exhausted by everything, he is calculating every outcome. "Hmm... that should do. Make sure the funeral doesn't seem rushed. It needs to look natural—like a proper farewell. No one should feel that something is off."

Sidharth leaned back in his seat, his fingers tapping against his knee impatiently. He let out a tired sigh before asking, "What's the time?"

Celine glanced at her phone. "4:09 AM."

Sidharth nodded slowly. "The time of death has been recorded as 3 AM... so everything lines up. Call Father Rafael now and tell him exactly this—"

He cleared his throat and began dictating, his voice calm but firm.

"Father... Artin had started drinking a lot over the last few weeks. I tried to stop him, but he wouldn't listen. Last night, he came home late... barely able to stand. He just stumbled into bed, and I was so angry at him for coming home drunk again that I didn't pay much attention.

Around 2 AM, he went to the bathroom to vomit. At first, I didn't think much of it—I was still mad. But then... the vomiting stopped, and there was complete silence. I waited a little while, but something felt wrong. When I went to check... he was lying there... unconscious.

I rushed him to the hospital, but it was too late, Father... Artin passed away from a cardiac arrest..."**

Sidharth paused, looking at Celine with narrowed eyes. "And make sure you sound like you're actually crying. He needs to feel that grief in your voice, like you're truly devastated. Can you do that?"

CHAPTER LIV

Celine swallowed hard, her grip tightening around her phone. Her voice was steady, but her eyes held a flicker of unease. "I'll do it."

Celine's fingers trembled slightly as she scrolled through her contacts, her breath uneven. She found Father Rafael's number and stared at it, hesitating. Her mind raced, silently rehearsing the words she needed to say.

She inhaled sharply, held her breath for a second, and exhaled slowly. Just say it exactly how Sidharth told you.

Her thumb hovered over the call button. She glanced at Sidharth.

"Put it on speaker," he mouthed, his eyes locked onto her with a quiet intensity.

Celine nodded stiffly and pressed the button.

The phone rang.

Each ring felt heavier, dragging on longer than it should. Her heart pounded in her chest.

Then, a faint, groggy voice answered.

"Hello?"

It was Father Rafael—his tone confused, laced with sleep.

Celine's mouth parted slightly, but no words came out. She froze, gripping the phone tighter.

Sidharth's eyes widened slightly, silently urging her to speak.

Her lips trembled, her throat tightening.

Celine swallows hard, forcing herself to steady her breath. She clears her throat, trying to suppress the tremor in her voice before finally speaking.

"Hello, Father... it's me, Celine."

There's a pause.

Father Rafael's voice, still groggy from sleep, responds with mild confusion.

"Which Celine?"

She hesitates for a split second before replying, "Artin's girlfriend."

The change in his tone is immediate. His voice, now filled with concern, comes through the speaker.

"Oh, Celine! What happened, child? Why are you calling so early? Is something wrong with Artin?"

Celine grips the phone tighter. She forces herself to inhale, then exhales shakily.

"Yes, Father..." she says, her voice laced with distress.

She pauses—just long enough for the weight of what she's about to say to settle in her chest. Something presses against her throat, making it harder to speak.

Her breath wavers as she continues, "For the last couple of weeks, Artin... he's been drinking a lot. Almost every night, he comes home late... drunk."

Her voice weakens, her words beginning to break apart under the weight of the lie she's weaving.

"We fought about it—constantly. Last night, it was the same. He came home late again... completely drunk. He just stumbled into bed, but I... I didn't speak to him. I was angry."

She sniffles, the panic in her voice more real than she expected.

"Around 2 AM, he got up and went to the bathroom to vomit. He always does that when he drinks too much, so I didn't think much of it. But then... after a while... everything just—"

She swallows, struggling against the lump forming in her throat.

"Everything went silent."

Her breathing shudders.

"I didn't check on him right away. I... I was still upset. But then, after some time, I got worried. I went inside and..."

Her breath hitches, and suddenly, she feels something genuine clawing its way up from inside her—a sinking, suffocating feeling pressing down on her chest.

"...he was lying there, unconscious."

Her voice cracks, her composure slipping.

"I—I tried to wake him up, Father, I really did, but he wouldn't wake up..."

Her words dissolve into a painful whisper.

"I rushed him to the hospital, but—"

She stops, squeezing her eyes shut, and then, finally, the words break through.

"It was too late."

A deafening silence follows.

Then, in a frantic, panic-stricken voice, Father Rafael asks,

"Celine... what are you saying? What happened to Artin??"

Celine's breath catches in her throat. Tears spill down her face as the final words escape her lips, trembling and shattered.

"Father... Artin is gone."

She breaks. A raw, uncontrollable sob rips through her.

Sidharth watches in silence, his eyes widening slightly. He hadn't expected this.

Not the trembling hands.

Not the real tears.

Not the way her shoulders shook as she cried into the phone.

Sidharth watches as Celine crumbles under the weight of her own words. For a moment, he hesitates—then, without thinking, he leans in, wrapping his arms around her trembling frame. He holds her tightly, feeling her body shake against his chest.

On the other end of the line, Father Rafael's voice is thick with grief.

"Where are you? I mean... which hospital is he kept at?"

Celine's breath shudders as she wipes her wet cheeks, trying to compose herself. Her voice, though strained, remains steady enough to reply.

"Medicity Hospital, Father."

A pause.

"Okay, I will come there, child. Don't cry." Father Rafael's voice is pained—his voice breaks, he is struggling to not cry. Grieving, yet still, he tries to comfort her.

But before he can hang up, Celine speaks suddenly, her voice hollow yet urgent.

"Father... one more thing."

She swallows hard.

"I don't really know much about Artin's relatives. If you can... can you please inform them? Because, Father... I just... I just can't talk anymore."

Father Rafael replies, his voice gentle yet burdened.

"Don't worry, child. I will inform everyone, I will come there as fast as i can."

The call disconnects.

CHAPTER LV

Celine drops the phone from her ear, her fingers still gripping it tightly. Then, she breaks down completely. A raw, quiet sob escapes her lips as she clutches onto Sidharth's hand, seeking an anchor in the storm of emotions swirling inside her.

She looks up at him, her bloodshot eyes filled with something deeper than just grief—something darker, something heavier.

"I just don't know, Sidharth..." she whispers. "Are we going too far?"

Sidharth's grip on her tightens. He looks at her, his expression unreadable. Then, in a voice firm and unshaken, he speaks the words that have always guided him.

"It takes a lot of sacrifices to rule the world... just think of this as one among them."

CHAPTER LVI

5:00 AM – The Hospital

Father Rafael arrives at the hospital, accompanied by the parish clerk, Peter. The moment he steps out of the car, a heavy weight settles on his chest. His boy—his Artin—is gone.

He pulls out his phone with trembling hands and dials Celine's number.

"Celine, I'm here at the hospital. Where is my Artin kept?" His voice is raw, barely holding back his grief.

A few feet away, Celine steps out of a black car, discreetly signaling Sidharth to keep his distance. She hesitates before answering, her throat tight.

"Father, please wait at the reception. I'm coming."

She makes her way toward the hospital entrance, but her legs feel weak beneath her. Every step is heavy, burdened with the weight of her guilt and grief.

At the reception, Father Rafael stands gripping Peter's hand tightly—not just for support, but because his body feels like it might collapse under the sorrow. His sightless eyes search the space around him as if hoping that somehow, against all reason, Artin might still be there.

Celine approaches. "Father, it's me... Celine."

The moment her hand reaches his, his fingers tighten around hers—the strength of his grip is overwhelming, full of unspoken pain. His voice trembles.

"Artin always wanted to introduce you to me as his other half. He spoke of you so fondly, always with love. But now... he's gone." His lips quiver. "Where is my son's body? I want to hold his hands one last time."

Tears spill from Celine's eyes. "Father, I'm— s-sorry."

She turns to the receptionist, trying to steady her voice. "I'm Celine, Artin Samuel's..." She pauses, struggling. "Dr. Ali should have informed you."

The receptionist nods. "Yes, you may proceed to the mortuary. I'll have someone escort you."

A hospital staff member steps forward, leading the way.

Celine holds Father Rafael's hand as she guides him down the quiet, dimly lit corridor. For the first time since everything happened, her composure breaks. Tears fall freely as she walks beside him, the weight of her actions suffocating her.

The hospital, even at this early hour, is alive—doctors and nurses move about, whispers echo in the halls, machines beep faintly in distant rooms. But the mortuary is silent.

CHAPTER LVII

Inside the Mortuary

Artin's body lies on a stretcher, covered by a simple white sheet.

Peter hesitates at the doorway, choosing to remain outside, giving Father Rafael his moment.

A hospital staff member gently pulls back the sheet, revealing Artin's face.

Father Rafael kneels beside him, reaching out with trembling hands. His fingers brush against Artin's cold, lifeless skin.

Memories flood his mind—the first time ten-year-old Artin clung to his hand, the boy's laughter, his stubborn determination, the warmth of the child he raised like his own.

And now, that warmth is gone.

Tears slip down the old priest's face, soaking into his beard as a deep, sorrowful cry escapes him. For the first time in years, he weeps openly, grieving for his son.

Celine watches from the side, silently crying. She doesn't move, doesn't speak—just watches, feeling her chest tighten until she can barely breathe.

Father Rafael takes a deep breath, trying to steady himself. He finally wipes his tears, his voice hoarse as he speaks.

"I will inform everyone and arrange the funeral. I will lead the mass for my son. Don't worry, child. I know your heart aches like mine. But those who love us never truly leave us. They stay with us, in the love they gave, in the lives they touched."

Celine sniffles, nodding. "Father... thank you for being here." Her voice breaks. "I will prepare everything for the funeral."

Father Rafael nods, rising slowly.

Peter steps in, gently taking his hand to lead him out.

Celine stands in the cold, lifeless room for a moment longer, staring at Artin's face. Regret claws at her, but it's too late.

He's gone.

The funeral preparations begin.

CHAPTER LVIII

Artin's body is carefully dressed in a crisp white shirt and black pants, a solemn yet dignified final attire. His face, now lifeless, is gently cleaned and prepared. The workers move with precision, their voices hushed, their movements careful—as if any sudden noise might shatter the fragile silence hanging over the room.

Celine stands at the side, clutching Artin's wristwatch in her trembling hands. The same watch he wore every day. It was a part of him, a simple thing, but now it felt so heavy in her grasp. Slowly, she hands it over to the worker. "Put this on him." Her voice is barely above a whisper.

As the worker fastens the watch around Artin's cold wrist, a storm rages inside her. The weight of everything—the lies, the betrayal, the guilt—presses down on her chest until she can barely breathe.

She can't stay here anymore.

Without another word, Celine turns and walks out of the room.

Outside – The Car

Sidharth is inside, dozing off from exhaustion. The quiet hum of the city in the early morning lulls him into a restless sleep. But then—

The car door swings open, and a sobbing Celine climbs in. The sound of her crying jolts him awake. Her entire body trembles, her hands gripping her lap so tightly her knuckles turn white.

Sidharth rubs his eyes, adjusting to the sudden chaos. "Celine...?"

Her voice comes out in broken gasps. "Sidharth... this is all a mistake. I regret everything. Everything." The words pour out between sobs, her breath hitching as she shakes her head violently. "I can't—I can't live with this. I can't—"

Her cries grow louder, her body curling into itself, rocking slightly as if trying to hold herself together.

Sidharth exhales sharply, running a hand through his hair. "Celine, it's fine. You need to calm down."

She shakes her head. "No. No, it's not fine. None of this is fine! What have we done?"

Sidharth grips her shoulders gently, forcing her to look at him. "Celine, you know why we're doing this. Don't fall apart now." His voice is low, firm, reassuring—but there's an edge of urgency.

She looks at him through tear-filled eyes, her breath coming in sharp, panicked gasps.

He glances at the dashboard, then opens it.

Inside, a small bottle of Divertine pills sits untouched. A quick fix. A way to settle the storm.

He picks up the bottle, shaking out a single pill into his palm before offering it to her.

"Take this. It'll help you regain your composure."

She hesitates, her tear-streaked face full of uncertainty. But then—her trembling fingers take the pill.

She swallows.

Her eyes flutter shut for a moment.

And when they open again...

The storm inside her is quieter. The weight on her chest feels lighter. Her breathing slows, steadies.

With newfound composure, Celine sits in the ambulance beside Artin's embalmed body.

The ambulance lurches forward, its sirens silent, only the soft hum of the engine breaking the stillness. The city lights flicker in the rain.

CHAPTER LIX

The ambulance came to a halt, and the doors swung open. Celine exits the ambulance and accompanies a devastated Shirley (Artin's mother). Arun, his face contorted with grief, took the lead, gripping the coffin as if holding onto a part of Artin he wasn't ready to let go of. Sidharth, Peter (parish clerk), and a few others followed. Sidharth's shoulder was burdened not just by the weight of the coffin but by the weight of what they had done.

Artin's mother struggles to walk. Her frail frame trembled, her sobs barely contained as she clung desperately to Celine's hand and the steady grip of a nun. Every step toward the grave felt like it was pulling her deeper into her sorrow. She had already lost her husband. Now, she was burying her son.

A quiet murmur of prayers mixed with the sound of raindrops hitting the ground. Around them, Artin's old college friends, childhood friends, colleagues, and parish members stood in silence, their faces pale, their eyes hollow with loss.

The coffin was lowered.

A sharp, agonizing wail tore through the downpour. Artin's mother fell to her knees. Her cries filled the air, raw and unrestrained, drowning out even the sound of the rain.

Father Rafael, standing at the head of the grave, struggled to keep his composure. His hands trembled. His voice cracked. The weight of loss hung heavy in the air, pressing against his chest. He had raised Artin, guided him, watched him grow. And now, he had to bury him.

CHAPTER LX

One by one, the mourners approached. Each took a handful of dirt, their fingers trembling as they let it slip through their hands, watching as it landed atop the coffin with a dull, heart-wrenching thud. A final goodbye.

Tears streamed down their faces. Every handful of earth felt like a piece of themselves being buried along with him.

All except Celine.

She stood still, gripping her arms, her face unreadable. Her eyes, red-rimmed and swollen, held something different—not grief, but guilt. A flicker of remorse. A whisper of regret. But no tears fell.

The grave was now sealed—a cold slab of concrete trapping Artin beneath the earth forever.

One by one, the people dispersed, umbrellas shielding them from the relentless downpour as they walked away, leaving behind only a few stragglers.

Sidharth, his face void of emotion, exchanged a brief glance with Arun before they turned to follow Father Rafael. The three of them made their way to Artin's house by Arun's car , the journey shrouded in a heavy, suffocating silence.

Meanwhile, Celine took Artin's mother Shirley and drove to the house. Shirley barely had the strength to walk. The grief weighed on her bones, dragging her steps as Celine supported her. Together, they entered the house, where Celine had arranged for a few servants to handle the visitors.

Inside, the house felt different—emptier, colder.

Shirley was taken to a room where she could rest, but her sobs still echoed faintly through the halls. Celine, maintaining a carefully crafted demeanour with the help of Divertine, greeted each visitor, speaking with a composed sorrow. She played her part well.

"It was a cardiac arrest," she told them. "His body couldn't take the stress... It was sudden, but at least he didn't suffer much."

The words rolled off her tongue effortlessly, rehearsed and precise.

By evening, the house had settled into an eerie stillness. The visitors had left, the servants had begun tidying up, and the storm outside showed no sign of stopping.

CHAPTER LXI

Celine approached Arun, her voice softer than usual. "Arun, can you drop Father Rafael back to the church?"

Arun nodded, saying nothing. His hands trembled slightly as he helped the blind priest into the car. The vehicle hummed to life, its headlights piercing through the foggy, rain-drenched road.

The silence stretched between them as they drove, but Arun couldn't hold it in anymore.

"Father... I don't feel like this is a natural death," he admitted, his voice breaking.

Father Rafael exhaled deeply.

"I know, son. I know it's not a natural death by cardiac arrest," he said solemnly. "The day before he passed away, Artin came to me and confessed everything."

Arun gripped the steering wheel tighter. His knuckles turned white.

"Father, I don't trust Celine. Something about her... I feel like she was involved. And not just her—Sidharth too. There's something going on between them."

Father Rafael nodded. "Do not discuss this with her. She is not safe."

Arun's breath hitched. "He was my best friend, Father... I wish I could fight the battle he started, but I'm not strong enough." His voice wavered, and his eyes burned with tears.

Father Rafael placed a comforting hand on his shoulder. "Son, God is watching everything. Evil will not go unpunished. He will send someone to fight those forces."

The words hung in the air like a prophecy.

As they approached the church, the rain continued to pour, a relentless reminder of the storm yet to come.

The parish clerk stood by the entrance, waiting. As Father Rafael stepped out of the vehicle, the church bell rang—one, two, three solemn tolls, piercing the silence like an omen.

Father Rafael turned back to Arun one last time.

"Wait for the day."

CHAPTER LXII

As the night settles and the rain fades, the house falls into silence. Shirley sleeps in Artin's room while Celine takes the other. She deliberately avoids staying with

Shirley—there's no point in forming a bond. Artin is gone, and Shirley is just a stranger to her now.

By midnight, Shirley's exhausted body gives in, her pillow damp with tears. But Celine lies awake. Every time she closes her eyes, an unnatural presence lingers in the room. An uneasy weight in the air, a feeling that someone—something—is watching.

She grabs her phone and calls Sidharth.

"Sidharth, I can't sleep. Every time I close my eyes, I feel like someone's here."

His voice is groggy but alert. "Should I come over?"

Celine gets up, her bare feet pressing against the cold floor. She tiptoes toward Shirley's room, carefully easing the door open just enough to peek inside.

Shirley is curled up on the bed, her face still streaked with dried tears. Her breathing is light, fragile.

Celine watches for a second, then slowly shuts the door.

"Yes," she whispers. "His mother is asleep."

A short while later, headlights briefly illuminate the house as Sidharth's car pulls up. He calls her.

"Open the door."

She does. No words are exchanged. They slip into the bedroom, moving on instinct, on something darker than love. They lock the door behind them, sealing themselves away from the world.

In the other room, Shirley gasps awake.

Her chest tightens, her breath uneven. A nightmare—no, a memory.

She rubs her temples, disoriented, then forces herself out of bed. Her movements are sluggish and drained. She stumbles toward the bathroom, splashing cold water onto her face.

Her reflection stares back at her.

Hollow eyes. A mother robbed of her son.

Returning to bed, she reaches for her sleeping pills, but her hands are shaking too much. The pill slips from her fingers, rolling onto the floor.

She sighs, bending down to retrieve it—and then, she sees it.

A laptop.

Tucked away, hidden beneath the bed.

Her breath hitches. Artin's laptop.

For a moment, she just stares. Her trembling hands reach for it, hesitant, afraid.

She pulls it out, slowly opening it. Artin had taught her how to use his laptop back when he first got it. The lock screen appears. Shirley knew the password.

She types:

C-E-L-I-N-E.

The screen unlocks.

A soft gasp escapes her lips. Her son's world is now in front of her.

She clicks through the folders—photos, memories frozen in time.

Childhood pictures. Laughing, carefree moments. Artin with her. Artin with Father Rafael. Artin with Celine.

Tears spill onto the trackpad as she scrolls. Her chest tightens with unbearable grief.

Then—a file catches her eye.

A video recording.

Titled: "If I die, please watch this."

Her entire body goes cold. Her heart beats so fast it hurts.

She hesitates—just for a second—then clicks.

The screen flickers.

And there he is.

Artin.

But not the Artin she remembers.

The Artin in the video is sick. Exhausted. Hollow. His eyes, sunken and red, stare through the screen.

His voice is weak.

But what he says shatters her world.

He reveals everything.

Lionsfield Pharma. The illegal experiments. The horrifying consequences of their work. The truth no one was meant to know.

And then, his final words—the words that destroy her.

"If I die, it will be because of Lionsfield Pharma."

"If I die, promise me this video will reach everyone."
A weak, pained smile.
"I love you, Amma."
"I love you, Father Rafael."
"Arun, thanks for everything, bro."
The video ends.

CHAPTER LXIII

The room is silent.

Shirley's breath is stuck in her throat.

Her mind collapses. A thousand broken thoughts crash down all at once.

Her unstable mind, carefully pieced together after years of treatment, is falling apart again.

Then, suddenly—she moves.

She grabs the laptop and runs to the other room.

Oblivious to the fact that Celine and Sidharth are sleeping in the other room.

Then—

BANG! BANG! BANG!

A desperate pounding on the door.

"CELINE, OPEN THE DOOR!!"

They jolt awake, terror instantly gripping them.

Celine panics, signalling Sidharth to get in the bathroom.

"WHAT? WHAT HAPPENED?" Celine shouts, her voice still laced with sleep.

From the other side—Shirley's voice, trembling, raw, unhinged.

"THEY KILLED ARTIN! OPEN THE DOOR, CELINE! THEY KILLED ARTIN!!!"

Celine's stomach drops. The blood drains from her face.

"WHO?! WHAT ARE YOU TALKING ABOUT?!"

She stumbles out of bed, unlocking the door. The second it opens, Shirley barges in, clutching the laptop like her life depends on it.

"WATCH THIS!"

Celine's fingers tremble as she looks at the screen.

And then, she sees it.

Artin's final message.

Her heart slams against her ribs. A sickening wave of dread crashes into her.

Inside the bathroom, Sidharth listens. He is enraged by this as once he had felt deeply embarrassed when he had to hide in the bathroom, he feels the anger boiling within him.

His face darkens. His patience snaps.

Outside, Shirley spirals.

"WE HAVE TO GO TO THE POLICE! NOW! RIGHT NOW!"

She's frantic, screaming, sobbing, clawing at Celine's arms.

Celine doesn't move.

Everything they did—everything they tried to cover—is about to come crashing down.

Then—

The bathroom door bursts open.

Sidharth storms out, his face twisted with rage. Without hesitation, he grabs a shawl, lunges behind Shirley, and wraps it around her throat.

She thrashes. Her nails claw at his arms, scratching, fighting.

She can't breathe.

Celine stands frozen. Her body is screaming at her to do something, but she just... doesn't.

She just watches.

Shirley's struggles weaken. Her body jerks violently—then, finally, goes still.

A second of silence.

Then, she crumples to the floor.

Lifeless.

Sidharth and Celine stand frozen, covered in sweat, their chests heaving, their minds spiraling.

Shirley's lifeless body lies before them.

CHAPTER LXIV

The air in the room is suffocating, thick with the stench of sweat, fear, and something far worse—the irreversible reality of what they've done.

Celine's hands tremble violently, her breath coming in shallow gasps. She can still hear the faint echoes of Shirley's last desperate struggles. The way she clawed at Sidharth's arms. The fading strength. The stillness.

She clamps a hand over her mouth. Her stomach churns.

Sidharth steps back, his pulse hammering in his ears. His grip tightens around the bloodstained shawl still clutched in his fist. His mind races—panic, disbelief, the overwhelming weight of what he's just done.

His fingers fumble for his phone.

He needs help.

With shaking hands, he dials.

The phone rings once.

Twice.

Then, a voice answers. Brother Charles.

Before the man can even greet him, Sidharth blurts out, "Brother, something happened—something really bad happened—"

Charles sighs through the receiver, unfazed.

"What did you do?"

Sidharth swallows hard, running a hand through his sweat-drenched hair. "We killed her."

A pause.

Then, Charles chuckles.

"So you two are full-blown murderers now, huh?"

Sidharth grips the phone tighter. "I didn't have a choice, brother. She found out everything. She saw the video—"

Charles clicks his tongue. "Tsk. I told you, didn't I? Anything goes wrong, you call me. Now listen carefully and do exactly as I say."

Sidharth and Celine don't breathe.

"You said she was mentally unstable, right?" Charles' voice is eerily calm. "So make it look like she ran away. Destroy the body. No body, no crime."

Celine finally speaks, her voice hoarse. "H-How?"

Charles laughs—a short, cruel sound.

"Take the body to the new factory and dissolve her in acid."

Silence.

Celine's stomach twists into knots. Her mind recoils at the sheer horror of what's being suggested.

"A-Acid?" she whispers.

Charles continues, "Digest her body in acid. People will assume she disappeared after losing her son. She was already unstable, right? A grieving mother who snapped and ran away—makes sense."

Sidharth clenches his jaw. His fingers tighten around the phone.

Then, Brother Charles's tone shifts, dark amusement lacing his words.

"And next time, try not to make a mess. Cleaning up after you idiots is getting tiring."

The call ends.

Sidharth lowers the phone slowly. His hands are still shaking, but his mind is made up.

He looks at Celine. Their eyes meet—both filled with the same silent horror.

No turning back now.

ACT II

THE RESURRECTION

A blinding flash of lightning splits the sky, followed by a deafening crack of thunder—a violent rupture in the silence of the night. Moments later, the rain returns, heavier this time, pouring down in relentless sheets, drumming against the earth.

Meanwhile, at the cemetery, rainwater pools over the freshly turned soil, the storm's fury soaking the earth above Artin's grave. The wind howls through the trees.

Inside the burial chamber,

A hollow, muffled thud echoes from beneath.

Bang! Bang! The sound grows louder, more desperate.

Deep inside the burial chamber, something stirs. The coffin shakes. The wood groans under pressure—then suddenly, crack! A splintering snap rips through the silence.

A hand bursts through the coffin lid, fingers clawing at the darkness.

ARTIN.

HE. IS. ALIVE.

They thought he was gone—but fate had other plans.

What was meant to be his end has become his rebirth. The ODFC-4 drug, used to destroy him, has instead been embraced by his body. They sought to silence him forever, to erase him from existence—but ironically, they have made him more alive than ever.

ARTIN OPENS HIS EYES, DARKNESS, CRUSHING DARKNESS.

Artin gasps, but there isn't much air—only the stale, suffocating void pressing in from all sides. His lungs burn, his chest heaves, but every breath is swallowed by the coffin's oppressive walls.

His heartbeat pounds in his ears, faster, harder. Thud-thud!. Thud-thud!!. He claws at the wood, his fingers scraping, splinters stabbing under his nails. His body jerks, desperate, his limbs thrashing against the tight space.

His mind screams—I can't breathe. I can't move. I have to get out.

His pulse surges, panic drowning reason. He rams his shoulder against the lid, once—twice—harder. The coffin creaks but doesn't break. The air is vanishing. The weight of the earth above presses down, a silent, crushing tomb.

With every ounce of strength left in his oxygen-starved body, he lets out a muffled, rage-filled roar and slams his fist against the lid. The wood shudders. Again. Harder.

The hole cracks more, the coffin's lid is breaking apart.

With one more fiecre punch...

THE COFFIN LID COMPLETELY SHATTERS.

With a deafening crack, Artin bursts through the shattered remains of his coffin, his body surging upward with explosive strength. He gasps for air, his lungs inhaling the damp, earthy scent of the grave. His chest heaves, his throat burns. He is alive.

Disoriented, he instinctively reaches for his wrist—his smartwatch. The time 12:54 AM. With trembling fingers, he flicks on the flashlight. A dim, bluish glow flickers to life, cutting through the suffocating darkness.

The light reveals his burial vault. He is entombed in an underground burial vault, four sides of cold concrete press around him, trapping him in a space no larger than a coffin. Panic claws at his throat as the reality sinks in. He is not dead. Only buried alive.

His breath quickens. The air feels thinner. The silence is deafening, broken only by the frantic thumping of his own heartbeat—a drumming war cry of survival.

His hands tremble as he presses against the walls, dirt crumbling beneath his touch. Claustrophobia strikes like a knife to his gut. His chest tightens. Every inch of his body tingles with the raw, electric sting of fear.

Artin's screams rip through the suffocating darkness.

"HELP! SOMEBODY HELP ME! ARGGGHHH! I'M STILL ALIVE! PLEASE!"

His desperate cries are swallowed by the concrete slab above him, his voice reaching no one. His lungs burn, his throat raw from the effort—but the silence answers back, cruel and unyielding.

A violent cough racks his body, forcing up a thick stream of blood—but it's not red. It spills from his lips in a dark, viscous sludge, unnatural, inhuman. His chest heaves as he stares at the black liquid dripping from his mouth, the weight of his new reality crushing down on him.

Finally, he stops screaming. There's no use. No one is coming.

Suddenly, his foot catches on the jagged remains of his shattered coffin, sending him crashing to his knees. His body trembles from exhaustion, he sits down on the floor, after sometime he notices a glint of light flickers in the darkness.

His smartwatch's faint glow reflects off something metallic—the coffin's handles. His breath hitches. An idea sparks in his mind, igniting a flicker of hope amid the crushing dread.

Without hesitation, he grips one of the metal handles, his fingers tightening around the cold surface. He plants his feet against the wooden slab it's screwed into and pushes with all his strength. The wood groans, then—CRACK! The handle rips free, jagged edges of splintered wood still attached.

His eyes burn with a newfound determination. He won't die here.

Clenching the handle like a weapon, he rears back and slams it into the concrete wall, hoping it will create a dent on the walls. A sharp, metallic clang rings out, reverberating through the confined space. Again. And again. His knuckles turn white, his muscles scream—but he doesn't stop. He can't stop. If there's even the slightest chance of escape, he'll tear through the very earth itself.

He swings the handle with relentless fury, slamming it against the concrete wall with such force that a burst of sparks erupts in the darkness. The metallic clang echoes through the suffocating vault, the vibration rattling up his arms. Again. And again. His strikes grow more violent, fueled by desperation and raw instinct.

Finally, beneath the relentless effort, a small dent begins to take shape.

A surge of unyielding determination floods Artin's veins. He can't stop now. He won't. Gritting his teeth, he swings again, this time aiming just beside the first dent. A deafening clang. Then another. The concrete trembles, thin cracks splintering outward like veins of lightning.

His breathing is ragged, his knuckles white from the sheer force of his grip. The metal handle in his hand is warping, crumbling under the repeated blows, but he refuses to slow down. With one final, brutal strike, the handle snaps in half, leaving him breathless.

But this isn't over. Not yet.

His eyes dart around the dark vault, heart pounding. He spots another handle lying among the coffin debris. Without hesitation, he snatches it up, tightens his grip, and continues his relentless assault on the cracking walls.

With gritted teeth and burning resolve, Artin places his feet into the dents he created, his fingers digging into the narrow cracks like a predator clawing its way out of a trap. The walls are slick with moisture, the cracks barely big enough to hold onto, but he refuses to let go.

His shirt tears as his muscles strain, every fiber screaming, veins bulging against his skin as he pulls himself upward. The concrete is cold and unforgiving, biting into his fingertips, but he keeps climbing—inch by inch, struggle by struggle.

His breath is ragged, his body shaking with exhaustion, but his mind is set. He reaches higher, pushing past the searing pain.

With one hand gripping the narrow crack for dear life, Artin reaches down, fumbling for the metal handle in his pocket. His fingers brush against it—but in that split second, his footing gives way.

His legs slip against the damp concrete, and suddenly, he's dangling in midair. His entire weight wrenches down on his fingertips, a single grip, sending sharp, unimaginable pain through his fingers. His muscles scream, his joints threaten to tear apart, but he refuses to let go.

A desperate, pain-laced scream rips from his throat. His chest heaves as he fights the panic clawing at his mind. The jagged wooden shards of the broken coffin lay waiting below, their splintered edges ready to impale him if he falls.

With a surge of raw willpower, he lunges for the handle in his pocket, yanks it out, and drives it into the wall. The metal bites deep into the concrete, holding just enough for him to regain his balance.

His breathing is ragged, his limbs shaking from exertion, but he pushes on. He forces his legs back into the tiny crevices, regaining his footing. Then, gripping the handle tightly, he hammers it into the wall again and again, carving new dents.

Each strike echoes through the burial vault like a war drum, fueling his climb higher—toward the only thing standing between him and freedom: the concrete slab sealing his grave shut.

Finally, his head reaches the concrete slab. A fall from this height is beyond fatal. Dazed, Artin grips the handle tightly, his fingers aching from the strain. With desperate precision, he drives it into the cement, carving holes into the edges of the slab sealing the burial vault.

A deep, guttural crack splinters through the silence.

Suddenly, water surges in—a violent torrent from the rain-flooded graveyard above. The force of it crashes against Artin's head, blinding him, knocking the breath from his lungs. His grip slips.

The cold shock sends his body into a spasm. His fingers claw at the fractures in the concrete, but it's too late—his legs buckle, muscles failing him.

Gravity takes over.

Artin falls...

Then—impact.

His head smashes against the cold, unforgiving ground. A sickening crack. Darkness rushes in, his consciousness snuffed out in an instant.

Jagged splinters of wood tear into Artin's flesh as he crashes through the shattered remains of the coffin.

His arm takes the brunt of his landing, bending at an unnatural angle. The bone gives way with a sharp, wet snap—piercing through his skin, the broken bone sticks out, blood gushes out of his arm.

The rainwater flows into the burial vault slowly flooding it.

CHAPTER LXVI

Outside, the night weeps. Cold rain hammers against the earth, turning the graveyard into a wasteland of mud and shadow.

Through the drenched grass, a rat flees. Its tiny body, slick with rain, trembles with exhaustion as it hurtles forward, its every step a frantic gamble against death. Behind it, a snake glides, unhindered by the storm. The predator moves with silent purpose, its scales gleaming wet beneath flashes of lightning.

The rat's tiny heart pounds like a war drum. It leaps over gnarled roots, skids through puddles, its whiskers twitching wildly as it searches for an escape. Then—it sees it. A gap in the earth, a jagged opening between the roots of a half-sunken gravestone. It lunges for the hole.

The storm's roar fades as the rat vanishes into darkness.

But the chase isn't over.

The snake hesitates only for a second before following, its sinuous form disappearing into the abyss—

—And then both are falling.

The rat lands first.

With a soft, panicked squeak, its tiny body crashes onto something unnervingly warm. The cold of the burial vault is suffocating, yet the surface beneath the rat pulses—faintly, but undeniably—alive.

It scrambles, its claws scratching against flesh. The rat landed on Artin's body. The rat reacts first. It scurries, desperate to escape, diving into the nearest crevice it can find—beneath the body.The rat reacts, it scurries, desperate to escape, diving into the nearest crevice it can find—beneath the body.

The snake drops down, landing with a hush beside them.

As the water inside rises the snake tries to escaping, the rat still hiding beneath Artin's unconscious body.

CHAPTER LXVII

Inside Artin's unconscious mind his past unfolds like a dream—soft, golden, untouched by the darkness of the present.

A ten-year-old Artin laughs, his voice light and full of joy, as he chases after his mother, Shirley, in front of their home. The warm afternoon sun bathes them in its gentle glow, the scent of fresh earth and blooming flowers carried by the breeze. Shirley, radiant and full of life, catches him in a playful embrace, tickling him until he gasps for breath between fits of laughter.

Then, the low, familiar hum of an engine rumbles in the distance.

Artin's eyes light up as he turns toward the road. A sturdy motorcycle pulls in, its tires crunching softly against the gravel. His father, Samuel, arrives—his presence strong yet comforting, like an unshakable pillar of warmth and safety. The retired military officer, now a dedicated kalari master, dismounts with ease. His sharp eyes soften the moment he spots his son.

Artin dashes toward him, and before he can even slow down, Samuel lifts him effortlessly, spinning him once in the air before pulling him close. Artin giggles as his father's rough, dry lips press gently against his soft forehead in a warm, protective kiss.

"You been good boy?" Samuel asks, his deep voice full of affection.

Artin nods enthusiastically.

Shirley joins them, wrapping her arms around them both, her laughter blending into the perfect harmony of their happiness. A family—whole, unbroken, filled with love.

Inside their cozy home, the scent of spices fills the air as Samuel stands by the stove, cooking, stirring a pot with practiced ease. Shirley moves beside him, preparing the ingredients, sneaking playful glances his way.

Artin sits close by, watching them with eager eyes. He dips a spoon into the steaming dish and takes a bite—his face instantly lighting up with delight.

"Mmm! Perfect!" he exclaims.

Samuel chuckles, nudging Shirley. "See? My cooking is good."

Shirley smirks, rolling her eyes. "Let's see if you can still say that after I add my touch."

Their laughter fills the kitchen, mingling with the warmth of the food—the kind of warmth that isn't just in the meal but in the very air around them.

Later that night, the family sleeps in one bed, bundled together in an unbreakable embrace. Samuel lies in the middle, his arms protectively wrapped around both Shirley and Artin. His breath is steady, strong, anchoring them.

Shirley rests her head against his chest, her fingers gently curled around his hand. Artin snuggles closer, burying his face against his father's side, feeling the steady rise and fall of his chest. His small hands clutch at Samuel's shirt, as if holding onto the safety of this moment.

Outside, the world is silent, but inside this home, inside this bed, love radiates like a warm, unyielding light.

A perfect family. A perfect life. A love so pure—so whole.

A love never meant to be broken.

CHAPTER LXVIII

The following day there was a grand festival at church, they returned back home at night. It was a perfect night. The grand festival at the church had filled the family with joy, their laughter echoing as they rode home on Samuel's bike. The air was crisp, the full moon casting silver light over the quiet streets.

Reaching their modest home, they stepped inside, their hearts still warm from the celebrations. As they prepared for bed, a faint noise from the living room cut through the silence—soft, almost deliberate.

Samuel's instincts flared. His brows furrowed.

He stepped forward cautiously, his bare feet barely making a sound against the floor.

Then—chaos.

A deafening crash, followed by a gut-wrenching scream.

Shirley and Artin ran toward the noise. The moment they reached the living room, their breath caught in their throats.

Two masked men stood there, knives gleaming under the moonlight streaming through the window.

Samuel was staggering, clutching his stomach. Blood seeped between his fingers. His eyes burned with pain, but his voice came out loud and firm:

"RUN! TAKE ARTIN AND GO!"

Shirley froze, gripping her son's shoulders. The words didn't register. Her mind refused to process what was happening.

One of the intruders lunged at Samuel, blade flashing. The other rushed toward Shirley and Artin.

But Samuel wasn't done.

With lightning reflexes, he caught the attacker's wrist mid-swing, twisting it violently. A sickening snap rang through the room as the knife clattered to the floor. Before the man could react, Samuel's fist smashed into his face—a brutal, bone-crushing strike.

The intruder's body crumpled, hitting the ground hard, unconscious.

Samuel wasted no time. He snatched up the fallen knife and turned.

Shirley was trapped.

The second intruder had backed her into a corner, his knife raised.

Samuel struck first.

With a sharp, precise slash, he sliced through the attacker's knees. The man shrieked, his legs buckling beneath him. Before he could recover, Samuel drove his foot into the man's face. The force of the kick sent the intruder's head snapping back, killing the man.

Shirley gasped, pressing a hand over Artin's eyes, shielding him from the carnage.

Samuel exhaled, chest rising and falling with exhaustion. Blood dripped from his fingers, but he was still standing.

Then—

"LOOK OUT!"

Shirley and Artin's screams pierced the night.

The first attacker—the one Samuel had knocked out—was back on his feet. His shadow loomed behind Samuel.

Steel flashed.

The blade plunged deep into Samuel's back.

His body arched from the impact, eyes wide, breath hitching in his throat. Blood dripped from his lips as the attacker twisted the knife deeper.

Samuel gasped, stumbling forward, his knees nearly giving out.

Shirley let out a broken, trembling cry. Artin stood frozen, his small frame trembling.

Samuel collapsed to his knees, but he wasn't done.

With the last of his fading strength, he drove his knife into the attacker's foot.

The intruder howled in agony. His knee buckled, forcing him to kneel.

Samuel's grip weakened. The world tilted. His vision darkened.

The man wrenched the knife from his foot and, in pure rage, plunged his blade one final time—straight through Samuel's throat.

The sharp edge tore through flesh and muscle. Samuel's body convulsed before finally going still.

The attacker laughed. A cruel, twisted sound that sent chills through Shirley and Artin.

Samuel—a husband, a father, —was dead.

Shirley sobbed, clutching Artin, but her son was no longer trembling.

His small hands found the fallen knife.

He gripped it.

The killer turned, still grinning. But before he could react.

Artin moved like a ghost.

The knife tore across the man's throat.

A thick spray of blood splattered across Artin's face. The attacker gasped, eyes wide in shock as he clutched his throat, stumbling back. His body convulsed, choking on his own life.

Artin didn't flinch.

He stood there, panting, blood dripping from his fingertips, the knife still clutched in his hands.

CHAPTER LXIX

The aftermath of that night shattered Artin and Shirley.

The house that once echoed with laughter and warmth became a hollow shell of grief. Samuel's absence was a wound that refused to heal, his bloodstains long washed away but never truly gone from their minds.

Then came Father Rafael.

A distant relative of Shirley, he arrived at their doorstep like a man sent by fate. His presence was calm, his voice steady, his faith unshaken. He took one look at Artin's hollow eyes and Shirley's fractured mind and knew—they needed help beyond prayers.

With the church's support, he brought them to a mental hospital run by the clergy. It was a place not of sterile white walls but of warmth, of whispered prayers, of attempts to mend broken souls.

For Artin, the sensation of taking a life—the weight of the knife, the warmth of the blood, the fading light in the man's eyes—clawed at his sanity after years of therapy, medication, and hypnosis followed. The memories of that horrific night. Locked away deep within a hidden part of his mind. His consciousness no longer had access to them, but the echoes remained, hidden beneath the surface.

Shirley, however, was never truly the same.

She was lost in a world of her own. Some days, she was the mother he remembered—gentle, loving, even laughing at small things. Other days, she stared blankly at walls, murmuring Samuel's name over and over, her hands trembling as if reliving the moment he fell. She was finally stable after years of treatment but the problems lingered within her mind.

They lived under the care of Father Rafael's church-run care home, where life slowly began to take shape again.

Days went by, Artin continued his schooling once he became well, As he reached 11th class, he met Celine and instantly fell for her. By the time their school was over they began their relationship.

After finishing school, Artin got his first laptop. It was a gift from Father Rafael. Instead of keeping it to himself, he sat down with Shirley and taught her how to use it.

When asked for a password, he typed a single word:

C-E-L-I-N-E.

A quiet promise, a reminder of the one person who made him feel whole.

Then Artin left for college. A fresh start.

He visited Shirley rarely—not because he didn't love her, but because it was easier to pretend the past didn't exist when he was away.

Five years passed.

Artin and Celine—now scientists—walked through the towering glass doors of Lionsfield Pharma.

CHAPTER LXX

Artin's eyes snapped open.

He was lying flat — but not in the damp stone of the burial vault. This place was different. Wrong. Around him stretched a narrow, decaying alleyway, lit only by the trembling glow of scattered flames dancing on the walls. The air was thick — not with fog, but with ash and the charred smell of flesh. Shadows moved where they shouldn't.

He pushed himself up slowly, breathing heavily. His hands trembled.

Then he saw it — a door.

Old. Ancient. Wrong. It pulsed faintly, as though alive. Mysterious, archaic symbols crawled across its surface, glowing faintly red, as if inked in embered blood. He walked forward.

His fingers touched the door — with a creak, it opened.

And there it was.

Fifteen bodies. Hung upside-down from rusted hooks jammed into the ceiling beams, spinning slightly, their limbs twitching as if they still clung to the last threads of life. Their skin was pale and waxy, slashed and punctured. Eyes gouged out. Tongues ripped. Some had symbols carved into their torsos. The stench — a thick, rotting perfume of death — hit Artin making him puke.

But then... a sound.

A soft, choked sobbing.

In the middle of the room sat a child, curled up, drenched in blood. A bloodied knife clutched in his trembling hands. His face buried in his knees.

Artin took a step closer, breath shallow. The boy's shoulders shook with each cry.

He reached out.

"Hey..."

His fingers brushed the boy's shoulder.

The sobbing stopped.

The boy raised his head slowly.

And Artin's blood ran cold.

It was him.

Ten-year-old Artin. But twisted — his eyes too dark, his skin stained, his mouth twitching like something inside wanted to tear free.

The boy opened his mouth — and screamed.

Not one voice. Hundreds. Men, women, children, beasts. All screaming through one mouth, tearing through Artin's mind like knives. He collapsed to the floor, clutching his ears, howling in agony.

When he looked up again, the child was changing.

Bones cracked and popped. Flesh tore. The boy's body contorted, growing. Expanding. Wings exploded from his back in sprays of blackened blood. Horns sprouted, twisting upward like ancient branches. His face twisted — first into the head of a bleating goat, then melted and reformed into something demonic. Unholy. Laughing.

Then — with a wet, sickening sound — the corpses fell from their hooks. One by one.

Thud.

Thud.

Thud.

They hit the floor, twitching. Crawling.

One face among them made Artin scream.

Diya.

The girl who had died in front of him. Her mouth gaped open like it wanted to scream, but only blood poured out.

The bodies began slithering. Not walking — crawling, squirming like maggots, tendons snapping, bones cracking, dragging themselves across the floor with broken fingers and torn limbs. Toward him.

He tried to crawl back.

Too late.

They reached him.

Dozens of decayed, semi-living hands grabbed him — pale, wet fingers clawing at his arms, legs, throat. Pinning him down. He thrashed, but there was no escape. The corpses pressed into him, their cold breath panting into his ears, moaning words that didn't exist.

And the demon stood above.

Smiling.

Then — with slow, sick delight — it plunged its clawed hand into its own chest.

The flesh didn't resist. It split open like fruit. Ribs cracked as the demon dug deep and pulled out its own heart — a throbbing, blackened mass, still beating.

Artin's scream was silenced by the corpses forcing his mouth open. Their bony hands pried his jaws apart until it felt like they would snap. He couldn't move. Couldn't breathe.

And the demon, grinning wide, raised the dripping heart high...

Then squeezed.

Blood burst forth in thick, hot gushes — spraying into Artin's mouth, drowning him in the taste of rot, rust, and ash. It poured over his face, down his throat. He was bathed in the blood.

He screamed his lungs out.

CHAPTER LXXI

Artin jolts awake, his eyes snap open once more—this time, surrounded by the familiar darkness and suffocation.

Its the burial vault. He breathes heavily as he realises it was just a nightmare.

Water sloshes around him. His body shudders uncontrollably.

A sharp squeal is heard as the rat scurries away, leaping onto a floating wooden piece of the shattered coffin.

The cold water laps at his legs. It has risen.

And Artin is still trapped.

The light from his watch falls on something moving.

A shadow beneath the water.

Artin's breath catches in his throat as his eyes lock onto it. A snake.

Its long, coiled body writhes beneath the surface, desperately seeking an escape, its forked tongue flicking, tasting the air. The sight sends a violent jolt through Artin's exhausted body. He backs up in fear, trying to move away from the snake.

But the moment he tries to drag himself backward—agony.

A searing, unimaginable pain erupts from his right arm. A scream rips from his throat.

Gritting his teeth, he forces himself to look. His arm.

Bent in half at an unnatural angle. The jagged, white end of his broken bone sticks out from torn flesh. Blood streams down his forearm, mixing with the filthy water.

A choked sob escapes him. His mind spins.

He presses his back against the cold concrete wall, struggling to steady his breath. But then—memories flood in.

His father. The break-in. The blood. The screams.

The images come crashing down, no longer locked away.

His hands tremble. His breathing quickens. The past is no longer buried.

Then—a splash.

His head snaps back to the water.

The snake has spotted the rat.

The small creature trembles atop a floating splinter of coffin wood, its tiny black eyes darting around in terror.

The snake's predatory instincts take over.

It rears back, spreads its hood, its jaw widening to reveal glistening, venomous fangs.

The snake strikes.

But before the fangs can pierce flesh—Artin's hand snaps forward.

He catches it. Mid-air.

The snake thrashes violently in his grip, its muscular body writhing and twisting. Its head lunges, fangs bared, trying desperately to sink them into Artin's flesh.

But Artin's fingers tighten.

Tighter.

Tighter.

His knuckles turn white. The snake's movements slow, its head immobilized by his grip. Its hissing grows weaker.

And then, with no hesitation, Artin bites off its head.

Blood—warm, explodes into his mouth. The headless body jerks violently in his grasp.

He spits out the head like it's nothing. His chest rises and falls rapidly, his breathing its rapid, almost primal.

With a deep, shuddering breath, he grabs his own broken bone.

And pushes it back in.

A guttural scream rips through him as another wave of pain crashes over his shattered arm.

The pain is beyond anything he has ever felt.

But he does not stop.

The convulsing body of the snake still writhes in his grasp. With one final act of sheer will, he wraps the serpent's body around his mangled arm—

A crude, makeshift bandage.

His eyes turns red, the pain is so unbareable, his nose starts to bleed but he still pulls to tighten it.

Tighter.

Tighter.

He pulls.

Blood seeps through the gaps in the snake's coiled body.

Artin gets up and rips off his shirt, his chest rising and falling like a beast starved for air. His muscles—taut, rigid—pulse beneath his skin, veins bulging as if they might burst free. His entire body twitches, not with fear, but with something far more primal. A hunger. A rage.

His eyes dart across the burial vault and lands on the metal handle.

He snatches it from the ground, gripping it so hard the metal creaks under his fingers. With a guttural snarl, he lunges at the wall, both hands working in tandem as he climbs.

This time, he is a beast.

His muscles bulge and coil, raw strength propelling him upwards. The pain from his broken arm lances through his body, but he doesn't stop. His flesh scrapes against the gritty concrete, tearing, blood smearing against the wall as he ascends.

Higher and higher.

His head slams against the concrete slab above. The last barrier. The final obstacle.

CHAPTER LXXII

Breathing hard, Artin raises the handle and hacks away at the cement on the edge of the slab. Pieces crumble, dust filling the stagnant air.

He pulls himself up, pushing the slab upwards. His eyes pierce through the tiny crack of freedom.

Then—suddenly.

He loses his balance again.

The slab drops.

Right onto his fingers.

A sickening CRACK.

Artin screams.

Agony floods his body. His balance shifts, his body dangling freely. Only his trapped, crushed fingers keep him from plummeting into his death.

He sobs.

But then... something snaps.

The sobs warp—twisting, distorting. His breathing quickens. His teeth clench. A sound bubbles up from deep within him.

Laughter.

A low, eerie chuckle at first. Then it grows. Twisting. Darkening.

Hysterical. Maddening.

The floodgates in his mind shatter. The memories come crashing in again—his hand gripping the knife, the warmth of blood gushing over his skin, the gurgled cries of the man whose throat he had slit.

His smartwatch blares an alarm: "Warning! High heart rate—211, 212, 213..." The numbers climb rapidly before the screen flickers and dies, the battery completely drained.

His fingers, trapped and broken, twitch.

His laughter explodes into howls.

He kicks against the walls, over and over. The brutal impact shatters his toes, dislocates them. But he doesn't stop. The pain feeds him. Fuels him.

Finally a foothold forms, his feet lodges onto them.

With newfound, monstrous strength, he presses his head against the slab and pushes.

His muscles scream. His skin burns. The slab moves.

His crushed fingers—numb, shattered—grip down tighter.

His eyes turn red, they dont look human, its filled with murderous intent, blood starts dripping from his mouth. With a final, soul-ripping roar, he hoists himself. Finally making concrete slide.

The grave opens.

Artin has freed himself.

A lightning strike rips through the sky.

For a fraction of a second, the world is bathed in blinding white—illuminating the figure standing atop the shattered grave.

Artin Samuel.

Very much alive.

CHAPTER LXXIII

The storm rages around Artin, rain hammering down on his skin. But as it touches him, it hisses and evaporates— transforming into mist that coils around his body like smoke rising from a furnace.

His breath comes in slow, steady waves. His fingers—mangled, twisted. His toes—dislocated, barely clinging to form. His expression remain unreadable.

Artin slowly lifts his gaze to the heavens, closing his eyes. The storm's fury reflects the chaos within him. Then, with a deep inhale, he moves.

Crack.

His left hand—barely functional—grips his right fingers and wrenches them back into place.

Crack.

His jaw tightens, muscles clenching, his teeth grinding against the unbearable agony.

Crack. Crack. Crack.

One by one, he fixes them.

A tremor rips through his body, every nerve set ablaze. Excruciating pain. His skin prickles, his hair stands on end. But then...

A devilish smile spreads across his bloody face.

A raw, unhinged grin.

With his newly restored right hand, he grips the left—his broken fingers twisting, snapping, realigning. The pain is savage. Merciless. But he endures.

Then, he bends—sitting on the grave that was meant to be his tomb.

One by one, he fixes his toes.

The storm howls. The wind shrieks. The lightning crackles—revealing the blood-smeared, monstrous grin stretched across his face.

Finally, he rises.

With deliberate force, he drags the heavy concrete slab back over the grave, sealing it shut.

He is no longer the man who was buried there.

He tilts his head to the sky—his chest rising, his veins pulsing, his reborn body seething with unrelenting power.

And then—

He lets out a war cry that shakes the very heavens.

The resurrection. The rebirth.

It is complete.

The drug ODFC-4 was designed to create superhumans.

But in every test before him, it had failed.

The human body was never meant to withstand its wrath. It was too toxic, too potent—a force beyond mortal comprehension. Every subject before him had fallen, their bodies unable to handle its potency. Organs ruptured, cells cannibalized themselves, nervous systems burned out like faulty circuits. Not just humans—no organism had ever survived it. Animals, lab-grown tissues—all withered and died upon exposure.

Until now.

Until Artin.

His body hadn't just endured the drug—it had embraced it. ODFC-4 had fused with his very essence, rewriting his biology at the most fundamental level. His blood, now laced with the cursed D-Factor, surged through his veins, pushing against his skin, bulging like thick cables, pulsating with unnatural life, expanding, mutating—twisting him into something beyond human.

His muscles swelled, tightening, coiling like tempered steel. His breath came slow, controlled—each inhale dragging in the very essence of his rebirth. All the wounds on his body already started healing.

Something within him had changed.

Something irreversible.

The drug that had claimed countless lives had found its first true vessel.

Artin Samuel was no longer just a man.

CHAPTER LXXIV

Artin's eyes, cold and unblinking, scanned the darkness. Then, his gaze fell upon a damp cloth, half-buried in the mud. He knelt, fingers closing around the fabric, lifting it with an eerie slowness. Without hesitation, he draped it over his body, concealing the raw, monstrous rebirth he had just endured. A ghost wrapped in shadows, a revenant born of blood and vengeance.

The wind howled as he turned away from the grave—from his past, from his old self. Step by step, he moved forward, emerging from the cemetery's iron gates like a phantom. His soul burned. His mind screamed.

He was starving—starving for revenge.

He walks away from the church, unsure of where to go. Father Rafael wouldn't be able to comprehend any of this. He wanders aimlessly, his legs trembling with each step, but he doesn't stop.

It's nearly 2 AM. The streets are deserted, except for the homeless, curled up on the sidewalks. Exhaustion crashes over Artin. He lowers himself beside them, pulling the damp cloth around his body. Curling up against the cold, he closes his eyes, his mind racing.

What now?

Artin slowly drifts into sleep... but as his consciousness fades, a sudden pull yanks him back—not in reality, but in his mind.

The darkness around him twists, morphing into cold, suffocating walls. He is back. Back in the burial vault. Back in the grave that had swallowed him whole.

His eyes snap open. He is in the coffin again—drenched, broken, trapped. The stench of death clings to the air. The water has risen, cold and unforgiving, lapping at his skin. The crushed fingers. The snake's corpse. The weight of the concrete slab pressing down on him—it's all still there.

Artin jolts awake, gasping for breath, his body drenched in sweat. His heart slams against his ribs. His body trembles, the weight of the nightmare pressing down harder than the grave itself.

His mind spirals. His pulse surges. His body, though reborn, still carries the trauma of death.

CHAPTER LXXV

Artin sits up on the sidewalk, his body heavy, his mind restless. His eyes wander aimlessly, searching for something—anything—to anchor him to reality. Sleep refuses to come. His pulse still pounds from the nightmare, his breath uneven.

Then, a thought breaks through the fog—Arun. His best friend. His biggest support.

A spark of determination flickers in his exhausted eyes. He has to see Arun.

With a sluggish groan, he pushes himself up. His limbs protest, his body aching from the ordeal it has endured. Every step feels heavier than the last, but he keeps moving.

The streets are quiet, wet from the rain. Dim streetlights cast long shadows as he trudges forward. His instincts sharpen when he spots CCTV cameras mounted along the roads. He tilts his head down, keeps his face hidden, slipping into the blind spots like a ghost.

The night air is cold against his damp skin, but he doesn't stop. He drags himself forward—step by step, street by street—toward the only person who can help.

Artin finally reaches the front of Arun's home. The sky is still cloaked in darkness, the air sharp and cold against his skin. He steps into the compound, his movements sluggish, and walks toward the front door.

He raises a trembling hand and rings the doorbell. Once. Twice. Again.

CHAPTER LXXVI

Inside, Arun stirs from a restless sleep, his face sunken with grief. He glances at the clock—3:00 AM. A dull ache settles in his chest. He's been mourning Artin the whole night.

Dragging himself out of bed, he makes his way to the front window, peering cautiously through the curtain. Outside, a shadowy figure sits hunched on the steps, back turned, soaked in rain.

Arun's heart races. He grabs an iron rod from behind the door, gripping it tight with shaking hands. The doorbell rings again—louder this time, more urgent.

He rushes back to the window—

But suddenly stumbles backward and falls to the floor, startled.

The figure is now right beside the window.

Face barely visible. Skin pale. Blood dripping from his hands.

A bloody palm presses against the glass, leaving a dark crimson print—then the figure collapses.

Panic claws at Arun's throat. The blood. The eerie presence. His instincts scream call the police. He scrambles for his phone, tries to dial—but the call doesn't connect

He hesitates. Something about the figure feels... wrong. Familiar.

Clutching the iron rod, he slowly opens the door, his breath shaky. He steps out into the cold air, eyes fixed on the unmoving body.

Cautiously, he pokes it with the rod. No reaction.

Steeling his nerves, he kneels beside it and pulls away the damp cloth covering the figure's face.

Time stops.

His breath catches in his throat.

It's Artin.

Drenched in blood, face bruised—but alive.

"Wha... what the hell?" Arun whispers, his mind spiraling.

He quickly checks for a pulse—it's there. Faint. But real.

Without another thought, Arun grips him under the arms and drags his unconscious friend inside, his heart pounding.

Arun's entire body trembles as he stares at the impossible—Artin, bloody and broken, lying unconscious in his room. The weight of what he's witnessing crashes down on him like a tidal wave. This shouldn't be real. It can't be real.

With every ounce of strength he can muster, Arun lifts Artin's limp body onto the bed. It's a struggle—the body is heavy, lifeless, like it's been through hell. Up close, it's even worse. Artin is severely dehydrated, covered in bruises, caked in dried blood, and riddled with half-healed wounds. His skin is pale, his lips cracked.

Arun's mind kicks into overdrive. He rushes to the storeroom and frantically gathers supplies—tubing, a needle, some leftover dextrose sugar. He improvises a makeshift IV, mixing the solution with urgency, hands shaking.

He bolts back to the room and sets up the IV, slipping the needle into Artin's vein. As the fluid starts to drip, he grabs a mug of water, fills it, and splashes it gently onto Artin's battered face.

Artin flinches.

A twitch. A flicker of life.

Arun leans in, grabbing a cotton towel, carefully wiping away the grime and blood from his friend's face.

"Come on, Artin... wake up..." he whispers, voice trembling.

Artin stirs. His eyelids flutter weakly. His body, though craving rest, tries to respond. His eyes open—just barely.

In a muffled haze, he hears Arun's voice, broken and full of disbelief:

"Artin...? Artin?"

But Artin's body can't hold on. The effort is too much.

His eyelids drop shut again. He slips into a deep, healing sleep.

Arun remains kneeling by the bed, eyes fixed on Artin's bruised, unconscious face. His mind is spiraling.

"Should I call the police? Should I take him to a hospital? Should I tell someone—anyone?"

A hundred thoughts bombard him at once, crashing into each other, leaving him paralyzed in uncertainty. His chest tightens. The logical thing would be to call for help. But something deep inside tells him not to.

He glances at the blood, the wounds, the sheer state Artin is in—and the impossible fact that he's even alive.

"They'll take him away..." Arun whispers to himself, trembling.

"They won't understand."

And he's right. They'll ask questions he can't answer. Arun doesn't know what's happened to his friend, but whatever it is—it's beyond anything the world is ready for.

So finally, with a heavy heart and a thousand unspoken fears, Arun decides to stay silent.

He will protect Artin. No matter what.

Arun removes the smartwatch on Artin's wrist and heads to charge it.

CHAPTER LXXVII

Some time passes. The sun rises, casting a soft golden hue across the city—the world beginning its day, unaware of the miracle that just took place. The clock strikes 6:00 AM. In the quiet kitchen, Arun stands, clutching a mug of steaming coffee, hoping the warmth will calm the storm still raging inside his mind.

Then—a sound.

A faint shuffle, the creak of a bedframe. Arun freezes. He sets the coffee down, heart thudding, and rushes toward his room.

He stops dead at the doorway.

Artin is awake.

He sits hunched on the edge of the bed, the makeshift I.V still trailing from his arm. His body is weak, trembling. His veins still darkened. His skin pale. But his eyes—red, sunken, tired—are open. Alive.

They meet Arun's concern eyes.

A single tear rolls down Arun's cheek, disbelief flooding his expression. His friend is really here. Alive.

Artin's expression is unreadable—blank, worn—but he tries to speak. His voice raspy, broken, tired.

"I'm alright, bro."

He tries to stand, swaying. Instinctively, Arun rushes forward, catching him, supporting his weight.

Artin breathes out a faint chuckle, trying to lighten the moment despite everything.

"I need a bath, bro... I smell like shit, don't I?"

And just like that, Arun's heart aches. Amid all the horror, all the scars, there's still a trace of him in there—the real Artin. A fragile shard of his humanity, still intact.

Arun nods silently, unable to speak, and gently guides him to the bathroom. He hands Artin a fresh set of clothes.

Artin takes them without a word, gives a small nod, and slowly closes the bathroom door behind him.

CHAPTER LXXVIII

Inside the bathroom, Artin stands silently beneath the cold stream of water, his head bowed, letting the droplets cascade over his battered body. His breathing is steady, but shallow—like he's holding something in.

Then, out of the corner of his eye, he catches his reflection in the fogged-up mirror.

He turns to face it.

What he sees shakes him.

His face—bruised, gaunt, drained, yet laced with an eerie strength. His arms, once lean, are now vascular, dense with muscle, veins bulging and twitching just beneath the surface. His chest rising and falling rapidly. He looks dangerous. Alien. Not himself.

As he stares, the mirror begins to betray him.

The tiles behind him warp, shift—the walls of the bathroom morphing into the stone and rot of the burial vault. The place where he clawed his way out of death. It's happening again—inside his head.

His mind screams.

His heart races.

His pupils widen. His face begins to tremble.

Tears well up in his eyes—but so does something else.

A grin.

A sick, trembling grin begins to stretch across his face, tears rolling down his cheeks as his lips part to reveal teeth gritting tightly, almost biting into themselves.

It's not just pain anymore. It's something darker. Something broken.

This face doesn't belong to him.

This isn't him.

This isn't human.

His trembling arm curls into a fist. He flexes—every muscle tightening, grotesquely defined, pushing violently against his skin like they're trying to burst out.

Veins throb, his body seethes with heat and pressure.

He opens his mouth, to scream, to laugh. But nothing comes out. That split second of stunned paralysis before the emotional dam bursts.

He stares again at the reflection—at the thing he's becoming. It's scaring him.

A wave of emotion crashes over him. The grin falters. He starts to sob. His knees buckle.

He drops to the ground under the still-running shower—the water now mixed with tears, his body curled up on the cold tiles as he lays on the floor.

He weeps.

Not just from pain, but from fear.

Fear of the beast within him.

Fear that he's already too far gone.

After some time Artin slowly rises from the cold, wet floor, water dripping from his skin as he steadies himself. His body still aches, his mind still foggy—but the storm inside him has quieted, just for a moment. He takes a shaky breath and looks around, grounding himself. He's still in the bathroom. Still in Arun's house. Still alive.

He turns toward the mirror again, his reflection staring back at him—**half man, half something else.**

He's not ready to accept what he sees.

Not yet.

He doesn't want this monstrous strength, this cursed power that now lives in his veins. **He's not ready to embrace the beast inside him—** but he knows deep down...

They both want the same thing.

Revenge.

His eyes sharpen, locking with his own reflection. His breathing slows. A cold determination replaces the chaos.

He leans closer to the mirror, water still dripping from his hair, and whispers through clenched teeth:

"Whoever did this to me... whoever made me crawl through hell—

I swear, they'll bleed for it.

And Lionsfield...

I'm going to burn it to the ground."

CHAPTER LXXIX

After bathing and changing into fresh clothes, Artin stands in front of the mirror in Arun's room. His reflection still feels like a stranger. He takes a deep breath, then slowly walks toward the kitchen.

Arun stands by the stove, tense and alert. He turns the moment he hears footsteps.

Arun asked, "How do you feel now?" — his voice laced with concern.

Artin replied, "I'm okay," his tone distant, worn.

Before Arun can ask another question Artin asked, "What all happened while I was gone?"

Arun paused for a moment then he looked up, tension in his eyes. "Remember the PredaXine sample?"

Artin nodded slowly.

"It got processed."

Artin's brows furrowed. "By you?"

Arun shook his head. "No... Dr. Vivek handled it."

He continues. "And around 100 liters of raw PredaXine is set to be shipped to the new Sitrom factory—either today or tomorrow. I'm not exactly sure."

Artin leaned in, his expression tightening.

"You know what that means, right?" Arun added. "From 100 liters, they can easily manufacture over 1000 liters of the finished drug."

Artin's voice broke through, filled with confusion. "Why the hell would they need that much PredaXine for?"

Arun replied in a tense tone, "I have some theories..."

He paused, then leaned in slightly, lowering his voice.

"Do you remember how the current BDP government has a feud with Sitrom Logistics and Lionsfield ?"

Artin nodded slowly.

"Well... I think they're trying to change the government."

Artin's eyes narrowed. "How?"

Arun swallowed hard. "You know PredaXine makes a normal person go completely aggressive... like wild, out-of-control crazy. Now here's where it gets twisted—I found out that the UJA party and our company... they're allies."

He exhaled sharply, clearly rattled. "The elections are just three months away, and there's this big public outrage going on—protests against the police and the government. People are furious about the missing girls and the suicides... and the police have no leads."

Artin clenched his jaw. "Go on."

"So, apparently the UJA party is teaming up with protesters. They're planning a massive march toward the Secretariat next week. A peaceful one—at least that's the plan."

Arun's voice dropped. "But I think... the police are going to be drugged. With PredaXine. If they snap during the protest, go rogue and start attacking everyone—including the protesters and UJA people—"

He looked straight into Artin's eyes. "Then the blame falls on the ruling BDP party government. It'll look like they ordered the assault."

Artin's expression darkened as the pieces started to connect.

Arun continued, "That chaos will flip public opinion overnight. The BDP government loses the election, UJA wins all those who died will become UJA's martyrs... and finally Lionsfield gets to run the show with no one stopping them."

Artin clenched his fist, his voice low but firm. "We need to do something—fast."

Arun replied in a firm voice, "Artin stop..!!"

Arun stepped forward, eyes narrowed, emotions bubbling just beneath the surface. "I'm not able to comprehend what the hell is going on, Artin," he said, his voice laced with fear and tension. "You were dead. I carried your coffin. And now you're just... standing here. What the hell happened to you?"

Artin leaned against the wall, his face expressionless, but his eyes told a different story.

"I was killed, Arun," he said quietly. "It was Charles... Charles Lionsfield."

The moment the name left Artin's lips, Arun froze. His face went pale.

"Brother Charles?" Arun asked, almost instinctively, his voice cracking.

Artin nodded slowly. "Yeah. It was him. He injected me with ODFC-4... in front of everyone."

Arun collapsed into a nearby chair, the weight of everything pressing down on him.

"We were working on that damn drug together," Arun said, his voice barely holding together. "I knew that was dangerous but... this..."

Artin's eyes fell to the floor. "I don't know how or why I'm alive. But I am. And something inside me has changed."

Artin looked up, his voice low but sharp.

"Celine..." he continued, eyes narrowing. "She was cheating on me. And she's part of this too. She knew everything."

Artin's mind raced, thoughts colliding in chaos—then suddenly, a spark. His eyes widened. "My watch... it was recording."

He turned to Arun. "Did you see my watch?"

Arun nodded quickly, realization dawning. "Yeah! I put it on charge."

"Get it now, it was recording when all this happened" Artin said, urgency cutting through his voice.

CHAPTER LXXX

Arun rushed to the room and returned with the watch. Artin took it, his fingers moving swiftly as he powered it on. He navigated to the voice recordings, then tapped on the most recent file.

[Recording begins]

Heavy breathing. Muffled movements. Then—metal scraping against concrete.

Artin's voice, barely audible:

"Ngh... wh-where..."

There's a rustle. The sound of straps tightening. Metal clasps click into place, locking down wrists and ankles.

A low, detached voice—unfamiliar and cold:

"Vitals monitor. Plug it in."

Beep. Beep. Beep... The rhythmic pulse of a heartbeat monitor comes online. It stutters. Faint. Weak.

Suddenly—

The unmistakable roar of engines. Two of them. Doors slam shut. Boots on concrete. A door creaks open.

A panicked whisper:

"He's here..."

Then, silence. No footsteps—just a presence. The air in the room feels heavier even through the recording.

Footsteps finally echo. Slow. Calculated. Then—

A voice, slick and venomous, enters:

"Ah... Artin."

It's him. Brother Charles. His tone is lazy, almost amused. The sound of a cigar lighting up follows. A long inhale. Then—

"You want to destroy my company?"

A short chuckle.

"This isn't a company, you fool."

Another step closer. A loud sizzling noise. Flesh burning.

Artin:

"Aghhh..."

A soft whimper. Then silence.

Brother Charles, now colder:

"This... is a family. The Lionsfield Family."
A pause. A sharp intake of breath.
"And when someone touches my family..."
His voice lowers to a dangerous murmur.
"I finish them off."
Another silence, then a wet sound—spit. Followed by a deadly silence.
A sudden blow. THWACK.
Artin's grunt, blood hitting the floor. Someone gasps in the background.
Brother Charles, now enraged:
"Bring me another ODFC sample!"
Scuffling. A drawer opens. A syringe gun clicks—three chambers loaded.
Steps. Then—
THUNK.
The gun slams into Artin's chest.
Click.
Artin:
"AAAGHHH!"
Click.
"AARRGGHH!!"
Click.
No sound now. Just Artin's body convulsing. The vitals monitor beeping wildly.
Beep-beep-beep—faster, climbing.
210... 220... 240... 270... 300—
Long, sustained beep. Flatline.
A trembling voice—one of the scientists:
"He's... he's dead."
Silence follows. Then Brother Charles speaks, calm as ice:
"Good."
A pause. He exhales slowly, like a man satisfied after a good smoke.
"Get the body. Take it to Medicity Hospital. Say he slipped in his bathroom. Cardiac arrest."
Chains clink as the body is unstrapped.
Charles continues, casual now:
"Sidharth i will be staying here for five day. On the third, I'm hosting a party. We need to clean up the chaos this bastard caused. I'll be inviting government officials, powerful people, my mercenaries..."
"Bring your men and the scientists too. They'll love it."

A colder tone returns.
"After the officials leave... we'll have a ritual."
Sidharth, in a low whisper:
"A ritual...?"
Brother Charles, with eerie finality:
"We need a sacrifice. For protection.
"Oh... and no weapons. No one brings weapons inside."
Beat.
"Understood?"
[Recording ends]

CHAPTER LXXXI

Arun sat frozen, the last echoes of the recording still lingering in the air. He turned to Artin, eyes wide with shock.

Artin's eyes were closed. But when he opened them—they were different. Filled with fire. Grief. Rage.

Artin continued, his voice gaining weight. "But this life—whether it was given by God or the Devil... I don't care. Because whatever brought me back didn't do it for peace. It gave me this body... this strength... to destroy that wretched company. I want to end them, Arun. Every single one who tried to end me."

"What do you mean 'end them', Artin? Are you going to f—king kill them?!" Arun's voice cracked, fear crawling into his chest as he took a step back, disturbed by the eerie calm in Artin's voice.

Artin didn't even flinch. His eyes, cold and hollow, locked onto Arun's.

"Yes," he said, voice low and venomous. "I want to kill the people who killed me."

"But Artin—" Arun stammered, "You didn't die, bro! You're alive! I get that you're angry, I get that you're broken—but killing them? That's not justice... that's—"

Artin exploded, voice shaking the walls.

"I AM VERY F—KING MUCH DEAD, ARUN!" he bellowed, eyes burning like coals.

"There's nothing alive in me anymore. They didn't just kill my body—they butchered everything I was. The person I used to be is gone, buried, rotting in a coffin. What came back... this—" He gestured at himself with a trembling hand, "—this is not human anymore. They made me into something else."

Then, his tone dipped into something even darker.

"You want to see what they've created?" he growled.

Without warning, Artin grabbed the collar of his shirt and ripped it open, the fabric tearing like paper. His chest rose and fell with rage, and his skin swelled with dark, twisted veins, pulsating violently as if something alive and evil throbbed beneath.

Arun froze. His eyes widened in terror. It wasn't just rage. It wasn't just trauma.

There was something monstrous inside Artin now.

Artin stepped forward, veins bulging, eyes wild.

"THIS is what they turned me into! A F—KING MONSTER!"

He grabbed a chair and flung it across the room. It shattered into pieces.

"I CAN NEVER GO BACK! My life is OVER! My soul—gone! You still think I'm alive?!"

Then silence.

A long, crushing silence.

And then... he broke.

Artin's voice cracked. His body trembled. His eyes welled up.

"They... they killed those girls in front of me, Arun. I watched. I just stood there, helpless. They screamed. I heard every second of it. And I did NOTHING. I couldn't. I can still hear their screams in my head. They... they kill hundreds every year with their 'recreational' drugs using us as their instruments and now they're about to kill millions with the abomination that's surging through my veins right now..."

He collapsed into the chair, burying his face in his hands. The sobs came—shaking, bitter, helpless.

Arun stood frozen. His chest rose and fell rapidly. Then, slowly, he walked over and placed a hand on Artin's shoulder.

"You're right.." Arun said quietly. "You're f-king right. His voice gets deeper as he spoke. They don't deserve to walk free. Not Charles, not Sidharth, not Celine. They've lost the right to live. And Lionsfield—this whole company—it has to burn to the ground. We'll tear them down. Brick by brick. Body by body. You're not alone in this, Artin. I'm with you... till the very end."

Artin looked up, his bloodshot eyes meeting Arun's. His breathing slowed, just a little. The storm within him calmed—not gone, but contained.

And in that moment, the monster inside him was not alone.

Artin slowly lifted his face from his hands—eyes bloodshot, jaw clenched, but something had returned behind them. Focus. Purpose. The storm was still raging inside, but now it had direction.

Arun tightened his grip on Artin's shoulder, his voice steady but burning with adrenaline.

"Artin... what's the plan? Let's f—king end this. Let's burn that whole thing down."

Artin took a deep breath, cleared his voice. Regaining his composure. He spoke,

"We finish what we started. No second thoughts. No more fear.

CHAPTER LXXXII

After a brief pause, he looked at Arun and spoke, voice low:

"We need to get into the party. I think that's where they're laying out their whole plan. The meeting will be where the UJA party leaders and Charles Lionsfield plan out everything."

He stood slowly, pacing, the gears in his mind spinning fast.

"It's happening at the new Sitrom factory, tonight right?"

"Yes" Arun replies confirming Artin's suspicious, he continues, Sidharth told me there's a party tonight.

Artin paused, eyes narrowing.

"That's the moment. That's when Charles, Sidharth, Celine—every last one of them, devoid of any weapons—will be in the same room. I can do the most damage then."

Artin takes a moment to think. Then he speaks,

"Since you're invited, you'll be able to get into the party without raising suspicion."

He paused, the gears in his mind clearly turning, hesitating for a moment. Then—

"I have an idea, Arun..."

Arun didn't even flinch.

"Tell me, bro. Whatever it is—I'm all in."

Artin stepped closer, his tone growing darker, more calculated.

"The 100 litres of PredaXine... it's being stored in the new Sitrom factory, right?"

Arun nodded, catching on quickly.

"Yeah, I heard Sidharth talk about it."

Artin's voice lowered to a near whisper, like he was speaking something sacred and deadly.

"I have seen the new Sitrom factory once and i noticed something, can you get me the blueprint of that factory. Every room. Every corridor. Every possible blind spot."

Arun's brows furrowed as he thought aloud.

"Hmm... getting into the internal systems won't be easy, especially since it's a new site. But... wait—give me a sec. There might be a way. Yes!! There is a way," Arun exclaimed, a spark of excitement lighting up his face. "Sitrom submitted the factory blueprint to the municipal corporation for approval. And guess what—I have a friend named Sajin working there. Through him, we might just be able to get our hands on it."

He paused for a second, then grinned. "Wait... I've got a better idea."

Without wasting a second, Arun unlocked his phone, opened his online payment app, and swiftly transferred   ₹5000 to Sajin.

Then he tapped on Sajin's contact and hit the call button.

The line rang for a moment, but Sajin didn't pick up the call.

Arun spoke with disappointment, "maybe Sajin isn't awake by now... whatever let's wait for some time and call him again."

CHAPTER LXXXIII

Both of them sat on the chair, minds racing ahead. Then Artin speaks, his voice weighed down by despair.

"Arun... I don't know how to make others understand all this," he mutters, staring blankly ahead. "There's no use in going to the government. I don't even know how I'm going to tell my mother... or Father Rafael... that I'm still alive. I don't even know if I should tell anyone that I'm alive. I don't even know if I'm Artin Samuel... or just a monster wearing his body."

There's a long pause.

Arun gently places a hand on Artin's shoulder, anchoring him in the present, grounding him.

"Artin... calm down. To me, you're very much still my old Artin," he says with quiet assurance.

Artin breathes in, trying to find comfort in those words.

After a short silence, Arun speaks again, his voice softer. "Did you... confess everything to Father Rafael?"

Artin nods slowly. "Yes... everything. From my fight with Celine... to the deaths."

Arun takes a moment, processing that. "Hmm... Father Rafael did tell me you'd confessed... but I didn't know you told him everything. Well... he does suspect Celine. He feels like she's hiding something."

Artin clenches his jaw slightly and nods again.

Then—suddenly—his expression changes. A thought sparks behind his eyes like a flash of lightning in a storm.

"Dr. Gopinath Chandran."

The name slips out like a revelation.

He turns sharply to Arun. " Arun...did you see Dr. Gopinath in the office yesterday?"

Arun shakes his head. "No. He's been absent for some time now. Why?

Artin leans forward, urgency rising in his tone.

"do you remember where all of this started? The day that test subject girl died?"

Arun's face darkens with pain, old memories returning to the surface like scars reopening.

"Yes... how can I forget that day. Our lives changed forever."

"Exactly."

Artin's voice is intense now. "That day... just before I left the facility... Dr. Gopinath gave me a pendrive. He said it contained the answers I was looking for."

Arun's eyes widen, a mix of fear and curiosity tightening in his chest.

"What was in that pendrive?"

Artin replies firmly, his voice hushed as if the walls themselves were listening.

"Mephisto. An AI developed by our company—designed to manage a database of all their illegal activities. All B-grade and A-grade scientists are allowed access to it... but here, in our facility, only A-grade scientists seem to have that kind of clearance."

"Using that pendrive... I uncovered so much about the company, Arun. This isn't the first time they've done things like this. It's been going on for years."

He pauses, his tone now laced with unease.

"But after he gave it to me... I haven't seen Dr. Gopinath ever since."

Arun, his mind rapidly connecting the dots, murmurs, "That's 's actually true. Dr. Gopinath has been absent for five days now."

He frowns, concern shadowing his face.

Artin leans in slightly, eyes locked with Arun's. "Do you know where he lives?"

Arun thinks for a moment, nodding slowly. "Yes... I think I do. Somewhere on Dhanwanthari Road."

Artin's voice sharpens with resolve. "We need to find him. Maybe he can help us."

But Arun, ever cautious, raises a painful possibility.

"What if he's already... killed off, like you were?"

Artin's expression hardens.

"Hmmm... whatsoever, we need to at least go to his house. We can't ignore this."

Suddenly Arun's phone rings. It's Sajin Nair. Arun quickly picks up the call and speaks first.

"Hello, is this Sajin Nair?"

"Yes, who's this?" came the reply.

"It's Arun. We met once at the bar, remember?"

"Ohhh Arun! Yes, yes, I remember! How are you, man?"

Sajin said, his tone warming.

"Doing good, Sajin," Arun replied casually. "Listen... I called you for a small favour."

"What is it?" Sajin asked, curious.

"It's... kinda confidential," Arun said, voice lowering.

"Okay? What is it?" Sajin asked again, now slightly cautious.

Arun hesitated for a beat, then went for it.

"Sorry to bother you but can you get me the blueprint of the new Sitrom factory? The one that was sent for municipal approval?"

There was silence for a second.

"Uhhmm... Arun, that's a risky job, you know... I don't know if I can really pull that off," Sajin said, his tone uncertain.

Arun smirked and leaned back.

"No, but Sajin... don't cut the call just yet. Check your messages. The job might suddenly feel a little... easier."

Sajin glanced at his phone. A notification blinked: ₹5000 credited to your account.

"...Okayyy, Arun," Sajin said, voice now lighter. "I'll get you the blueprint by 8 AM. I reach the office around then, and once I log into the system, I'll send it over. Sound good?"

"Ohh, perfect! Thank you so much, Sajin!" Arun replied, relieved.

"Alright, man. Take care. Bye."

The call ended.

CHAPTER LXXXIV

Arun turns to Artin and says, "So yeah... we'll get the blueprint."

There's a quiet intensity in his voice—one that matches the storm brewing behind Artin's eyes.

Artin gives a slow nod, eyes fixed ahead, the pieces of their plan beginning to fall into place.

But then his expression darkened, the weight of something deeper settling in.

"We have to execute all our plans tonight but before any of this, I need to make sure my mom... and Father Rafael are safe."

He stood, pacing a little, his voice tightening with concern.

"Father Rafael is relatively safe. Not many people know about him, and they'd never suspect a blind and innocent priest like him. But my mom..."

He paused, jaw clenching.

"They could use her. Hurt her to get to me."

He looked at Arun, determination in his eyes.

"I won't let that happen. I have to secure her safety first—only then can we go through with this."

Arun nodded in understanding, quietly watching his friend shift from strategist to son.

There was no turning back now.

Artin sits on the chair, brows furrowed with concern.

"The thing is... I don't even know where my mom is right now. I don't know if she's at my house... or if she went back to the care home after the funeral."

Arun glances up.

"I think she's at your house... probably with Celine."

Artin replies,

"Hmm hey, I have the number of the care home. Can you call them and check."

Arun nods quickly.

Artin provides Arun the number, "Okay, here's the number—9347395157. Call them and say you're a relative, just checking in after the funeral."

Arun dials the number, then puts the phone on speaker.

"Hello, Akashaparva Care Home, Kottayam. How can I help you?"

"Hi, this is Arun from Cochin. I'm a distant relative of Shirley Samuel. I recently heard about her son's passing... can I talk to her and offer my condolences."

There's a pause.

"One moment, sir."

The receptionist covers the receiver, calling out:

"Rejina, can you bring the phone to Shirley Samuel?"

A woman's voice responds in the background:

"Ma'am, Shirley hasn't returned yet... she left for her son's funeral and hasn't come back."

The receptionist returns to the call.

"Sir, she hasn't returned to the care home yet. But I'll let her know you called when she gets back."

"Thank you," Arun replies, then ends the call.

Artin turns to Arun.

"Looks like you were right. She's probably still at my house... with Celine."

He clenches his jaw and continues.

"Then I have to go there. I have to get her out of that house."

Arun looks at Artin, his brows furrowed with concern.

"But Artin... we still haven't figured out how you're gonna get into the party."

Artin thinks for a moment.

"Arun, I have a plan—but for that, you need to go to the office. Everything has to look normal. If we raise even a bit of suspicion, they'll know something's wrong. Just act like it's a regular day.

During that time, I'll go find Dr. Gopinath."

He continues.

"Near my workstation, there's a small drawer. Inside, there's a spare key to my house. You gotta return early from work. Bring that key when you come back."

"Got it. Then?" Arun asks.

"Keep an eye on Celine and Sidharth. Watch their movements at work, see if they talk about the party or the schedule. Anything could help us."

Arun nods again.

"Okay... so after work, I come here with the key."

Artin confirms.

"Yeah. Then we'll head to my house together. You'll go inside and get my mom. Drop me off just a bit away from the house, I will stand outside... mom shouldnt see me, she won't be able to handle seeing me—not yet. If the door's locked from the outside, use the spare key to get in."

"And after that?" Arun asks.

"Once we have her, you'll take her straight to Father Rafael. Tell him she is not safe with Celine and let her stay with him for the time being. I'll stay back at the house and wait for Celine to return, when she returns I will give her a surprise."

"Wait, what? You'll stay in the house?"

Artin nods, eyes cold and focused.

"Yes. Otherwise, she'll know something is wrong the moment my mom isn't at home."

He pauses, his voice low and resolute.

"Through Celine... I'll get into that party."

"But... how?" Arun asks with confusion.

Artin gives a faint smile.

"Trust me, Arun. I got this."

Arun exhales, still uneasy but trusting.

"Okay..."

Artin sits, eyes closed, while Arun waits for Sajin to send the blueprint. The weight of what lies ahead settles between them—but so does the unspoken promise:

This time, they won't let evil win.

CHAPTER LXXXV

8:11 AM.

A sharp ping echoes in the silence.

Artin's eyes snap open. Arun, still seated nearby, glances at his phone—and his face lights up.

"It's the blueprint," he says, excitement cutting through the tension. "I'll grab the laptop!"

He bolts from the room, feet thudding against the floor. Artin slowly sits up, tension rising in his chest. Moments later, Arun returns with his laptop in hand. He powers it on, connects his phone, and opens the blueprint on the larger screen.

The glowing display reveals the detailed layout of the new Sitrom factory.

Together, they lean in.

The blueprint shows a four-storey facility with a basement-level parking lot. The facility contained a VIP meeting room and a smaller store room. Each floor is tightly sealed—heavy-duty security doors, motion sensors, and industrial-grade smoke detectors, sprinklers, and extinguishers wired across every hallway and lab.

Ground Floor – Reception & Meeting Hall

"This," Artin mutters, pointing to the central hall. "This is where they'll host the party. And maybe..."

His eyes narrow.

"...the ritual."

Second Floor – Grade B Laboratory

A larger space, sprawling with workstations. They study the layout, scanning for anything unusual—but it looks relatively standard compared to what they see next.

Third Floor – Grade A Laboratory

This section is smaller but far more secure. High-clearance entry points. Reinforced glass. And there—

Something catches Artin's eye.

He taps the screen. "That looks... odd. What is that structure?"

Arun leans closer. "Wait... I've seen that before."

His fingers dart over the keyboard. He types quickly, pulling up the Sitrom Medical Devices website. A few scrolls later—

"Here. It's a Bio-Fluid Infusion Chamber. One of the most advanced in the market."

He clicks into the model.

Product: Sitrom iX Biochemical Chamber Mk.IV

Specs:

— Built-in thermal stabilizer (cooling system)

— Infusion rate: 1 litres in 5 mins

— Operates via Central Venous Catheter Network (CVCN)

— Used in advanced biomedical transformation and chemical testing

Arun whistles low. "That thing can inject an entire human with six litres of whatever's in that tank... in minutes. And they're keeping it in the Grade A lab? That's no accident."

Artin's face hardens. "They're getting ready for mass-scale human testing... or worse."

Then they scroll to the piping blueprint.

Two large storage tanks are located outside the facility, behind a sealed barrier. Both are connected via insulated pipe systems leading directly into the building.

One tank is labeled CHEMICAL STORAGE. The other—WATER RESERVE.

Arun zooms in.

"Look at this," he says, pointing at the junction. "The pipelines from both tanks are routed through the same lever control system. That's extremely risky."

Artin stares. "That's not a design flaw. That's a feature."

He traces the chemical pipes—they flow directly into processing units in the Grade B lab. And the water tank's pipes? They feed into every tap, fire extinguisher, smoke detector sprayer, and sprinkler head in the building.

Then the realization hits him. Artin leans back, exhaling slowly.

"Yes. This what I was exactly looking for. We can switch the contents."

Arun's eyes widen. "Wait... you mean—?"

Artin nods. "If we reroute the chemical tank into the sprinkler system, we could infect the entire building. Once the fire systems are triggered..."

"Wait—you mean you're going to infect everyone at the party with PredaXine while you go in to finish them all??"

Arun's voice trembles, a mix of panic and disbelief clouding his words.

"That's literally suicide, Artin. You do know what happens when someone's exposed to PredaXine, right? They turn into animals—mindless, rabid. They'll tear apart anything standing in front of them. We dont even have any weapons Artin!"

Artin doesn't flinch. His voice is low, calm—eerily composed.

"Arun... in a forest filled with savage animals... an abomination is always more dangerous."

He stands up, the dim light catching the edges of his shadowed face.

"They'll try to kill me. They'll bring death like they always do...

But what can death do... to someone who's already defied it?

I am the weapon Arun."

Artin's eyes lock onto Arun's.

"I will walk out of that room alive. And whoever is left behind—they'll kill each other because of the drug. It's not suicide, Arun.

It's mercy.

It's justice.

It's a favor to the world... not foolishness."

Arun stares at him, shaken.

There's something terrifying in Artin's resolve—but beneath it, the same fire they both shared when this fight began.

"But still... it's dangerous, Artin. I don't want to lose you again," Arun says, his voice barely above a whisper.

Artin's tone softens, but his resolve doesn't waver.

"You remember what we promised, right? That we'd take all of them down—every last one. This is how it has to be."

Arun takes a breath. The fear is still in his chest—but so is the promise. So is the rage.

He nods slowly.

Artin places a hand on his shoulder.

"Now theres only one last critical task for you Arun. Once you're inside the party, you need to pull the diversion lever. It's near the back corridor, just behind the wine cellar."

He leans in.

"There are no cameras there—it's a blindspot. One pull, and PredaXine will flow through all the taps, sprinklers everywhere.

"Hmmm... I'll do it," Arun says, his voice steady, reassuring.

Artin nods slowly, then glances at the clock on the wall.

"It's almost 9AM," he says. "Time for you to head to work."

"Hmm," Arun agrees with a sigh, rising to his feet. He adjusts his shirt, then looks back at Artin.

"While I go to work... you're going to meet Father Rafael, right?"

Artin nods silently.

Arun pauses, eyes scanning Artin's torn clothes and pale skin.

"You might need better clothes... and something to hide yourself."

Without waiting for a reply, he goes into his room.

CHAPTER LXXXVI

Moments later, he returns—arms full.

A black hoodie, black pants, a black mask, and a pair of dark sunglasses.

"Take this," he says, handing them over. "Get ready quick. We got some real shit to deal with."

Artin nods silently, accepting the clothes.

He walks toward the other room to change, while Arun turns to his room, adjusting his collar and preparing to leave for work.

Artin exits the room, now wearing the black hoodie, mask, and sunglasses—his face completely hidden from the world. Only the sleek smartwatch on his wrist remains visible, silently ticking toward the storm ahead.

Arun waits by the door, eyes scanning him. Without a word, he pulls out a small earpiece and hands it over.

"Here, take this," Arun says. "This'll be our mode of communication. Since you lost your phone, this earpiece connects directly to your smartwatch. We won't let this plan fail. This plan is perfect."

Artin accepts it, fitting the earpiece with a sharp nod, his eyes burning with purpose beneath the glasses.

No more fear. No more hesitation.

They step into Arun's car, the engine roaring to life as both of them strap in—driven, focused, ready to face the chaos they've chosen.

The city blurs past as the car speeds through the morning streets.

They ride in silence—two souls stitched together by guilt, loyalty, and revenge.

Soon, they reach Dhanwanthari Road.

Arun pulls the car to a halt.

Artin's hand lingers on the door handle, hesitating for a second.

"Arun..." he says, voice low but firm, "No matter what happens—I'll make sure your mom's treatment goes well. I swear it."

Arun turns to look at him, eyes soft but resolute.

"It's fine, bro. I don't want this blood-stained money to heal my mother. I'd rather treat her with my sweat-stained money instead."

Artin stares at him for a moment... then gives a small, grateful nod.

"You're like a brother to me," he says. "So your mother is my mother."

Arun smiles faintly.

"I know, bro... Till the end, we stand together."

Artin grips his shoulder once, firmly—then steps out of the car. He turns, gives Arun a final nod, and with that same faint smile still lingering behind the mask... Artin walks away.

The mission has begun.

CHAPTER LXXXVII

As Arun drives off toward the Lionsfield Pharma office, Artin begins his walk down Dhanwanthari Road, scanning his surroundings with purpose.

He moves quietly, eyes flicking from one nameplate to another, searching for any sign of Dr. Gopinath's residence.

Each step is measured, deliberate—like a tiger stalking its prey.

Artin keeps his head slightly bowed, avoiding eye contact, blending in with the crowd that passes by.

To them, he's just another pedestrian. But beneath the mask and sunglasses, his mind races.

He walks like a shadow—silent, invisible, but searching.

Artin walks further down, turning into a less crowded, quieter stretch of Dhanwanthari Road. The chaos of the city fades behind him.

Then—he sees it.

A rusted nameplate hangs crookedly outside an old compound wall:

"DR. GOPINATH CHANDRAN."

Artin halts. His eyes sweep across the street.

No one nearby.

No footsteps behind.

The house seems abandoned. A stack of old newspapers lies untouched near the front gate—proof that no one has exited or entered for days. The car porch stands empty.

Something's off.

Artin slips around the side of the compound, staying low, silent. When he reaches the back, he studies the wall, then climbs over it with minimal effort, landing inside the property like a phantom.

He approaches the back door and tries the handle. Locked.

He glances around once more. No eyes on him.

With one sharp kick, a dent caves into the door's center.

Another—BANG!—and the door crashes inward with a jarring thud.

Quickly, Artin steps inside and repositions the door into its frame. With a firm punch, he wedges it back, masking the break-in as best as possible.

The house is dark. Cold. Silent.

He treads forward with caution.

The kitchen is wrecked—drawers flung open, plates shattered, the fridge door swinging slightly.

He enters the living room—worse.

Broken vases, a smashed TV, ripped cushions. Even the CCTV camera has been ripped off and left hanging, wires exposed like veins.

A chill runs down Artin's spine.

This wasn't a robbery. Something worse happened here.

He pushes open the bedroom door.

Chaos.

Everything's trashed.

Furniture overturned, books torn apart, drawers ransacked. No blood. No body. Just destruction.

A hollow silence that screams something terrible had happened.

Artin begins combing through the room, hands moving fast but precise.

Burned papers lie in the corner—charred remains of files. Someone tried to erase evidence.

But Artin doesn't stop. He keeps searching—flipping through drawers, reaching behind shelves—until finally...

He freezes.

His fingers grip the edge of a file, almost burned half-buried under a fallen cabinet.

He pulls it out.

The name written on the file sends a jolt through his entire body—

"AZAZEL'S BLOOD OR D-FACTOR."

Artin stands frozen.

His breath catches.

A cold bead of sweat rolls down his temple, trailing past the mask as the words burn into his eyes.

His heartbeat pounds louder than the silence in the room. Hands trembling slightly, he flips through the pages—hoping, praying for answers.

But the file is almost entirely destroyed.

Only fragments remain.

Scorched edges, ink smeared and unreadable. Pages blackened into ash.

His fingers twitch with frustration.

"Damn it..."

Artin tears the half-burned page from the file and quickly stuffs it into his pocket. His hands are still trembling, but his mind is locked in—sharp, focused, relentless.

He spends the next hour scouring every corner of the house. Drawers, closets, under furniture—nothing. No hidden drives, no notes, no traces of where Dr. Gopinath might have gone. Only silence and the haunting wreckage of what once was.

By the time he checks his smartwatch, it's almost 12 PM.

With a sigh of frustration, he makes his way back to the kitchen. He yanks the broken door open and steps out, then forcefully pins it back into its frame like before—just enough to not draw attention.

He looks around the street.

Still calm.

Still no one.

Like a shadow, Artin leaps back over the wall, landing silently in the alley behind the house. He dusts himself off and slips into the road, blending back into the world.

Raising his wrist, he activates the earpiece through his smartwatch and speaks calmly, his voice low but urgent.

"Arun, pick up."

The call finally connects. Artin speaks first, his voice calm, unwavering—cold with purpose.

"I think they dealt with Dr. Gopinath the same way they did with me. Or... he escaped. Either way, he destroyed everything he was researching. But one thing's clear—he knew a lot about whatever the hell is flowing through my veins."

A pause. Then Arun's voice crackles through the earpiece, frustration heavy in his tone.

"Dammit... we have no other leads left."

Artin exhales slowly, his eyes scanning the crowd around him as he walks.

"Don't worry. We'll proceed as planned."

A beat of silence, then his voice softens slightly.

"I want to go to the church, Arun... I just don't know if I should."

Arun replies after a moment of thought.

"Hmm... it's almost 1 PM. Everyone's heading out for lunch. I'll call you back after it's over, alright?"

Artin nods faintly, though Arun can't see it.

"Okay."

The call ends.

CHAPTER LXXXIX

Artin walks through the streets and blends into the sea of people.

No longer a man.

Just a shadow in motion.

A ghost walking among the living.

Artin finally reaches St. Paul Church. He walks in slowly, quietly, like a ghost returning to familiar ground. The interior is dim and silent, bathed in a faint golden light from the stained-glass windows. He slips into the last bench, eyes weary, heart heavy.

Up ahead, seated in the front row, is Father Rafael—kneeling in prayer.

Artin sees him.

His heart sinks.

A longing rises within him—a need to run forward, fall at his feet, embrace him. But he doesn't. He can't. Not yet. If he does, everything will fall apart. His plans will crumble. Father Rafael would never let him walk this path of vengeance and fire. He would never let Artin fight again. He would never let him be taken away again.

Father Rafael remains bowed in prayer, but his senses are sharp. The blind priest feels it—someone has entered the church. Someone is now seated at the last bench.

But something's wrong.

That presence—it isn't holy. It isn't peaceful.

It radiates darkness.

The priest's face tightens. A cold sweat forms on his brow. His spine stiffens. The presence behind him carries the weight of evil—familiar, yet unnatural. He doesn't turn. Not yet. He continues praying, lips moving, but the unease grows heavier with every second.

Finally, he reaches for his old phone, tucked beside him. With trembling fingers, he dials the parish clerk.

"Peter... can you please come to the nave. Now," he whispers, voice low, barely above a breath.

Peter responds instantly.

"Yes, Father. On my way."

Father Rafael doesn't move. Not a single twitch. He holds his breath, waiting.

A few minutes pass.

Peter enters the nave, stepping lightly.

He looks around and walks up to the priest.

"What is it, Father?" he asks gently.

Father Rafael's face is pale.

"Is someone sitting behind us?"

Peter glances back, scanning the rows of pews.

His face contorts with slight confusion.

"No, Father... it's just you and me here."

A cold silence falls.

Father Rafael feels something twist deep inside him. Something unexplainable. An eerie sensation crawls across his skin.

He rises slowly, gripping his cane, leaning slightly toward Peter.

Without saying a word more, the two of them quietly exit the nave, leaving behind the stillness of the holy place—haunted now by a presence neither of them can see.

Artin exited the church before anyone could notice him. Like a phantom slipping through shadows, he vanished into the sunlight. As he walked away, the time is 2 PM Artin's smartwatch buzzed. He tapped his earpiece to connect the call.

Arun's voice came through, slightly anxious.

"Artin, Celine and Sidharth just left the building. I have no clue where they're headed."

Artin replied calmly,

"Okay. You do one thing, you leave too, lets go to my house. I'll wait near St. Joseph Chapel Road—pick me up from there."

"Got it. Leaving right now," Arun responded.

He grabbed the spare car keys from Artin's desk and hurried toward the basement to start the vehicle.

Meanwhile, Artin moved quickly through the streets, weaving through the crowd toward the designated spot.

At the same time, Celine and Sidharth were unknowingly driving toward the same location—heading to a mall just off St. Joseph Chapel Road.

Suddenly, another call buzzed in. Arun again.

"Artin—they're heading to the same road. I can see their car right ahead of me!"

Artin's voice remained flat.

"Don't worry. They won't see me."

"Artin, just be cautious," Arun urged.

Artin finally reached St. Joseph Chapel Road. He stood on the opposite side of the mall, blending into the moving crowd, his presence cold and silent.

Then, a sleek black Mercedes pulled into view. Inside sat Celine and Sidharth—laughing, relaxed, unaware. Artin watched them from a distance, expressionless, unreadable. But his eyes... burned with something darker.

Celine's gaze wandered—then froze.

She locked eyes with him.

That figure. That stare. That impossible face.

It was him.

He didn't move. He just stood there. Menacing. Cold. His eyes boring into hers like a curse reborn.

Her breath caught. A chill swept through her body.

"ARTIN!" she gasped.

"It's him—I saw him! Sidharth, reverse the car!"

Sidharth, startled, looked at her.

"What? What are you talking about? It's probably just someone who looks like—"

"No! Reverse the car!" she cried again, her voice trembling.

Sidharth complied, reversing out of the parking lot in confusion. They jumped out, eyes scanning the crowd frantically.

But he was gone.

Just like a ghost, Artin had vanished. Arun had arrived just in time and picked him up, disappearing into the flow of the city.

Inside the car, Artin leaned back in the seat, watching the mall fade away behind them. A small smile crept onto his face—subtle, cold, victorious.

He knew exactly what that look had done to her.

They drove in silence toward Artin's house. The clock ticked close to 2 PM.

Arun finally broke the silence.

"So... Dr. Gopinath is a dead end?"

Artin nodded, eyes fixed ahead.

"Yes."

Arun hesitated, then asked,

"Do you feel anything, like pain? Any side effects from the drug?"

Artin replied coldly,

"No. Nothing so far. Let's just hope I don't die soon."

"Artin... don't say that," Arun murmured.

"Okay," Artin replied softly, then pulled a torn piece of paper from his pocket. He handed it to Arun.

"I found this at Dr. Gopinath's place."

He read the words aloud:

"D-Factor, or Azazel's Blood."

Arun's eyes widened slightly.

"That sounds exactly like something that could bring someone back to life."

Artin nodded, his voice low.

"Yes. But we'll deal with that later—after we handle them tonight."

(Referring to Brother Charles, Sidharth, and Celine.)

As they neared Artin's house, he signaled Arun to stop the car.

"I'll stay out here. You go in," Artin said calmly.

Arun nodded and drove up to the gate. It was shut.

He stepped out of the car, scanning the surroundings. The afternoon sun cast long shadows as he opened the gate and stepped inside. Artin's car was still in the porch, untouched.

He rang the doorbell.

Ding dong...
Silence.
Again.
Ding dong...
Still nothing.
A faint unease began to creep up his spine.
He cupped his hands and called out,
"Shirley Aunty? Shirley Aunty!"
No response.
Frowning, he reached into his pocket and pulled out the spare key Artin had given him. He unlocked the front door and stepped inside.
"Shirley Aunty?" he called again, voice echoing through the house.
Nothing.
No footsteps. No voice. No sound.
Something was wrong.

CHAPTER XCII

A terrible sense of dread settled in Arun's chest. His hands shook slightly as he pulled out his phone and called Artin.

"Come here, right now" his voice laced with panic.

Within moments, Artin stepped into the compound. As he approached the porch, he saw Arun sitting there in silence—staring blankly into the air.

Artin's tone sharpened instantly.

"Arun. What happened?"

Arun didn't respond.

Artin's voice hardened.

"Arun, WHAT HAPPENED?"

Arun finally spoke, eyes still distant.

"Shirley Aunty... she's not here."

Artin froze.

His pulse surged. A storm swelled behind his calm expression. Anger and fear churned in his chest.

His voice dropped low and dangerous.

"Arun. When does the party start?"

"3 PM," Arun replied quickly.

Artin checked the time.

"It's 2:30 now. Go. Stick to the plan. Everything will go as planned. Go!"

Arun hesitated, worried.

"But Artin how-?"

Artin looked him dead in the eyes.

"I'll manage. Do what I told you. We don't have time. Leave. Now."

Arun reluctantly agreed. He got in the car and drove off toward the new Sitrom factory where the party was being held.

Artin watched the car disappear, then turned and entered the house. With a firm hand, he locked the door behind him.

The living room was dark. Curtains drawn. No sunlight. No sound.

Artin walked forward slowly and sat down in the dark, in the heart of his home... waiting.

Waiting for Celine in the silence.

But Artin's mind was in overdrive.

Where is my mother?

The question echoed like thunder inside his skull. Over and over. Each repetition tightening something inside him, winding his anger like a ticking bomb.

He sat in the darkness, fists clenched, his breath steady—but his thoughts anything but.

His jaw tightened.

His mother's voice, her smile, her presence—all suddenly felt like memories he was trying to hold onto before they slipped away into the void. That void that followed wherever they went.

His hands began to tremble—not in fear, but fury.

They had crossed the line.

Taking her... if they had touched even a strand of her hair...

His blood boiled. His heartbeat was no longer a rhythm—it was war drums.

The silence of the house no longer felt empty.

After a while, the faint hum of a car reaches Artin's ears. His ear twitches. His muscles tense like coiled steel.

The sound grows clearer—wheels coming to a stop just outside.

Celine and Sidharth step out, laughing, unaware of the storm waiting inside.

Celine holds a bottle of expensive champagne—meant for tonight's party. Their footsteps approach. Their laughter grates in Artin's ears like nails on glass.

Two clicks.

The key turns. The door unlocks.

Celine steps inside first and flips on the lights—

Her smile vanishes.

Her eyes widen in raw terror.

Artin.

Sitting still in the center of the room, legs crossed in a figure-four lock, head slightly tilted, arms resting like a statue. Expressionless. Cold.

Their eyes meet.

Celine drops the champagne.

CRASH!

Glass shatters, champagne floods the floor like blood from a wound.

Sidharth bursts in, alerted by the sound.

His eyes freeze. His breath catches in his throat.

"Ar-Artin..?!" he gasps.

He instinctively reaches out, grabbing Celine's hand. Artin slowly rises from the couch—into full view under the light. His face hollow, his stare inhuman.

Panic overtakes Sidharth. He pulls Celine, lunging for the door—hoping to trap Artin inside.

Foolish.

If Artin could get in undetected, he could get out the same way.

In a flash, Artin's hand grabs the flower vase on the table.

WHAM!

The vase crashes into Sidharth's head with ruthless precision. The blow sends him staggering, blood spilling down his face.

Celine shrieks, horrified.

Artin walks forward, eyes bloodshot, steps deliberate—his presence monstrous.

"SOMEBODY HELP!!!" she screams.

Artin keeps moving, his face twitching, his rage boiling over.

His voice is not his own anymore—it's something deeper, darker:

"WHERE IS MY MOTHER?"

Celine panics and bolts toward one of the rooms—but Artin's hand snatches her wrist mid-run. With a terrifying force, he hurls her across the room.

She crashes onto the floor, a cry of pain escaping her lips.

But Artin doesn't stop.

He towers over her.

"WHERE IS MY MOTHER?" he repeats, each word heavier than the last.

Sidharth, blood pouring from his head, groans from the floor.

"ARTIN... if you kill us, you'll never find out where she is..."

Artin's eyes slowly shift. His breathing heavy, his face locked in a predator's gaze. He turns to Sidharth.

He grabs him by the collar and slams him against the door.

Sidharth avoids eye contact.

Artin's presence is suffocating.

Suddenly—

Celine lunges, holding a jagged piece of the broken vase. She stabs it into Artin's back.

CRACK!

The shard snaps—half of it embedded deep inside him.

Unfazed he turns to her slowly.

His hand grips her throat.

She chokes, her feet lift slightly off the ground as his grip tightens.

Sidharth sees his chance.

With trembling fingers, he pulls out a silver canister—the sedative spray. In one swift motion, he breaks the top off, shattering the atomiser. Then he jams it against Artin's nose and pushes.

A violent blast of gas hisses out—right into Artin's face.

Artin blinks. His grip weakens. His knees shake.

Celine falls to the ground, coughing, gasping for air.

Artin stumbles backward.

His eyes flutter.

And then—
He collapses.

Sidharth and Celine breathe profusely, their chests heaving—shattered, traumatized by what just happened. Celine is speechless, her mind fractured from the near-death experience. Her limbs tremble uncontrollably. She stares at the unconscious figure on the floor—Artin. Or... something that looks like him. Is this really Artin? A ghost? A demon? Her life, once filled with comfort and shallow luxury, now feels like it's plunging headfirst into an eternity of torment—for the sins she committed, for the man she betrayed.

Sidharth, just as shaken, tries to collect himself. His voice trembles but carries urgency. "Get me a rope," he orders, trying to mask his fear with control.

Celine nods shakily and stumbles off, returning moments later with a rope. Her hands are trembling as she passes it to him.

Sidharth crouches and binds Artin's limbs tightly. The body he ties down is not the man they once knew. His physique—muscular, dense, powerful—was nothing like before. His face... it held a fierceness beyond human. The only thing that still looked like him was the smartwatch on his wrist. Everything else had transformed.

Sidharth wastes no time. He pulls out his phone and calls Brother Charles.

"Hello, Sidharth," Brother Charles answers, his voice calm as always.

Sidharth gulps. "Sir... I don't know how to explain this. It—it seems... Artin's body has accepted the drug."

There's a pause on the line—brief, but chilling. Then, for the first time, Brother Charles's voice isn't calm. It spikes in alarmed disbelief.

"WHAT?! How?!"

Sidharth recounts the chaos: the confrontation, the blood, the impossible survival. He speaks of the way

Artin stood, the strength in his muscles, the rage in his eyes before falling unconscious again.

And for a few moments—Charles, Sidharth, and Celine—none of them speak. All three are still in disbelief at what they've just witnessed.

This should not be possible.

A person could survive the ODFC-4 drug for up to two days—only in extremely low doses. And even that left them fractured. The test girls died because they were given a higher dose—and because they were young. Their systems couldn't bear it. That was the rule. That was the science.

But Artin? He had been injected with three times the deadly dose. And yet, he came back.

He didn't survive.

He won over death.

Brother Charles is the first to break the silence, and when he speaks again, it's no longer calm. It's euphoric. Hysterical.

"Heh... heh... HAHAHAHAHA!" His laugh bursts through the phone. "Bring him here. Bring him here immediately! This... this is going to be the best party ever!"

Charles's voice grows more manic with every word, sending shivers down Sidharth's spine.

"His blood... it's a gift to Father Mortis! With his DNA, we'll do what science, what God failed to do! This is the moment I've waited for! We can bind any dark factor compound to a human now! Do you realize what this means?"

He laughs wildly again, unhinged. "The dawn of a new race is upon us! Father Mortis's dream—our dream—it's finally real!!"

Sidharth, breathing heavily, nods silently. The fear in him now replaced with fanatic excitement.

He hangs up and immediately makes another call, summoning his goons to the house. They arrive swiftly, lifting Artin's body like a precious relic and loading him into their van. Behind them, Sidharth and Celine follow in their own car, heading straight to the new Sitrom factory for the party of the century.

The ride is silent at first. Celine, still trembling, wipes her tears. Her voice cracks as she whispers, "Will we win...?"

Sidharth turns, eyes gleaming with madness. "YES. We're going to rule over the world!!"

He sees the emptiness in her gaze and reaches into the car's hidden compartment, pulling out a strip of ecstasy pills. He hands them to her.

"Celine... take this. And listen to me."

She hesitates—but her trembling fingers accept the pill. With a reluctant motion, she puts it on her tongue and swallows. Moments later, her pupils dilate, her breath deepens, and her fear begins to morph into a dark euphoria.

Sidharth smirks. The drug's effect kicks in.

"From Artin's DNA," he growls, voice thick with delusion, "we'll find a way to bind our blood with the dark factor. And then... we're no longer humans."

His knuckles whiten around the steering wheel as he continues, "We'll be gods to them. Not kings. Not rulers. Gods. We'll create a new race. A race without pain.

Without weakness. Without any flaws."

The madness is infectious. Celine screams ecstatically, her voice laced with pleasure, "AHHHHH YESSSS!!!"

Their laughter fills the car. Twisted. Hysterical. No trace of sanity remains.

They're not human anymore.

They never were.

Eventually they reach their destination. The Sitrom factory no longer looked like an industrial complex—it had been transformed into a den of decadence. Surrounded by guards holding weapons. Its front was decked out in dazzling lights, pulsating with bass-heavy music. Liquor flowed freely. Pole dancers performed on glittering platforms. Lines of luxury cars gleamed in the moonlight, their engines silent but their presence screaming wealth, power, and corruption.

Sidharth and Celine stepped out of their car after parking in the VIP zone. Their faces were lit by the neon glow, no trace of fear or guilt—only hunger. Hunger for power, for the future they were about to carve with blood, money, and faith in Father Mortis.

Behind them, the black Sitrom van rolled to a stop. Two masked goons yanked open the doors and carefully pulled Artin's unconscious body out. Still tied, still unmoving—yet still breathing. They carried him into the side entrance of the factory and suspended him upside down in the storeroom.

Back outside, Sidharth and Celine made their way to the front of the building. The entire facade had transformed into a massive party venue. Spotlights painted the sky. Electronic music shook the ground. Drugs were offered openly—cocaine lines on mirrored trays, ecstasy pills in crystal bowls. Pole dancers spun on golden rods, cheered on by groups of intoxicated elites.

Many people greeted them—scientists, corporate goons, pharma executives, foreign guests, and other Lionsfield staff, all smiling under the influence of substances and delusions.

Among the crowd stood Arun, frozen.

His eyes locked onto Sidharth and Celine as they walked in, grinning like royalty. His pulse quickened. His heart screamed: Where is Artin? Where is he?! But he couldn't speak. Couldn't act. He was surrounded. Outnumbered. Just one honest man caught in a pit of wolves.

Suddenly, a convoy of black SUVs screeched to a halt outside the gate. The music dimmed slightly as heads turned.

Brother Charles had arrived.

A fleet of vehicles followed behind him—cars marked by flags, badges, and insignias of power. High-ranking government officials. Police commissioners. State-level intelligence heads. Business magnates. And then most notably—key leaders of the UJA party.

The DJ took the mic, voice booming through the speakers:

"Ladies and gentlemen, please welcome the captain of Lionsfield Pharma India... Mr. Charles Lionsfield! The man behind tonight's celebration!"

The crowd erupted into applause and cheers.

Brother Charles stepped out of the car, surrounded by elite bodyguards and shadowy men in suits. His long coat billowed as he walked. Dark glasses. Expression unreadable. Around him, mercenaries from different global mafias flanked him—followers of the Mortis cult, each bearing a unique tattoo under their sleeve.

Sidharth approached him reverently. Without hesitation, he bent down and kissed Charles's hand.

Celine followed, doing the same.

Charles smiled faintly. Like a prophet being honored by his disciples.

This party wasn't just celebration.

It was a conversion.

Tonight, they would slowly turn every Lionsfield employee, scientist, and investor into a devotee of Mortis. One by one. Drink by drink. Ritual by ritual.

Sidharth climbed onto the elevated stage and took the mic, raising his glass high.

"LET THE PARTY BEGIN!!!"

The crowd roared.

Music blasted.

The bass thumped so loud it shook glasses on the table.

People swarmed the dance floor. Some flocked toward the drugs, eyes glittering. Some were mesmerized by the pole dancers. Others were already drunk, laughing and howling like animals in a circus.

But while the party exploded outside—inside, deeper within the factory—the real event was about to begin.

Brother Charles, Sidharth, Celine, and his top mercenaries led the government officials, senior police officers, and U party leaders into the VIP meeting room—a vast, soundproof space lined with gold-trimmed walls, LED screens, and a long black conference table.

This party was the cover.

The real purpose was this meeting—and the ritual to follow.

As everyone took their seats, Sidharth leaned in toward Brother Charles.

"Sir," he whispered. "I have brought him."

Brother Charles didn't look at him. He simply nodded once.

"Good. We'll take care of it after this meeting." He exhaled sharply. "It was extremely difficult to bring all these people here at the same time. We finish the meeting fast, then we will deal with him."

He paused.

"Because if this meeting is successful..." he grinned devilishly, "...we're going to get 500 crores from the UJA party. And with the example of what's going to happen in kerala—from what we've created—we'll sell PredaXine to the world. Militaries, black markets, terrorist regimes. At a price we set. On our terms."

Sidharth's breath hitched with excitement.

He whispered with reverence: "Hail Father Mortis."

Brother Charles turned toward him, smiling.

"Hail Father Mortis."

And just like that—the meeting began.

The heavy steel doors of the VIP room sealed shut behind them with a hiss.

A dark silence hung for a moment, broken only by the muffled echoes of music and debauchery from outside. The room was lit dimly by overhead lights shaped like inverted crosses. At the far end stood a large projection screen with the logo of Sitrom Chemicals slowly fading into the Mortis cult symbol.

Brother Charles stepped forward to the head of the obsidian conference table. All eyes turned to him.

He didn't sit.

He stood.

He placed both hands on the table and looked around the room—locking eyes with the police commissioners, the BDP party MLAs, the pharma investors, and UJA party leaders seated across from each other. Behind them stood elite guards with earpieces and concealed firearms.

Charles's voice cut through the air like a blade.

"Good evening, gentlemen... and welcome."

A pause.

"As you all know, we are here to finalise the PredaXine deal."

He turned to the UJA party leaders.

"We set the price tag at 700 crores for the promised volume of PredaXine."

Then shifting his gaze to the pharma investors seated to his right, he continued.

"From that sum, 7% will go directly to our pharma investors."

The four investors exchanged subtle smiles, mentally calculating—56 crores each. A silent victory.

Just then, one of the BDP MLAs stood up. Tall, well-dressed, his voice carried the weight of many backroom dealings. He adjusted his watch before speaking.

"On behalf of the BDP MLAs who are prepared to resign and join UJA—we place our demand."

"Six crores for each MLA. In addition, a confirmed ticket to compete in the next election. The morning after the massacre, we'll resign. That will collapse the government. And the state will be pushed to elections."

He sat back down, crossing his legs, his fingers drumming lightly on the table.

All eyes turned toward the man at the far end—Mr. Pratap Shekaran, the sharp-eyed, silver-tongued leader of the UJA party.

He tapped the table twice—clack clack—before rising.

He looked amused.

"Well, well... the 700 crore price tag..."

He chuckled.

"...is a bit too steep for us. But—"

"—we accept your demand."

A beat. He turns to the MLA.

"Six crores per MLA, though? I'm not a fan of bargaining, but let's be honest... five crores is more than generous."

His tone was casual, but his words were razor-sharp.

"Even if you don't switch sides... your government will fall anyway."

He flashed a politician's smile.

"So yes. Five crores. Final offer."

The MLA leaned back, contemplating. The room held its breath.

Finally, he nodded.

"Agreed."

Pratap grinned wider.

"Haha, good! So... how many MLAs are we talking?"

The MLA laughed.

"How many MLAs do you need, Pratapetta?"

That sealed it. Quiet chuckles rippled through the room. Even the commissioners smirked.

The deal was struck.

The conversation spiraled into further details—vote banks, media cover-ups, distribution logistics, trial demos, and the upcoming massacre that would serve as both a warning and a testimony to PredaXine's power. The police commissioners joined in—assuring tactical cover and silence from key stations across the state.

Everything was falling into place like dark clockwork.

Finally, Brother Charles stood again. The room stilled.

"Thank you, gentlemen, for making this meeting a success."

He paced slowly around the table.

"I promise you all—especially the UJA party—this 700 crores is not a payment. It's an investment. What we've forged here tonight is not just a deal. It's a legacy."

He pointed outward—toward the partying masses.

"Together, we will conquer Kerala. Then India. Then the world."

He raised his glass of wine.

"To Father Mortis. To power. To a new era."

Everyone in the room stood and clapped. The claps grew into loud, confident applause. Glasses were raised. Eyes sparkled.

The meeting was over.

The future had just been sold.

Brother Charles stepped out of the meeting room, his white coat swaying as Sidharth and Celine followed close behind. The heavy steel doors groaned shut behind them, sealing in the smell of cigars, power, and betrayal.

Inside, the VIPs stood up, ready to leave now that the business was done. Guards stood at attention, but most were now reassigned—Brother Charles had issued new orders.

Discreetly, black SUVs were summoned to the rear gates.

"Get the MLAs out of here—quietly," Charles murmured to his comms. "Take them to the Elysian Resort. No one sees them. No media, no slip-ups."

His voice was cold and precise.

The MLAs, cloaked and hurried, were quietly herded into the waiting vehicles by the guards—guards who would now be absent from the main complex. The facility's security count had dropped significantly... but the transportation of those MLAs without raising suspicion was more important than any immediate risk.

Soon, the VIPs left, their vehicles disappearing one by one into the shadows of the night. The guards left with them.

Everyone was gone.

Everyone except Mr. Pratap Shekaran, who remained in the lounge, sipping a final glass of whiskey.

Charles turned to Sidharth, he gave the next command.

"End the party. It's time."

Sidharth nodded and walked to the stage. He picked up the mic.

"Soo... thank you all for attending the party," he said with a sly smile. "It's 11 PM. I request all of you to return home. The party is... officially commencing."

The employees—secretaries, lower-rank scientists, chauffeurs, and assistants—began to leave, their laughter and chatter fading into the darkness.

But not everyone left.

Those who remained:

The pharma investors

Sidharth's goons

Brother Charles's elite mercenaries

Brother Charles himself

All A-grade scientists

Two B-grade scientists, one of whom was Arun

Arun had been called to stay back. The reason wasn't clear at first—but he suspected it had something to do with the whispers he'd been hearing all night.

He stood awkwardly near the labs, anxious.

Just then, Sidharth approached him, smirking.

"Arun," he said smoothly. "Ten lakhs for an unofficial work. That's what you'll get tonight."

Arun's throat dried. "Ten lakhs?! for... what work exactly?"

Sidharth leaned in, speaking low. "You're going to extract and process DNA from a test subject. That's it."

But as Sidharth walked away, Arun followed from a distance—and overheard a chilling exchange between him and Dr. Vivek.

"...we'll isolate the DNA... Artin's... we start once the chanting begins..."
The blood drained from Arun's face.
They had Artin. Alive. Somewhere in this facility.
They were going to use his DNA.
Panic hit him—but so did clarity.
He had to play along. He agreed. Not for the money. Not for survival.
But to save his friend.

Meanwhile, Brother Charles ordered the first floor to be cleared and transformed.

"Make the arrangements. Begin the setup. The ritual starts in 30 minutes."

The room was emptied, then slowly converted. Velvet curtains were drawn. Ancient symbols drawn in crimson chalk coated the floor. Lights—black, red, and bone-white—lined the perimeter.

The air turned heavier. Charged.

One by one, the participants began to gather in the now-transformed ritual chamber.

Robed men filed in silently—faces hidden, movements mechanical. Among them were:

Brother Charles, in ceremonial robes.

His mafia mercenaries, standing like dark statues.

Dr. Vivek, holding a leather-bound tome.

And finally, Sidharth, who entered holding the hand of none other than Mr. Pratap Shekaran.

The truth revealed itself.

Sidharth Pratap.

Son of Pratap Shekaran.

And Mr. Shekaran was not just the UJA Party President—but also a secret investor in Lionsfield Pharma.

That's why he agreed to the 700 crore deal so quickly.

Because a huge sum of money would eventually reach his own pocket—all while maintaining the illusion of politics. Looting his very own party.

They stood together at the front of the chamber.

Pratap didn't speak. He didn't need to.

Together, they began chanting—the first verses of the ancient ritual echoing off the marble walls.

The rest joined in. Deep, guttural, inhuman. Like the voice of something ancient awakening.

Charles, midway through the chants, turned and signaled Sidharth.

"Bring the guards. Open the storage."

He turned to Pratap and the mercenaries.

"Lead the chant. Don't let it stop."

Then, with purposeful steps, Brother Charles, flanked by a handful of guards, Sidharth, and Celine, made their way down the corridor toward the lower levels.

Toward the storage room.

Toward Artin.

They enter the storage room—Brother Charles, Sidharth, Celine, Arun, a B-grade scientist, and the guards. The air is heavy with ritualistic chants that echo through the concrete walls, strange symbols glimmer in red on the floor. Arun's mind twists in horror as the atmosphere claws at his sanity. His heart drops as he enters the storage room.

An unconscious Artin hanged upside-down. His body limp, suspended like a broken doll.

Brother Charles walks towards Artin. A guard hands him a baton. Without hesitation, Brother Charles slams it into Artin's stomach. Then his chest. Again. And again. The thuds are sickening. Artin jerks awake with a wet cough. His head spins.

"Drop him," Brother Charles orders.

The guards unhook the chains. Artin crashes to the cold floor. His arms and legs are still bound with steel chains. He groans, barely able to open his eyes. His lips twitch, dry and cracked.

"...Where... where's my mother? Please... let my mother go..."

Brother Charles chuckles. He lifts the baton and slams it into Artin's head—once, twice, a third time. The metal clangs against his skull. But there's no blood.

Brother Charles growls and strikes with full force. This time, blood trickles from Artin's forehead.

"Now it bleeds," he mutters, pleasured.

He spins around, eyes burning. "YOU TWO!" he barks at Arun and the scientist. "Take the blood sample. NOW! What the hell are you gawking at?!"

He hurls the baton across the room. It clatters against the wall like a gunshot.

Arun stumbles forward with the other scientist. Hands trembling, his face pale. The scientist unzips a small black medkit and pulls out a vein viewer, a butterfly needle, syringes, a blood collection bag, and a portable centrifuge unit. Wires and vials tangle in their arms as they work fast.

The needle pierces Artin's vein. Blood seeps into the collection tube. Arun watches, eyes wide, as the thick, red-black blood swirls in the vial. His and Artin's eyes lock—one filled with guilt and helplessness, the other with broken sorrow. Arun tries to hide the tears.

"Process it. Right now," Brother Charles orders. "If I don't see results soon, both of you will hang."

Four guards escort Arun and the scientist out. Only seven remain inside.

Artin, barely conscious, whispers again, "...Where is my mother...? You got what you wanted... you can kill me... but please... let her go..."

His voice breaks.

Brother Charles grins wide. "You want to see your mother?" He gestures. "Sidharth, bring me the tablet."

A guard hands the tablet to Sidharth, who passes it to Brother Charles. He turns the screen to Artin and taps play.

"There. That's your mother."

Artin squints—and then his heart stops. The footage shows his unconscious mother, Shirley, draped over the shoulder of the Chief Goon—the same monster who killed the girls. Behind him stands Celine and Sidharth.

A massive tank of acid glows under the dim light.

The goon throws Shirley's body onto a metal platform. Sidharth presses a button.

The platform tilts.

Her body drops into the acid.

Artin screams.

"AMMA!! AMMAAA!!!"

Brother Charles kneels beside him. "Oh, forgot to tell you. Celine and Sidharth strangled her. My idea was the acid. Efficient, isn't it?" He chuckles. "You couldn't even get to see her one last time."

Artin's eyes fill with tears, but slowly they bleed. Crimson streaks stream from his tear ducts.

Brother Charles delivers a brutal kick to Artin's face.

Artin falls unconscious.

"Sidharth," Brother Charles says, rising. "My gift to you... for making our dream real." He places a hand on his shoulder. "He's all yours."

He exits the room with three guards, their footsteps echoing like a death march.

Sidharth turns to a guard. "Bring him outside. We finish this there."

He looks at Celine. "Come. I want you to see how powerless he really is."

Celine breathes fast—adrenaline burning in her chest. She nods.

Two guards drag Artin by the chain on his legs. His body trembles slightly. His eyes stay closed, but his mind reels—acid sizzling... his mother's body dissolving... his father's death... the blood-soaked knife... the girls' screams... Diya... Ameya... the burial vault... the snake... his smile in the mirror...

His heart races. The watch on his wrist flashes: 299 BPM... 300... 301. It bursts apart, sending sparks.

They stop. The guards force him onto his knees.

A third guard hands Sidharth a gun.

Artin is motionless. Veins bulge across his skin. His muscles flex violently against his tattered shirt. The veins throb. Popping out, pulsating.

Sidharth stands in front of him. Two guards hold Artin's shoulders.

Sidharth aims the barrel at Artin's head.

His finger touches the trigger.

BANG!

But suddenly,

Just before it hits—Artin moves.

The bullet hits above his collarbone. It tore through his skin but doesnt fully penetrate. Blood oozes, his eyes snap open.

Bright red. Bleeding red. Demonic red.

The chains binding his arms behind him suddenly snap—shattering them like its nothing. His hands slam the guards beside him by the legs—flipping them mid-air like ragdolls.

He jumps—breaking the chain at his ankles. Steel shards blast into the air like shrapnel.

Sidharth stares in disbelief. Artin kicks him—with unimaginable power—launching him off the ground. Sidharth crashes across the dirt, his gun flying from his hand.

Artin stands tall. Veins bulging, muscles hard like stone. The glass shard loged on his body from the earlier fight ejects out from his back, launched like bullets. The bullet from his shoulder falls to the ground.

He smiles—a grin full of wrath—and turns to Celine.

Celine doesn't see Artin anymore—she sees death itself standing before her. Her whole body trembles in pure, soul-tearing fear.

Only one guard has a gun left. He points it at Artin, glancing toward Celine as if for one final order, he pulls the trigger. But Artin moves—before the bullet reaches him, he ducks with inhuman speed. The bullet misses, slicing through air.

Artin grabs the leg of a guard still groaning on the ground and hurls him like a ragdoll at the one who fired.

They both collapse in a heap.

The guard who handed Sidharth the gun lunges forward, roaring as if brute rage could stop what's coming. Artin's fist meets him halfway. One devastating punch cracks into the guard's face with a sickening thud, sending blood and teeth flying.

The man hits the ground hard, dazed—but Artin doesn't stop. He yanks the man back to his feet, his hands gripping with monstrous strength. With a terrifying crunch, Artin breaks the guard's collarbone—snap. The scream comes out loud. Artin drives his elbow into the man's neck like a guillotine. Bone crushes, spine gives, and the body goes limp in his grip.

He lets the corpse drop like garbage.

Then he turns—and pauses.

Sidharth is standing right in front of him. Trembling, blood dripping from his lips, barely able to hold the gun in his shaking hands.

But while Artin stands still for a second, something moves behind him.

Celine.

She'd crept up like a snake, grabbing a knife from a fallen guard's belt. Her hand shakes violently, but she grips it tight, knuckles white. Her breath is fast and shallow, her heartbeat thunder in her ears. She raises the blade with trembling resolve.

Sidharth sees his moment. His finger finds the trigger. He pulls it.

Bang!

But Artin... Artin is no longer human.

He moves with the speed of an apex predator, dodging the bullet with uncanny precision.

And then—

Silence.

Sidharth's eyes widen. The gun falls from his hands, clattering to the dirt.

Behind Artin...

Celine stands frozen, the knife falling from her grip.

A bullet wound blooms across her chest. Blood leaks from the center slowly at first, then in torrents. Her eyes, wide and wet with terror, fill with tears—not from pain, but from the overwhelming horror of her final moment.

She looks at Artin—straight into his eyes. Her lips quiver, but then... forge the faintest smile.

And she collapses to her knees.

Her breath catches—gasping, gurgling.

Her eyes lose their focus.

She falls to the earth.

Lifeless.

A silence falls. Heavy. Dreadful.

And now—Artin stands tall.

His eyes blood-red. Veins pulsating. Muscles hardened.

Sidharth stands still, crying he doesn't move.

Because he already know—

Death is here.

Artin walks slowly toward Sidharth, who's now on his knees, weeping. There is no sympathy in Artin's eyes. No mercy. Just cold, deathly silence.

He reaches out.

With a single brutal twist—crack—Sidharth's neck spins a full 180°.

The body drops to the ground like discarded meat. His face frozen in horror... looking behind him forever.

Inside the facility, in the dim red glow of the ritual chamber, Brother Charles leads the chanting. Hooded men sway rhythmically, voices low and haunting.

Suddenly, a guard from the Grade A labs leans in, whispering into Charles's ear:

"Sir... they've finished the processing."

Brother Charles's eyes widen. He stands abruptly, eyes gleaming with fervor.

"It's finally ready." He turns to Mr. Pratap.

"Keep chanting. Louder. Shake the heavens if you must. I'm finally going to take Azazel's blood."

He exits with the guard, his long robes brushing the floor.

Mr. Pratap raises his hands high:

"LET OUR CHANTS SHAKE THE HEAVENS AND EARTH! LOUDER!!"

The room echoes with thunderous chanting as Brother Charles heads for the Grade A lab. The heavy reinforced door closes behind him with a hiss.

Outside, Artin stands over the dead. He picks up a pistol, then grabs Sidharth's limp body by the collar. With one hand, he drags the corpse along as if it were weightless.

Only eight guards remain in the facility. Four are inside with Brother Charles. Four stand ahead of Artin.

They spot him.

But they hesitate.

Too late.

Artin raises the pistol—untrained, erratic—and fires. Two guards go down instantly, bullets ripping through armor.

The gun jams.

No hesitation—Artin hurls the pistol at the third guard. It slams into his skull with sickening force, cracking through bone. The man drops like a puppet with cut strings.

One guard remains.

He fires. Artin dodges.

Another shot—it hits his chest, but does little. Artin only flinches.

Now face-to-face, the guard stares up in horror.

Artin grabs him by the throat, lifts him, and slams him into the concrete.
CRACK.
Dead.

Artin breathes out slow, steady. He checks the guard's pocket and finds a lighter... and a cigarette. He lights it. Smoke curls lazily from his lips as he resumes walking—dragging Sidharth's corpse through blood-soaked corridors.

He reaches the door to the first floor ritual chamber.

From behind the thick walls, the chants grow louder—eerie, maddening.

They agitate him.

Artin pauses.

He exhales... then kicks the door open.

It shatters inward.

The chanting stops.

Every head turns. The room goes silent.

Artin steps inside, dragging Sidharth's corpse behind him.

He throws the body to the floor—right at Mr. Pratap's feet.

Pratap drops to his knees, his face contorted in panic and disbelief.

"Sidharth...? SIDHARTH!"

He grabs the corpse, hands shaking violently, checking for a pulse. He weeps.

No one speaks. No one breathes.

Behind Artin... on the wall...

A poster reads:

"R.I.P. Artin Samuel – B-Grade Scientist, Lionsfield Pharma."

The faces in the room shift from confusion—to horror.

They look at the poster... then back to him.

It's the same face.

Not the same man.

Something else now stands there. Something reborn.

Artin steps forward.

They all step back.

Meanwhile upstairs,

Brother Charles stands in the Grade A lab.

The Bio-Fluid Chamber glows cold blue, ready.

"Make it ready," he growls.

The A-Grade scientist loads the newly processed vial of ODFC-4.

Charles removes his robes. Naked, pale, scarred from previous fights—he steps into the machine. Needles pierce his skin.

He gasps.

The transfusion begins.

Silvery black fluid flows into his bloodstream.

But behind them—Arun watches.

Quiet. Steady.

He moves to the control panel.

Turns off the coolant system.

A silent sabotage.

The temperature in the chamber starts to rise.

Charles doesn't notice.

Not yet.

Downstair Artin stands still.

A god among men.

The cigarette flickers between his fingers.

He raises it—slowly—to the smoke detector above.

Mr. Pratap rises, fury taking over his grief.

"KILL THAT SON OF A—"

Six men charge.

But—

The smoke alarm SCREAMS.

Sprinklers activate—

Not water.

But PredaXine.

A fine mist descends—over everyone.

Their dress. Their faces. Their hair.

Everyone stops.

They sniff. They wipe it but they feel it.

Something is wrong.

Then—

Screams.

One man slams his fist into the man beside him.

Another bites into a shoulder.

One begins to howl.

Another smashes his own head into the wall until it cracks.

All six who charged at Artin... start fighting each other.

Savage. Brutal. Animalistic.

Then the crowd turns on itself.

Executives, cultists, scientists—they all snap.

Claws. Screams. Blood.

A flesh circus explodes in the chamber.

Artin smiles—a devil's grin.

He walks forward.

Into the chaos.

Not to fight...

But to tear it all down.

One man turns toward Artin.

Eyes wild.

Muscles twitching from the effects of PredaXine.

He charges.

Artin doesn't flinch.

THWACK!

Artin's fist crashes into the man's face—so hard, the jaw dislocates sideways, snapping with a wet crack.

The man stumbles back, gurgling.

Artin steps forward—rams his knee upward into the man's ribs with bone-shattering force.

CRACK!

The man is launched backwards, limbs flailing, body crashing into a pillar. He lands in a heap—dead before he hits the floor.

But there's no time to stop.

They're coming.

From all sides.

Ravenous. Mindless. Howling like beasts.

But Artin stood as a corpse reanimated by rage. By pain.

By the screams of innocent lives.

Artin becomes a lifeless human surrounded by mindless ones.

One lunges.

Artin spins—his elbow smashes the skull in. Bone shatter.

Another leaps at him. Artin ducks and grabs the man mid-air, swinging him around and using his body to knock down two others like bowling pins.

Blood sprays. Bones crunch.

He pivots. Punch. Punch. Punch.

Each strike is faster than a whip crack—faster than sound—so fast, the air hisses with every blow.

Fists become iron. Arms become sledgehammers.

A woman with blackened eyes screeches, charging with a broken wine bottle.

Artin catches her arm mid-swing.

Twists it.

SNAP!

Her own bone erupts through her skin. She screams.

He lets her scream for half a second before driving his fist into her throat, crushing her windpipe.

She drops, twitching.

Artin's chest heaves, soaked in blood—not of his.

Around him—madness.

People tear out each other's body.

One man rips off his own ear and throws it like a weapon.

But none of them reach Artin.

Every time one tries—

He breaks them.

One man—twice his size—grabs him from behind.

Artin grabs the man's wrists and pulls them forward, dislocating both arms in one jerk.

The man screams. Artin headbutts him once, shattering his nose, then drops him with a spinning heel kick that sends teeth flying across the floor.

He's surrounded.

But he doesn't care.

Each kill makes Artin more fiecre.

His mother's face flickers in his mind.

He throws another punch—shattering someone's ribcage from the outside.

He remembers the innocent screams and cries.

He grabs another by the throat and crushes it like glass.

He lifts a man—by the leg—and swings him into the wall, splitting the man's skull wide open.

Artin's body moves like a machine fueled by an evil fury.

Blood spatters his face.

His knuckles are raw.

But he doesn't stop.

Mr. Pratap grabs a man by the hair, yanks it so hard it tears from the scalp, and slams a fist straight into his face—again and again—until bone caves and blood splashes out.

Across the chaos, Dr. Vivek gets kicked by a frenzied scientist, the blow sending him hurtling backward—

CRASH!

He lands over Mr. Pratap, flattening him momentarily. Mr. Pratap roars in fury, shoving Vivek off like a wild bull.

Dr. Vivek lunges back at him.

A savage brawl erupts between the two—no more alliance, no more plan, just raw madness. Mr. Pratap grabs Vivek by the collar and rams his head into the wall—once, twice, five times—

CRACK.

CRACK.

CRUNCH.

The wall splits open—so does Vivek's skull. Blood trickles from his nose and ears as his body slumps.

But the chaos doesn't stop.

Artin is still in the eye of the storm.

He punches in all directions—brute force exploding from his fists.

He twists arms until they snap, shatters fingers, elbows throats, breaks jaws.

But they keep coming.

He starts getting overwhelmed—swarmed by beasts in human skin.

He roars. His rage combusts.

Steam rises from his body.

Muscles tighten, veins pulse like cables under skin.

He clenches his fists.

And then—

Boom.

Artin moves like a cannon blast.

His punches are bullets.

His kicks are wrecking balls.

His elbows are axes.

His knees are hammers.

He jumps and kicks three men in a single airborne spin.

Bodies fly.

Bones explode.

Blood sprays like fountains.

He stomps over corpses, doesn't slow down—not for a second.

Then—he sees him.

The Chief Goon.

The monster who murdered the girls. Who dropped his mother into acid.

The predator has found his prey.

The goon is in the middle of carnage, ripping off heads, clawing faces, howling with bloodlust.

Artin moves forward, eyes locked on him.

Anyone who steps in his path gets destroyed.

A Russian mafia mercenary steps up, cracking his knuckles, a wall of muscle and rage. He slams his fist into Artin's stomach—

It lands.

But Artin doesn't move.

Not even a blink.

Artin stares him down.

Then slips behind him with inhuman speed—

Grabs him by the belt and shoulder—

Throws him overhead—

SLAMS the mercenary's skull into the marble floor with a violent crunch.

Neck breaks. Body twitches once. Done.

Artin keeps moving—every breath a warning, every step a kill.

One man tries to stop him—Artin grabs him by the throat, lifts him, and slams him down so hard the tiles crater.

Then finally—he reaches him.

The Chief Goon turns, just in time to see a red-eyed monster charging through the madness.

Artin roars.

And unleashes hell.

His elbow crashes into the goon's face—BAM!

Teeth shatter. Blood flies.

Artin's fingers pierce into the man's chest—tearing through skin and bone—cracking ribs apart like firewood.

The goon roars in pain—but Artin grips his throat, lifts him off the ground.

HEADBUTT.

HEADBUTT.

HEADBUTT.

Teeth explode from the goon's mouth.

One tooth lands in Artin's mouth.
He bites down and spits it out with disgust.
The goon's face is unrecognizable now—just pulp and blood.
Artin lifts him.
Drives his head full force into the wall—
BAM.
Again.
And again.
Until the skull splits open.
The goon drops.
Dead.
At last.
But the chaos hasn't stopped—not yet.
All around him, people has tore each other apart—bitten, stabbed, corpse laying.
Arms ripped off. Eyes gouged. Guts spilled.
Artin pauses, his breath ragged, chest heaving like a beast.
He sees Mr. Pratap and what's left of Dr. Vivek dismantled on the ground, everyone has died.
Artin turns.
And walks over the corpses.
He reaches the main hallway.
His body soaked in blood.
He kicks open the exit door—BOOM.
Cool air floods in.
He steps into the hall.
Breathing hard.
Eyes burning.
Chest rising.
Back cracked.
Knuckles split.
But still standing.
He turns his head upward—
Toward the A-Grade Lab.
Toward the final nightmare.
Toward Brother Charles.

Upstairs, in the Grade A lab...

Inside the biofluid chamber, the thick liquid begins to bubble—violently. The ODFC-4 coursing through Brother Charles's veins forces his body into a rapid transformation, packing on nearly 40 kilograms of pure muscle in just under thirty minutes. The process is immensely exothermic. Without coolant, both his body and the biofluid begin to boil.

Charles's eyes snap open. He feels the searing heat consume him from the inside. His veins light up like burning wires. Panic takes over. His body shakes violently within the chamber. A scream escapes his mouth—even though it's submerged beneath the fluid.

The other scientists scramble. One of them frantically punches in override codes on the chamber console. Another tries to restore coolant flow. Arun, playing dumb, keeps his expression neutral.

Bodyguards rush in.

"Do something!" one of them screams at the scientists. "Save him!!"

But it's too late.

The fluid now roils with thick bubbles. Charles's transformation continues uncontrollably—muscles tearing and reforming, bones cracking and expanding. Skin begins to melt off. The heat is cooking him alive.

Suddenly—BOOM!

The reinforced door blasts inward, ripping from its frame and smashing into one of the guards, pinning him down.

Artin steps in.

His body drips with blood and rain, a cigarette still smoldering between his lips. The three remaining guards raise their weapons. But Artin grins, eyes glowing with fury.

He lunges forward—lightning fast.

He grabs the first guard's gun and smashes it into the second guard's stomach.

Then he twists, takes the second guard's weapon, and shoots the third point-blank.

The first one tries to recover—Artin slams his head in with the empty gun.

The last guard fires—but Artin kicks him, then grabs and hurls him onto the metal door, knocking both unconscious.

Silence.

One of the scientists picks up a weapon, trembling as he aims it at Artin.

But Arun steps in, kicking the gun away. The scientist stumbles back.

Then—a deafening explosion.

The biofluid chamber shatters, glass and metal flying like shrapnel. Steam and boiling fluid gush out. One shard of reinforced glass pierces through the scientist's chest, killing him instantly.

What remains inside the chamber falls out—a horrific heap of burnt muscle and bone.

Brother Charles.

No longer human. His body is warped, overgrown, deformed beyond recognition. His skin has peeled away, and organs seem scorched from the inside. Huge veins twitch beneath what's left of his flesh. His limbs look inhuman, stretched and brutalized.

Heavy silence.

Arun, breath shaking, stares at the grotesque body.

"Artin... I think he's dead."

Artin, his voice low and almost inhuman, asks:

"Why?"

"I turned off the coolant... Sabotaged it. His body overheated during transformation. That's 40 kilos of mass forced into muscle. Look at him—he's mutated. His organs might have boiled from the inside out."

Artin nods slowly. They both approach the body with caution.

But then—Artin's eyes narrow.

A vein on the corpse's neck twitches.

His heart skips.

"ARUN! HE'S ALIVE!!!"

Before either of them can react, Brother Charles—or whatever he has become—rises.

He's enormous, skin melted, jaw twisted grotesquely. Two horns now crown his face. Veins and muscles bulge in unnatural patterns. A devilish smile stretches across his toothy maw—his lips are gone, torn off by the heat.

With one brutal kick, Charles launches Artin across the room.

He grabs Arun by the throat, lifting him off the ground.

Artin screams, "NO!!"

Charles slams Arun into the wall like a ragdoll.

Rage fills Artin's veins. He charges at the monster, swinging his left fist with everything he has. But the creature catches it mid-air.

Artin freezes.

It's the first time someone stopped his strike.

Fear creeps in. For the first time since his rebirth, Artin feels powerless.

Charles's smile widens. He twists Artin's arm, bones creaking. Artin screams in pain. The monster's other hand wraps around his throat, squeezing.

Artin chokes. He feels death in the monster's grip.

But then—his heart races. His body heats up. Veins bulge, eyes burn red. Steam rises from his skin, scorching the monster's hand.

It yelps, recoiling.

Artin lets out a guttural growl. He attacks—kicking the monster's abdomen repeatedly, forcing it to its knees. He leaps in with a knee strike to its jaw—shattering it.

Charles roars. Blood gushes from his mouth.

Enraged, the creature throws a flurry of punches. Artin dodges—left, right—but one punch connects. CRACK. Artin crashes to the floor.

The monster grabs Artin's leg and swings him through the air, then slams him into the ground—once, twice, again. It grabs his throat once more, opening its massive jaw, ready to bite off his neck.

But suddenly—its body seizes.

It drops Artin, twitching violently.

Charles falls to his knees. His back arches as more horns sprout along his spine, piercing his own flesh. His joints twist at impossible angles. Blood sprays as more bone shards erupt through his body.

He screams—a monster in pain.

Artin sees his chance.

He lunges forward. With everything he has, he grabs the monster's arm, slams it into the wall, shattering several horns. He climbs onto the beast's back, locking his arm around its neck, and his legs around its torso.

They both collapse to the floor.

The monster thrashes—but Artin's grip only tightens. With a roar, Artin pulls back with all his strength, using his knee to bend the monster's spine.

Both scream—one in rage, the other in agony.

"ARGHHHHHHHHHHHHHH!!"

CRACK!!!

The sound of bone breaking echoes through the lab.

Artin's hold loosens. He drops to the ground, panting heavily.

The monster's spine has split, its neck snapped, and its twisted backbone now sticks out through its abdomen.

Brother Charles—the monster—is finally dead.

Artin scrambles to his feet, lungs heaving, and rushes to Arun—his friend lying motionless. Blood trickles from Arun's mouth, his body barely responding, chest rising shallowly.

"Arun? Arun!" Artin drops to his knees, shaking him. "Wake up, man—we won! I killed him! It's over!"

Arun's eyes flutter open, glazed and faint. His lips tremble as he forces out a whisper, "Artin... I don't think I'm gonna make it."

"No! No, don't say that," Artin pleads, panic setting into his voice. He gently lifts Arun's head onto his lap, brushing blood from his face. "You're not dying on me. I won't let you. You hear me? I'm gonna save you, Arun. Just hang on—"

Arun coughs, a weak gasp escaping his mouth, followed by a groan of pain. "Artin... promise me... promise me you'll finish what you started. Promise me you'll burn it all down..."

Artin grips his friend's hand tightly, tears spilling down his face. His voice cracks, trembling under the weight of emotion. "I promise, bro. I swear I'll destroy this entire company."

Arun's gaze finds Artin's, locking eyes one last time. Artin speaks again, voice softer, steadier now. "Don't worry about your mom. I got it. You don't have to worry anymore."

A faint smile flickers across Arun's lips as he nods weakly. His grip loosens.

"No... no, please," Artin sobs, pressing Arun's hand to his chest. "I've already lost everything. Don't you leave me too... please, man... please don't go."

But Arun's eyes are already slipping shut. His breath fades out like a whisper on the wind.

Artin stares in disbelief, clutching him tighter. "Arun...?"

Silence.

The cold, irreversible silence of death.

Artin breaks. His cries echo through the ruined lab, raw and shattering, holding his best friend's lifeless body in his arms.

Artin gently lays Arun's body down on the cold, bloodstained floor. His fingers linger on his friend's lifeless face.

He rises slowly—legs trembling, soaked in blood of his own and others'. The flickering overhead lights hum like dying fireflies, casting long shadows across the massacre around him. Dead bodies, shattered glass, twisted steel—it all fades behind him as he limps forward.

He doesn't look back. Not once.

Every step is a battle. His breath ragged. His heart hollow. He walks through the halls of the facility where screams once echoed—now reduced to a haunted tomb soaked in red.

By the time he stumbles outside, the air is cold. The wind bites against his open wounds, but he doesn't flinch. Blood drips from his fingers. His shirt clings to his skin, soaked through with sweat, tears, and everything he's lost.

It's almost 2AM. The world is asleep. But Artin, he is wide awake in a nightmare he cannot escape.

He limps forward—no destination in sight. Just the cold earth beneath his feet and a void inside his soul. His vision blurs. Not from pain, but from the ache in his chest.

Artin limped down the broken sidewalk. The buzz of distant traffic felt like a world away. His breaths were shallow, his body numb. He didn't know how long he'd been walking—maybe minutes, maybe hours. Time had lost all meaning.

He passed the forgotten ones—figures curled up on the sides of the street, wrapped in torn blankets and the last threads of hope. Some of them looked up, most didn't. But no one questioned the blood on his shirt, the hollowness in his eyes.

One old man, seated by a cracked wall, murmured prayers beneath his breath. His frail hands clutched a string of worn-out beads, his voice trembling as though whispering to angels who never answered.

As Artin passed, he collapsed beside him—too tired, too broken to go further. He shivered—not from the cold, but from the weight of everything inside him.

The old man turned his head, noticed the trembling.

Without a word, he reached into the thin sack beside him and pulled out a ragged cloth—frayed at the ends, barely warm, but all he had. He held it out with a kind smile.

Artin hesitated... then took it.

No questions. No judgment. Just quiet mercy from a stranger who had nothing but still chose to give.

Artin wrapped the cloth around himself. It smelled of earth, of old woodsmoke, of someone who had suffered and survived. The man leaned slightly against Artin's shoulder as he slowly dozed off.

Artin didn't move. He let the silence wrap around him.

In that moment, more than ever, he wished it would all just stop.

After sometime he wished he could fall asleep like this. And never wake up.

To die quietly beside the stranger. A part of him... wants to stop. Right there. Collapse on the sidewalk and never get back up. Die. Just... disappear.

What's left anyway? Arun is gone. Everything he loved betrayed him. His hands are now again stained by death.

He looks up at the night sky. The stars blink like silent witnesses, uncaring. The wind whispers like ghosts in his ears. "End it... let go..."

But something pulls him back.

A face. A voice.

Father Rafael.

The old man with blind eyes who saw more than anyone else. The only person who ever saw the good in him when Artin couldn't even find it himself.

Artin clenches his jaw. Breathes in sharply.

He won't die.

Not yet.

With shattered strength, he carefully gets up, without disturbing the sleeping stranger beside him. He limps toward the only place that still feels like home—the church. Toward the only soul he can still call family. Toward the light.

The church stood still in the quiet veil of dawn.

It was 4:03 AM.

The world outside was dark and cold, but inside the House of God, a dim golden glow bathed the altar, casting long shadows that stretched like silent echoes. The air was thick with incense, heavy with memory.

Father Rafael knelt at the front pew, rosary in hand, eyes closed, lips murmuring the Liturgy of the Hours. He had begun his day, as always, in devotion—his soul reaching for heaven even as the earth weighed him down.

Then—he felt it.

A shift in the air.

The presence of someone fimilar. The same eerie presence.

His prayer halted mid-word.

"Who is it?" he asked softly, without turning, his voice steady but cautious. His heart quickened.

From the silence behind him, a familiar voice answered, cracked and soaked in sorrow.

"...It's me, Father."

Father Rafael froze in shock, he knows that sound.

For a moment, time itself stopped. The priest couldn't breathe—his heart thundered against his chest. He had led the funeral mass. He had wept for his soul.

Now, that soul knelt before him.

Artin collapsed to his knees and fell at Father Rafael's feet, clutching them desperately. A cry erupted from him—not just of grief, but of a soul shattered and seeking redemption. His tears fell fast, soaking the old priest's robe, dripping onto his feet.

Father Rafael sat frozen, eyes wide, hands trembling.

"Artin... is that you?" he gasped, his voice barely holding together.

Artin sobbed harder, wrapping his arms around Father Rafael's legs like a child clinging to the last thing he believes in.

Then, with trembling hands, Artin leaned forward, his head against the priest's feet. And in a quiet, sacred gesture—he wiped away his own tears from Father Rafael's feet using his face.

A gesture of unworthiness.

Of reverence.

Of repentance.

A broken man, bowing at the feet of grace.

Father Rafael's eyes filled with tears—tears of disbelief, of sorrow, and of fierce love. He gently reached down, lifting Artin's head. The priest felt Artin's face with his hand, the face resembled not a monster, not a sinner...

...but a son.

"My child..." he whispered, voice cracking.

CHAPTER CX

In the heart of a sleeping church, two souls wept—one for what he had become, and one for the miracle of his return.

Artin knelt at the altar, broken in body and soul, the smell of blood still clinging to his clothes, soaked into his skin, staining the very air around him. The ancient stone floor bore his weight as if it had held a thousand broken souls before. His hands trembled. His voice cracked as he confessed everything. Shirley's death shook father Rafael the most. Tears rolled of off his cheeks profusely.

Artin's tears fell freely, he was broken and lost not even able to lift his head.

Father Rafael stood frozen at first, overwhelmed, his old, weathered hands searching Artin's face, his heart caught between disbelief and compassion. The very boy he had raised like a son—the one he buried with trembling hands—was now weeping at his feet, alive and undone.

Slowly, Father Rafael wrapped his arms around Artin's trembling frame.

"My son..." he whispered, voice quivering with emotion, "your sins... are forgiven. In the name of Jesus Christ, our Lord and Saviour—who conquered death, who walked among the broken, who bled for the lost—you are forgiven."

Artin cried harder into the folds of Rafael's robes, the words cutting through the suffocating guilt.

Father Rafael sat in silence, still holding Artin's shoulders, but his eyes had drifted far, lost in thought. A deep shadow passed over his face. The weight of the moment was immense—he could feel it pressing down on his chest like a divine burden.

His mind raced.

What do I do now?

Who do I turn to?

The police? No. They're powerless against the forces Artin has crossed. Worse—some may already be under the company's thumb.

The government? Corrupt. Infiltrated. Helpless.

Should I let him fight? Continue this war he didn't ask for but now feels bound to?

He looked at Artin—bloodied, broken, barely breathing hope. No... that path would swallow him whole.

A shiver ran down Rafael's spine.

The powers within him...

He had felt it when he embraced him. A pulse. A heaviness. A dark aura trailing just behind his soul.

These powers... they weren't divine. They weren't gifts from heaven. They were something else. Something darker. Tainted.

Rafael clenched his jaw, heart pounding.

If the world finds out what he is... if the evil forces lurking in the shadows discover what he's become...

They will use him. Twist him. Turn him into the very monster he's trying to destroy.

He bowed his head and gripped his crucifix tightly.

No. He must be hidden.

Protected—not just from the world, but from himself.

He looked at Artin again, who sat quietly beside him, still lost in grief, unaware of the storm he carried within.

"I have to keep you safe," Rafael whispered in his mind. "You are not ready. The world is not ready."

With a firm voice father Rafael spoke to Artin,

"This life, it is over now. The death, the blood, the poison—they belong to the old you. What stands before God now is a man reborn."

Artin pulled back slightly, eyes red, voice hoarse. "But Father... I made a promise. I promised Arun I'd finish this war. I told him I would tear the company down. I have to."

Rafael's eyes sharpened with a holy fire. He placed both hands on Artin's face, steadying him.

"No, Artin. Listen to me."

"This is not the time. You are not ready. You are hurt. Hunted. Barely alive. If you keep fighting you will soon turn into a monster. God did not bring you back to die again. You will fight, yes—when the time comes. But not now."

He stood slowly, drawing Artin up with him.

"You will go where I tell you to go. You will hide. You will heal. And when the time is right... when the storm begins again... then, Artin, you will rise—not as the broken man you are now—but as the warrior God is shaping you to become."

Artin replied, his voice still laced with guilt.

"Alright, Father. I trust you."

Rafael placed a hand over Artin's heart.

"My son. You have a second life now. And Heaven is watching."

"What should I do now, Father?" Artin's voice cracked, the weight of the bloodshed still hanging on his tongue. His eyes were swollen, his breath uneven, his body barely holding itself up.

"You will have to stay away from Kerala," Father Rafael said softly, firmly.

Artin's head snapped up, his voice tense, desperate. "Where, Father?"

He wasn't just asking for a place—he was asking for direction, purpose, a reason not to collapse again.

Father Rafael paused, gripped the cross in his hand tightly as his thoughts swirled in prayer. Then he answered, "There's a Christian monastery... far away in the hills of Sikkim. A place untouched by the noise of the world. You will go there. And you will begin again."

Artin looked down, the urge to resist burning quietly behind his eyes. He wanted to fight. He wanted to finish what Arun died for. But Rafael's voice... his presence... reminded him of something bigger than revenge.

"I will go," he whispered, defeated but obedient.

"I'll get you a train ticket to Siliguri," Father Rafael continued, "From there, take a bus to Sikkim, and you will reach the monastery. There, they will take care of you."

Artin nodded, the weight of a thousand memories behind that small motion.

"Okay, Father," he murmured, still weeping.

"Come," Father Rafael said gently, placing a hand on his back. "You can use the guest room to wash. I'll get you something clean to wear."

The two of them walked slowly through the dim corridors of the church. The silence between them was sacred, heavy, yet strangely comforting. As they reached the guest room, Artin stepped in with his head bowed low.

Father Rafael turned away, retreating toward his own quarters. His hand gently brushed the cold walls as he walked, his fingers guiding him as much as habit did.

But inside, his mind was a storm.

Reaching his modest room, the dim glow of the lights still flickering by the crucifix, Father Rafael felt for the edge of the table and picked up his old phone. His fingers trembled slightly.

He dialed.

The phone rang for a few seconds before the voice on the other end croaked through a sleepy haze.

"Father? What is it?" asked Peter, the parish clerk, still wrapped in blankets on his small cot in the parish clerk's room.

"Peter... come to my room. Now," Father Rafael said curtly.

Before Peter could respond, the line went dead. The sudden silence on the other end made the air in Peter's room feel heavier. He sat up slowly, rubbing his eyes, muttering under his breath, "I don't know what's gotten into Father after that boy's death... He hasn't been the same."

Yawning, Peter shuffled through the quiet corridor.

As Peter reached the doorway, he gently knocked, but the door opened slightly on its own.

"Father?" he called softly.

Inside, Father Rafael sat at the edge of his cot, head lowered. His face, usually so calm and composed, was now shadowed with something Peter had never seen before, a mix of fear, urgency, and something deeper.

Peter stepped in, his voice turning serious. "Father... what happened?"

The priest jolted ever so slightly—his senses, dulled by the storm of thoughts, hadn't registered Peter's approach.

"Peter," he began, his voice low but sharp, "I have something very important to tell you."

Peter, concerned now, quickly pulled the old wooden chair closer and sat down. The air felt thick with the weight of unspoken words. He had never seen the old priest this shaken.

"Tell me, Father," he said gently, trying to steady the tension in the room.

Meanwhile, inside the guest room, Artin moved with slow, weary steps toward the bathroom. His hands, still trembling, reached for the old razor and pair of scissors lying atop a wooden table.

He opened the bathroom door, the scent of soap and old water lingering in the air. With no second thought, he peeled off his torn, blood-soaked clothes and threw them into the wastebin, watching as the weight of everything he had been soaked in — loss, death, rage — dropped away with each layer.

He turned on the shower. Cold water thundered down over his battered body, mingling with the dried blood on his skin. The blood slowly faded down the drain, swirling away. Some wounds stung with the water, others had clotted. Muscles trembled as the water pounded against bruises and open wounds. His head tilted upward, letting the stream hit his face, eyes shut.

Images flickered behind those closed lids.

Screams. Arun's body. A hallway soaked in death. His hands — shaking, covered in someone else's blood.

Finally, he turned the water off.

The room returned to silence — broken only by the soft drip of water from the faucet and the quiet beat of his heart.

He wiped the fogged mirror clean with his hand.

What remained wasn't a man.

Not yet.

Just a figure.

Broken.

Still breathing.

And then, he reached for the scissors.

His fingers were still shaking, but steadier than before. He brought the blade to his beard and began to cut — slowly, methodically. Strands fell in clumps, curling into the sink like discarded history.

Each snip wasn't just remains. It was the removal of something else — a past self. The face of the man who'd burned. Who'd fallen. Who'd bled his way out of hell.

Next came his hair. He cut without care. Chunks fell to the floor, stuck to his chest, fell into the sink like dead leaves in winter.

And then — the razor.

He ran it across his jaw. A line of blood slipped free, tracing a thin path toward his neck before being caught by the cold tap water.

He didn't stop.

He shaved until the last trace of the bloodied warrior was gone.

He washed his face.

Looked up.

What met him in the mirror wasn't someone reborn. Not yet. But someone changed.

Face clean-shaven. Hair cropped close.

But the bruises were still there. The exhaustion.

The eyes — still hollow. But now with something flickering behind them. Not fire. Not hope.

Resolve.

As he stood there, soaked in the dim light of the bathroom.

Outside, the guest room door creaked open slowly.

Peter stepped in, careful and silent. The bathroom door remained closed. He glanced at the floor, noticing the discarded, bloodied clothes inside the wastebin, and his eyes softened.

He said nothing.

He walked in, placed a neatly folded pair of fresh clothes — a plain grey shirt and black pants — on the bed. Then he turned and walked out, closing the door gently behind him.

Artin stepped into the guest room once more, now clothed in the soft, clean garments left for him. The grey shirt clung loosely to his chest, the black pants light and unburdened by blood. He took the black face mask resting on the table, paused, then pulled it over his face. The fabric hugged his skin, muffling his breath — not just to hide who he was, but to silence who he had been.

He stepped out into the nave. Shadows stretched long across the marble floor, cast by flickering candlelight and the pale hints of dawn struggling through stained glass.

Up near the altar, Father Rafael sat on the first bench, still and upright. His sightless eyes were aimed forward, but they shifted slightly as if sensing Artin's presence before his footsteps made a sound. A cloth bag sat beside him on the pew. In his hands, he held a photograph, his thumbs lightly brushing its edges as though reading it by touch alone.

Without turning his head, he spoke.

"Take this."

Artin approached, slow and quiet. He reached forward and gently took the photograph from Rafael's hands.

It was an old photo. In it, Artin stood between two figures. His father, Samuel, with broad shoulders and proud eyes. His mother, Shirley, with her hand on Artin's shoulder and a soft, radiant smile. The image was frozen in time, but the warmth inside it struck Artin like a blow. A past life. A vanished world.

Rafael's voice broke the stillness again, low and weathered.

"There's some money in the bag. A few clothes. An old phone." He nodded toward it. "When you get there... call me."

Artin didn't speak. He bent down, picked up the bag, and slung it over his shoulder. The weight was small, but it felt like something sacred.

"I've arranged everything," Rafael continued. "Peter is waiting outside."

Artin gave a silent nod, and the two of them walked down the aisle together, the sound of their steps swallowed by the old stone. Rafael's hand brushed gently along the edges of the pews as they walked — he didn't need sight to know the way.

Outside, the air was cool and still, tinged with the scent of dew and distant smoke. Peter sat waiting behind the wheels of the car, his face calm, unreadable. He said nothing when they approached, didn't even glance toward Artin. He simply unlocked the doors.

They got in.

The engine hummed to life, and the car rolled off. Peter didn't speak. He didn't ask questions. There was no need.

The streets passed by like faded dreams — lamp posts flickering in retreat, alleyways yawning like tired mouths. The sun hadn't yet broken the sky, but the blue of morning was beginning to stretch its fingers across the horizon.

Rain began to fall as the car rolled through the quiet streets — a slow drizzle at first, then a sudden, steady downpour. The raindrops hit the windshield in delicate rhythms. The world outside blurred under the rain.

In the backseat, Artin sat in silence, his fingers moving over a scrap of paper. He tore it from the small notepad he found tucked inside the bag Rafael had given him, then folded it carefully and kept it in his palm like something precious.

When they reached the railway station, the car came to a gentle halt.

They stepped out — Rafael, steady despite his blindness, guided gently by Peter's hand. Artin followed close behind. The station loomed before them, old and humming with early morning life. Distant chatter echoed mixing with the soft clang of metal and the hiss of far-off engines.

Inside, under flickering tube lights and crumbling banners, Father Rafael handed Artin the train ticket.

They stood together, waiting. The rain drummed on the tin roof above, a lullaby for the tired and the grieving.

Then, quietly, Artin broke the silence.

"Father..." His voice was low and weak. "Can you take care of someone for me?"

Rafael turned his face toward the sound, his brows gently furrowed. "Tell me, my son... what is it?"

Artin reached into his pocket and handed the folded piece of paper to Peter. "Transfer all the money I have to this account," he said, his eyes on Father Rafael. "Please... make sure this person gets everything they need. Food, medicine, safety. Whatever it takes."

Rafael's head tilted slightly. "And who is this person?"

A pause.

"Licy Thomas," Artin replied, his voice tightening. "Arun's mother..."

The silence that followed was heavy, reverent. Rafael reached out and placed a hand on Artin's shoulder, his expression gentle and grave.

"I will," he whispered. "You have my word."

Artin turned to Peter, who was still holding the note. Their eyes met. "Thank you," he said softly. "For everything, Peteretta."

Peter didn't speak. But a faint smile rose to his lips, barely there — the kind that speaks more than words ever could. A silent farewell.

A distant horn pierced the station. The train was arriving.

The platform shifted with movement, people stirring and bags clattering against stone. The train pulled into view, hissing and groaning as it slowed, its windows glowing dimly in the grey dawn.

Artin stood.

He turned to Father Rafael and embraced him. It was the kind of hug that carried a thousand unsaid things. A thank you. A farewell. A forgiveness. A prayer.

Rafael held him tight.

Artin then moved towards the train, he said nothing more. He didn't look back.

He climbed aboard.

Rafael, his cane in one hand, reached for Peter with the other. They turned and began walking out of the station.

255

Inside the train, Artin walked slowly, past passengers murmuring and shifting in their seats. His gaze flicked from face to face, searching. At last, he found an empty window seat.

He sat.

A quiet sigh escaped him as he leaned back. The train smelled of wet metal and rust. Across from him sat an old woman, draped in a shawl. She looked at him, her face lined and kind, and smiled.

Artin hesitated, then pulled his mask down.

He smiled back.

The train lurched forward.

The station fell away.

Artin sat in silence, the hum of the train blending with the clatter of the tracks. The memories fled back into his mind for one last time. As he looked outside the window, the rain poured steadily, tracing lines down the glass — each drop a fleeting memory, slipping downward and vanishing.

He leaned his head against the windowpane, his breath fogging a small circle on the glass. The world outside ran behind — trees, lights, distant figures.

Then, he reached into his pocket and pulled out the photo Father Rafael had given him. It was worn, the corners soft from years of being held.

For a long moment, Artin just stared.

And then... the ache found him.

Two tears welled up, slow and silent. They escaped his hollow eyes and rolled down his cheeks, warm against his skin. They dropped onto the photo.

The train rumbled forward through the rain. Around him, the world moved on — passengers chatted quietly, the old woman across from him folded her hands and looked away, giving him space without saying a word.

Artin folded the photo gently and placed it into the safety of his bag. He sat upright, wiped his face, and exhaled slowly.

Everything is finally over...

...for now.

And with that, he closed his eyes. But one question lingered in his mind, heavy and unanswered, Why did my body survive the drug?.

As the train rattled on through the storm, somewhere far from its tracks, in a hidden facility nestled in the heart of Laos, something darker was unfolding.

4:30 AM

The Sitrom factory, cloaked in secrecy and soaked in sin, buzzed with tension. In its coldest chamber, beneath fluorescent lights, an unconscious man lay shackled to a steel chair. Around him, wires slithered from the walls, veins of machinery feeding into his flesh. A tank beside him pulsed with thick red liquid — ODFC-5 — the fifth iteration of the Oncogenic Dark Factor Complex.

Behind a thick glass wall stood a group of scientists, their hands trembling behind clipboards and lab coats. But in their midst stood a man who did not flinch — Edgar Lionsfield, tall, merciless, dressed in black. His presence silenced the room.

The intercom crackled.

"ODFC-5. Administering minimum dosage. Initiating... in 3... 2... 1."

Click.

The liquid surged. The man's eyes shot open — pupils darting, skin convulsing with something slithering beneath it. Bones cracked. Flesh bulged. He screamed.

BOOM!!

His body tore apart, a sickening explosion of blood and tissue.

The glass wall was painted in red mist. The room fell silent.

Edgar's eyes remained cold. Disappointed.

Without a word, he turned and walked away. His bodyguards followed.

Outside, the rain had begun in Laos too. His black SUV waited. But before Edgar could open the door, his top henchman, Boun, approached cautiously, phone still warm in his palm.

"Sir..." Boun whispered, "There's news. From India."

Edgar stopped. "Speak."

Boun hesitated, then leaned in. A few murmured words later, Edgar's face changed. The predator paused — nostrils flaring, hands trembling slightly at his sides.

He didn't speak. He simply got into the car. A silent storm behind glass.

The convoy of black SUVs tore into the muddy roads, water splashing like blood under tires. Within the hour, they arrived at Lionsfield Mansion, an ancient estate cast in stone and shadow.

Inside, in a candlelit room that smelled of death and, lay Mortis Lionsfield — the man himself, strapped to machines and tubes, barely alive, yet terrifying.

Edgar entered quietly. The old man's bloodshot eyes opened.

"Edgar...?"

Edgar stepped forward, voice cracking like dry leaves.

"F-F-Father... Ch-Charles w-was... ki-killed..."

The old man's body jolted. His frail chest rose.

"W-WHO... WHO KILLED MY SON?!"

"I... I know who d-did it... I-I'll bring him to you... I-I'll b-bring his h-head... and... and p-place it at your f-feet..."

The old man's eyes filled with tears. Fury and sorrow danced in the flames.

Edgar turned sharply. Outside the chamber, Boun awaited.

"Prepare a team of mercenaries and get me a jet. I'm going to India. You handle everything here." Edgar ordered.

Boun nodded. "Yes, sir."

As Edgar turned to leave, Boun hesitated again.

"Sir... should I inform Father Mortis that we found a Pure Blood match?"

Edgar stopped.

His eyes burned.

"No," he said coldly. "I'll tell him myself — when I put that boy on his knees before him."

Boun swallowed hard and nodded. "O-Okay, sir."

The black SUV roared to life again, as Edgar stepped into the rain, into his car. The predator is out for hunting.

But far, far away, the train moved deeper into obscurity.

Artin sat by the window, sleeping with his head leaning against the fogged glass.

He was silent. He was still. The picture in his hand damp with tears. A man fading between life and myth.

No signal, no trail, no name.

As the rain soaked the tracks behind him, Artin was vanishing — into the folds of a world that no one could reach.

Gone.

But not gone forever.
THE END

Ethical Note

This book is a work of fiction. It explores themes of trauma, vengeance, and corruption through an intense psychological and action-driven lens. It is not intended to glorify violence or mental illness, but to reflect the cost of human suffering and the search for redemption.

www.ingramcontent.com/pod-product-compliance
Lightning Source LLC
Chambersburg PA
CBHW051220130726
47988CB00001B/161